Talking at the Woodpile

Talking at the Woodpile

stories by DAVID THOMPSON

CAITLIN PRESS
HALFMOON BAY, BRITISH COLUMBIA

01 02 03 04 05 06 16 15 14 13 12 11

Caitlin Press Inc.
8100 Alderwood Road,
Halfmoon Bay, BC V0N 1Y1
www.caitlin-press.com

Text design by Kathleen Fraser.
Cover design by Pamela Cambiazo.
Printed in Canada

Caitlin Press Inc. acknowledges financial support from the Government of Canada through the Canada Book Fund and the Canada Council for the Arts, and from the Province of British Columbia through the British Columbia Arts Council and the Book Publisher's Tax Credit.

Library and Archives Canada Cataloguing in Publication

Thompson, David (David William)
      Talking at the woodpile / David Thompson.

ISBN 978-1-894759-57-1

      I. Title.

PS8639.H625T35 2011   C813'.6   C2011-900469-0

For my wife Wendy.

Contents

Frozen in Time   9
Bear Man   19
Talking at the Woodpile   33
Yukon Justice   39
Piedoe   48
Victor the Gypsy   56
Buford's Tooth   68
Mimosa Nightingale   79
Time of Change   91
The Rock Creek Boys   104
The Man Who Thought His Wife Was an Alien   120
Joseph Copper and the Small People   138
Rambling in the Rambler   152
Brian's Epiphany   164
Jealousy among Friends   173
Winch's Meltdown   183
Hunker Creek Hideout   193
Dawson City's Ditch Digging Authority   210
Acknowledgments   223

Frozen in Time

In a cramped tunnel deep in permafrost on top of bedrock—fifty-nine claims above Discovery, where Adam's Creek meets Bonanza Creek—Wilfred Durant worked late into a sub-zero Yukon night.

Candles in tarnished tin holders cast shadows of his toil as he stooped in the low headroom. His breath rose in wavering columns to blanket the ceiling in a field of white crystals. The tunnel was bridged with rough timbers oozing amber sap that stuck to Wilfred's clothing and tools. He preferred to cut the sap out of his hair rather than wash it out.

The barber will straighten it once I'm in town, he thought.

The dank air smelled of wet wool, pine lumber and lately—barn animals.

Wilfred had an idea what the smell was. Parts of ancient horses, camels and a giant sloth—all well known to placer miners—had washed out in his sluice box over the years. He reached into his waistcoat pocket to take another look at the stained ivory carving he'd found a week ago. He planned to show it to Chief Daniel and the Han elders.

Wilfred shovelled tons of overburden and pay dirt into a wooden cart balanced on rickety lodgepole pine tracks that led to a vertical entrance. There the Arctic air dropped like an anvil onto his shoulders and back. He scooped the ore into beaten metal buckets and hand-cranked them forty feet to the valley floor above. His palms were sore from the manila ropes, and working back and forth from the relative warmth of the tunnel to the outside air inflamed his arthritis. He had just turned forty but at times felt ninety-five.

At two o'clock in the morning Wilfred put down his tools. He was played out; he could barely raise his arms. He trudged up the hill to the comfort of his cabin. The sparsely furnished single room was dim, since its rough log walls absorbed much of the oil lamp's light. A table and two chairs stood between two lumber-framed beds and the stove, and rough plank shelves supported cans of butter, sacks of dry goods and other groceries. Dog-eared magazines and newspapers lay stacked everywhere. A pastel doll-faced 1931 calendar girl invitingly held out a can of evaporated milk next to where Wilfred sat. He crossed off the days with a pencil hanging from a string he'd tied to a nail in the wall.

In the middle of the floor sat a galvanized washtub half full of silt-grey water. When Wilfred needed money, he thawed a bucket of frozen pay dirt and panned out the gold. Working by the light of the wood stove's open door, he would sort nuggets from the gravel—the wheat from the chaff.

Wilfred cooked his meals to last a week and scooped them from a cast-iron Dutch oven. He washed down his pork and beans with the blackest of coffee, then he boiled dried fruit and topped it with crushed arrowroot cookies and milk. Life on the creek was hard, but Wilfred had come to work and work he did. Comfort would come later. After stoking the stove, he climbed into bed and fell asleep. His mother said that Wilfred slept the sleep of the just.

When he awoke, the sun blazed in a clear sky, and its reflection off the snow hurt his eyes. Exposed rock absorbed the heat, causing wisps of moisture to rise into the air. The only sound in the valley was the throaty crackle-croak of a raven calling its mates, and the distant sound—five claims up—of an axe splitting firewood into kindling.

Leaning in the shelter of the doorway in his shirt sleeves, Wilfred soaked up the sunshine. He felt rested and relaxed after his breakfast. He'd used his last two eggs and the butt end of the back bacon, so he'd penciled "3 doz eggs" and "4 lbs bacon" on the shopping list tacked next to the calendar. He lingered, reluctant to leave the light of day for the dark, damp tunnel. Finally he went in to finish dressing.

Walking stooped under the low roof and banging the scabs on his spine—like buttons down his back—Wilfred headed for the tunnel face. A large clump of gravel had sloughed off during the night, exposing a mound of hair.

"What the hell!" He stood up suddenly and banged his head on the ceiling. He barely felt the gravel and ice trickling down his back.

A few scrapes of his shovel, and a massive head started to emerge. Wilfred resisted the overwhelming primeval urge to flee. He stood his ground, reached out his trembling arm and ran his fingers through the long strands of hair until he touched the frozen, granite-like body beneath. It was truly dead. He withdrew his hand; it was wet and covered in hair that was difficult to remove.

His brow was dripping with sweat, and he felt giddy from the fright. He stood up straight, took a step back and relaxed his shoulders. He said quietly, "It's a mammoth, it's a damn mammoth."

Gold could wait. A mammoth was much more interesting. Wilfred spent the day chipping around the carcass. In places the skin and flesh were missing and white bone shone through. The crushing permafrost had deformed the body grotesquely, but it was remarkably well preserved. Scattered throughout the thick coat were blades of grass, willow leaves and alpine flowers that still held their colour.

The animal was sitting up, suspended in the wall like a trophy. Wilfred could dig above and below the mammoth, which was resting on its knees with its trunk folded back along one side. He exposed the domed skull and the ends of the curved tusks. The eyes were sunken into black slits, and the mouth was slightly open to show a pale tongue clenched between gigantic molars. Every shovelful uncovered more.

Even in death, the behemoth's might was impressive. Wilfred had never seen anything like it. Finally he had to stop; there wasn't enough food in his cabin to scrape together another meal, and he needed help.

It was twenty-five below when he walked to Dawson along Bonanza Creek Road. He pulled a sled piled with firewood and a tent, stove and sleeping bag, his survival gear in case things went awry. He stopped once to boil water from snow and eat bread that he thawed by dipping it in hot sugary tea. He completed the five-hour journey between the rising and the setting of the winter sun.

It took half the night to warm his cabin on Eighth Avenue with a blazing fire before he could turn in. In the morning his first order of business was to call on William Pringle, an old soldier and friend. They had been business partners from time to time, and Wilfred knew he could count on William's advice.

"*Mammuthus primigenius*," William said after listening intently. "Wilf, my man, you've found an ancient elephant named after an old Russian word, *mammut*. More closely related to the Asian elephant than the African elephant. And a mature one, by the sound of it, maybe eleven feet tall at shoulder height and weighing sixteen thousand pounds. A rare find. This will be interesting. Could be ten thousand years old."

It was a scramble to pick up supplies, check the mail, hire Windy Sale with his horse and sleigh and take care of other small business. They got out of town by noon the following day, with perishables tucked under buffalo robes to survive the cold. The steady pull of the sleigh and the rhythmic clop of horses' hooves had Wilfred nodding off. He slept until the sleigh came to a sliding stop in front of the cabin. Windy dumped off men and supplies, turned around, and with a "Goodbye!" he was down the road and out of sight.

The cabin was dark and frozen. It had retained none of the heat from a few days ago. Wilfred lit the lamps and built a blazing fire with precut wood. Wilfred always played this game when he went to town: he would stoke the wood stove and set the air vents just right, thinking he'd get back before the fire went out and the cabin froze. But he never made it. This time a jar of blueberry preserves had frozen and cracked, oozing a sticky puddle on the table.

Wilfred muttered, "That's my favourite jam. And my best tablecloth."

William was barely able to contain his impatience. "I want to see this thing right away."

They made their way down the trail to the ladder extending above the shaft, gripped its icy rails and climbed down. An eerie silence beckoned them as they hurried along the tunnel with William leading the way. He stopped dead when the lamplight picked up the head hanging out of the wall. He stumbled, caught his balance and gasped for breath. Nothing had prepared him for this.

"What in hell is this, Wilfred? What in hell did you dig up?"

Wilfred was amused to see William's reaction and deadpanned, "It's the mammoth I told you about, William. Did you think I was kidding?"

William held the lamp closer and ran his fingers through the mammoth's hair. It stuck to him as it had to Wilfred.

When William had seen enough, they pulled up a couple of timbers and discussed their next move. Hours later, still unsure, they headed back to the cabin.

The next morning they returned and removed a large block of frozen gravel from under the animal's trunk, exposing its chest.

What they saw caused them to push each other backward. They stared at a human face and hands reaching upward as if begging to be pulled from under the beast.

"That is the weirdest thing I have ever seen," William said, leaning forward to get a better look. Brushing away the gravel, Wilfred saw a round face with marble-white skin accented by blue veins. Wide open, coal black eyes stared lifelessly, and bloodless lips curled back, exposing pale gums and perfect teeth.

Wilfred felt uneasy. He felt that way around bodies; he would make any excuse to get out of there. "Let's just leave this, William. Let's get a cup of coffee and think this through."

William ignored him and continued brushing gravel.

Wilfred turned to leave. "William, I cannot stand this. I don't want to disturb a body. I hate dead things. They make me sick. I hate the smell. When I studied at the Sorbonne in Paris, I visited the catacombs and I couldn't get out soon enough. Let's just bury this end of the tunnel and forget him. He's been here for thousands of years. Let's leave him be."

William didn't look up. "Go if you want to. I need your help, but if you can't stand it, I'll do this myself."

"Let's contact the government. They'll know what to do," Wilfred said.

"Those pencil-pushers? That's a pipe dream. You seem to have forgotten that I was in Flanders. I saw what bureaucrats can do, the mindless idiots." He pointed at the frozen man. "If they get hold of him, they'll dump him in a tank of formaldehyde and prance him around the country on a CPR train like a circus freak. They don't have respect for the living, so why would they respect the dead? Not a chance, Wilf, my friend. No civil servants are getting their greedy, grubby hands on this. We'll have to figure out something else."

Wilfred knew he was right. He sat on a timber and put his head in his hands. After a long while he broke the silence. "Okay. I will help but I'm not touching him."

William looked up from his work. "I knew I could count on you. This is unprecedented, a huge find. We have to move this guy. Nothing else will do. Let's do the best we can."

For the rest of the day they dug below and around the man and finally pulled him loose. He was fully clothed except for a moccasin that Wilfred retrieved later. His legs were bent up to one side, and like the mammoth, the man was flattened; bone was exposed in places. Overall the body was complete, and concealed underneath it was the link between the two. Protruding from the centre of the mammoth's chest was the broken shaft of a spear. Long ago these two had battled. Both had lost.

Carefully, respectfully, Wilfred and William laid the body on a blanket. Then, holding two corners each, they carried him to the cabin. They cleared the table, laid down a clean cloth, and brushed the gravel and debris off the body.

Wilfred closed the stove vents and opened the window. "We can't let him thaw, William," he said. "Whatever we do, we have to do it quickly."

William, who had studied natural science, began the examination while Wilfred took notes. First he washed the face and hands. Then he methodically described what he saw. "Amazingly well-preserved young male, perhaps twenty years old. About five foot six with a round face, a broad mouth, dark skin, and hair cut blunt over the forehead. His physique is compact and muscular."

The man's chest was crushed. Broken ribs protruded through his skin, and the clothing was bloodstained. William concluded that death had been sudden.

The examination went on late into the night. Wrapped around the body and tied with lengths of babiche—caribou rawhide cords—were light garments of scraped caribou skin. Over these the man had worn heavier outer clothing of caribou hide trimmed with wolverine fur. The pants went to his knees and were made of heavier moosehide. Fur lined his outer garments. His belt, decorated with pieces of bone intricately carved into star shapes, held a knife sheath but no knife. His footwear was trimmed with red and blue porcupine quills and came up over his knees. The insides of his moccasins were stuffed with grass. Around his neck was a decorative leather pouch that they left unopened. The man's hands and legs were tattooed with small birds and decorative bands. On his right shoulder a tattoo showed a man and a bear standing together; the bear's upper leg was extended. Wilfred sketched the scene into his notebook.

"Bear Man, that's what we should call him," Wilfred said, and William agreed.

The late-morning winter sun was rising when they finished and sat exhausted. Carefully they washed and dressed the body. Then they wrapped a Hudson's Bay Company blanket around him and tied it with twine. Wilfred inexplicably felt an urge to place the small ivory carving he'd recently found within the wrappings. Then they returned the body to the icebox of a tunnel for safekeeping.

"What's next?" William asked, drinking coffee as he sat with his back to the stove. He was trying not to yawn.

"I still think we should tell the government," Wilfred said. "We could go into Dawson and bring out the mining recorder. We could explain things and ask his opinion."

"We can't, Wilf, we've gone too far. We have disturbed an archaeological site. I'm afraid we'll have to cover our asses from here on in."

Wilfred reluctantly agreed. "It wouldn't look good if they declared this guy a national treasure or something after we dug him up and moved him."

Without another word, both men turned in to get some welcome rest.

About an hour later, Wilfred awoke. He wasn't in his cabin. He stood on the tundra, looking down at the Blackstone River. Wind blew the snow across the landscape in silence. A figure walked toward him; it was Bear Man. Wilfred saw that he was distressed and tired, and frost covered his beard and hood. Bear Man walked up to and past Wilfred without showing any sign of having seen him. Wilfred turned and watched him disappear into the wall of whirling snow.

Suddenly Wilfred was back on Bonanza—he recognized Adam's Creek near his claim—but it was fall, and the leaves had turned. A group of men walked toward him in single file with frost marking their breath. Slung on their backs were light packs suspended from a single, wide band around their foreheads. They carried spears and bows. Wilfred recognized the last one in line: Bear Man. The group filed past silently toward a willow thicket.

The leader turned abruptly, raised his clenched fist and appeared to shout something. The men in the front of the column ran in all directions, dropping their packs. Others quickly pulled arrows and fitted them into their bows. Bear Man dropped his pack with a dip of his head and faced the moving mass of brown willows before him. Out of the splintering wall blasted a mammoth, its trunk held high, mouth wide open and eyes blazing. Travelling faster than a man could run, the animal charged straight into the midst of the scattering group. Bodies tumbled and were thrown wildly about until Bear Man stood alone. The mammoth rushed forward.

Bear Man jammed the base of his heavy spear into the ground. He turned and for a moment met Wilfred's eye. Then he turned back to face the charging beast. The long, broad, razor flint sliced deep, tearing skin, flesh, cartilage and bone until it found its destined home in the massive heart. Bear Man and the mammoth crashed together and slid into a deep pool in the creek. The whole scene had taken but seconds.

Wilfred sat bolt upright in bed, soaked in sweat. William snored peacefully on the other side of the cabin, unaware of the drama that had just unfolded in his friend's dream. Wilfred threw off his covers and shook William awake.

"William, wake up! I know what we have to do. I had a dream. I saw Bear Man, the mammoth, everything."

With hot coffee cups in their hands, Wilfred recounted his dream and his plan. "We can ask Chief Daniel and the Han elders to take the body. Bear Man is one of theirs, an ancestor. We'll explain everything to them. With their help, we can get ourselves off the hook."

"Wilf, you're a genius. That dream was God-sent," William said.

One month later, on a spring afternoon, Wilfred and William stood high on the hills across the valley from the mouth of Bonanza Creek, once called Rabbit Creek, near the confluence of the Yukon and Klondike rivers. A sombre spectacle was taking place. A multitude of people stood in a silence so complete that distant sounds carried clearly. They had gathered to honour Bear Man. His oak casket, inlaid with copper wolves, was suspended over an open grave. Wilfred and William stood, hats in hand, at a place of honour. They had helped to carry the casket. Both shed tears unabashedly.

From across the clearing, within the fringe of trees, came the single rap of a drum. A high-pitched, plaintive woman's voice sang the first verse of the "Goodbye Song," followed by a loud chorus. Wilfred had heard this song many times before at funerals, and both he and William joined in.

A procession of dancers appeared, led by Tlingits in black and red button blankets; other dancers wore the full-feathered bonnets of the Plains people. Some were in Inuit garb, and many wore brightly decorated buckskin and headdresses. Han, Gwich'in, Iroquois, Cherokee, Dakota, Micmac, Paiute, Apache, Cree, Winnebago, Stoney, Hopi, Arapaho, Navajo, Haida and Blackfoot had all travelled far to be here today to honour the ancestor of them all. The unity of their diversity wove a flowing tapestry of colour and grandeur toward the burial site.

Commissioners, Members of Parliament, chiefs and people of many backgrounds were present. The elders spoke first, thanking

William and Wilfred for their wisdom and help in bringing Bear Man to where he was today. Sweetgrass smouldered, and elders dabbed attar of rose on foreheads. The great gathering sang, chanted and recited prayers. Then Bear Man was laid to rest.

A four-day potlatch followed. Friends were made, and many generous gifts changed hands. William and Wilfred had to call on Windy with his horse and cart to carry everything home.

After the potlatch, Wilfred and William returned to the claim to finish removing the mammoth. They had plenty of help. Federal civil servants, enraged that they didn't get their hands on Bear Man—but unwilling to challenge the elders—jumped in and took over. Wilfred and William didn't stop them but charged a hefty rent for the use of Wilfred's cabin. The bureaucrats took their prize, bundled it up and stored it in Richard Cooper's ice house to wait for the next boat back to Whitehorse. The narrow-gauge White Pass & Yukon Route railway carried it—packed in a thousand pounds of ice—to Skaguay; a ship ferried it to Vancouver. The Canadian Pacific Railway carried it in a freezer car to Ottawa.

Wilfred never heard from any of the bureaucrats again. "Ungrateful louts," he said whenever they were mentioned.

The mammoth remained in Ottawa until the 1980s, when the government shipped its bones and tusks to the Beringia Interpretive Centre in Whitehorse to be assembled for display.

If you visit the centre, walk past the sabre-toothed tiger and look to the left. There you will see William and Wilfred's mammoth. The display text doesn't say anything about them, but Wilfred and William could have told you the real story. If you look closely at the chest bones, you will see the deep, serrated spear cut inflicted by Bear Man so very long ago on that day on Rabbit Creek.

Bear Man

Angunatchiuk heard laughter as he awoke. Rolling onto his side, he propped himself up on one elbow. His wife Ayauniq sat with their two children Saluk and Qalu. They were laughing over a game; Ayauniq was keeping a feather aloft by fanning it with another feather. Every time the feather approached the floor, Ayauniq would pretend to panic and frantically wave her feather until it floated up again. The children fell over, limp with laughter, and Angunatchiuk laughed along with them. When Ayauniq saw that Angunatchiuk was awake, she put away the toys and laid the children down for a rest, covering them with a blanket made from feathery duck skins.

Their dome-shaped tent was made of caribou hide stretched over a birch-pole frame. The walls had windows of caribou intestine sewn into them and an opening in the roof to let smoke escape. Soft light filtered into the warmth of the interior, and clean-smelling fresh-cut pine boughs covered the floor.

Angunatchiuk and Ayauniq were married when Ayauniq was fourteen and Angunatchiuk was fifteen. Ayauniq was a member of the

Crow clan, Angunatchiuk a member of the Wolf. The children would take their mother's clan. Their parents had arranged the marriage at a large gathering held at the junction of the Whitestone and Porcupine rivers. Angunatchiuk delighted in Ayauniq. Her kindness and beauty pleased him, and their two children were healthy and happy.

Their winter camp on the Blackstone River was situated in the middle of the caribou winter range. Since early morning a caribou head hanging by a braided rope had been roasting over the fire. Smooth rocks shoved into its nostrils would keep it cooking evenly. Every so often someone nudged it to keep it spinning. When the skin cracked, it would be done.

The door flap was pulled back, allowing a gust of cold air to flow in. Angunatchiuk's father-in-law Yugunvaq had come to visit. He closed the flap behind him and stomped his feet to remove the snow. He took a seat by the fire.

"How are you, Angunatchiuk? And how are my favourite daughter and my grandchildren?" he asked.

The children threw the blanket off and ran to sit with their grandfather. Yugunvaq hugged them both while Ayauniq fetched dried caribou meat and a bowl of bear fat. Dipping the meat into the fat, they ate and talked.

Yugunvaq asked about everyone's health, and shared tidbits of news. His presence was dignified. He stood taller than most. He had thick grey hair, a creased and weathered face with sparse facial hair, high cheekbones and a broad nose. His eyes were penetrating and expressive. Yugunvaq was a respected elder who was known as a shaman. People said that he could fly, but he would never admit to it. How else could he leave one group of people and arrive so quickly over a long distance among another group? And how else could he say to people returning to camp from far away, "I saw you and your brother at the sandy creek, fishing"? The only thing they would remember seeing at the creek was a hawk flying high above them.

Angunatchiuk told how, when he first met Yugunvaq at the Whitestone Village, the elder picked him up and held him under one arm. Yugunvaq told him to close his eyes, then Angunatchiuk felt as though they were flying. When they stopped, Yugunvaq told him to open his eyes. They were in a different place. It took them the better part of a day to walk home.

At night, when the snow looked blue from the moonlight and the shadows in the pine forests were darkest, people could hear Yugunvaq chanting. One by one they made their way to his tent and filled it. When Yugunvaq finished, others took up their own prayers. It was hours before Yugunvaq spoke.

He told ancient stories about the great migration across "the sea that lost its water." He described how man had come to exist, how his place was set in creation and the purpose of that place. As morning grew near, Yugunvaq spoke with the authority of a shaman who saw the future. He spoke of things to come, when people with snow-white faces would travel to this land and cause difficulty because they had not listened to the Creator when He spoke to them.

"They kill their shamans and do not see or hear. This will cause much suffering. For many years, it will disrupt our lives. But this time of suffering will end, and from it a great spirit will develop, and our people will one day take their rightful place in the world, a place of wisdom and honour," Yugunvaq said.

"The times will be dark, but the future will be bright. This will take place in a time far from this time, when many families will have come and gone." He warned the people, "Tell this story often. Watch for this and don't lose heart. At the coming of the snow-faced people, the Frog Spirit Helper will appear as Ti'anaxeedakin, the Wealth Woman. This will bring many people to this country."

Yugunvaq stopped speaking, dropped his chin to his chest and covered his face with both hands. He looked up and said solemnly, "Tell your children to tell their children for as long as the rivers flow never to drink the firewater given by the snow-face, and always respect their elders." With that he stood up, took his coat and left. Those inside heard branches rustle in the pine trees above the tent. Yugunvaq was gone and would not return for days.

Weeks later Angunatchiuk fidgeted restlessly in the tent. He and his family were hungry for fresh meat. A hunter had seen a small herd of caribou migrating among a larger herd of mammoth that were travelling south on the hills beyond the camp.

As he buckled on his knife belt, Angunatchiuk told Ayauniq, "Your mother Alak asked for fresh meat, and I told her I would do my best. I'm going after those caribou and should be back before night."

His uncle Suyuk met him as he was about to leave and said, "Why are you going out, Angunatchiuk? We have enough food, and those caribou are too far away. You are wasting your time. Find something better to do."

Suyuk was powerfully built and wore his hair in a braid down his back. He looked strong, but he had one weakness: he was selfish and took care of his own interests first. Suyuk was the chief, but Yugunvaq was the spiritual leader that people turned to. Yugunvaq was training Angunatchiuk to walk in his footsteps. Angunatchiuk didn't like Suyuk, but he was a great hunter and held in high respect by people far and wide.

Out of respect, Angunatchiuk didn't argue. "I will try. If it is too far, I will return."

"Maybe I should send Malak with you. He's a good hunter," Suyuk said.

Angunatchiuk bristled at the suggestion that Suyuk's oldest son should accompany him. Malak was younger and less experienced than Angunatchiuk, and he was heavy and slow, with rotting teeth. Other hunters said, "His clumsiness makes it impossible to track game. When he lies on his belly he passes wind and the animals run off. He and Suyuk just laugh—they think this is funny—but it is more work for us. One time Ojuk, the elder brother of Alak, smacked him with his bow while they lay in the bushes and then had a big fight with Suyuk."

On their return Malak would criticize every move Angunatchiuk made to anyone who would listen.

"No, uncle, don't trouble yourself or cousin Malak. I will be fine," Angunatchiuk said, failing to keep the anger from his voice.

Suyuk heard the tone and snapped, "Go do what you want, waste your time. Don't listen to me. I don't know what I am talking about."

Angunatchiuk's snowshoes kicked up snow as he ran toward where the hunter had last seen the herds. The caribou and mammoth had trampled the ground, and willow bushes were torn up by the roots so that clumps of soil dotted the snow. He would keep his eyes sharp; mammoths were testy, and the thick willows hid them until they were almost on top of you.

Caribou were more plentiful; mammoth numbers had declined in recent years. Yugunvaq had seen great numbers of them dead on the plains, some with blood around their mouths, while the living staggered about wheezing as if they couldn't breathe.

Crawling over a hill, Angunatchiuk came upon a herd of caribou grazing lichen by scraping away snow with their hooves. He crept forward with his bow and paused to rub two pieces of wood together, mimicking the sound of antlers rubbing on trees. A curious bull approached Angunatchiuk's hiding place, and when it was close, he leaped out. The animal bolted and slipped to its knees. Angunatchiuk released two arrows in quick succession. Each found its mark deep in the animal's chest, and the caribou dropped to the ground. The herd scattered.

"Alak will be happy," Angunatchiuk said softly. He was exhausted. The burst of speed and excitement had drained his energy, but he was pleased at his success.

He turned the caribou over on its back and cut off the legs at the knee joint, then removed the head. He sliced, then pushed and pulled the hide away from the neck, stomach and legs. With the skin lying on either side of the carcass, he split the stomach, and the steaming guts spilled out, filling the air with the pungent smell of warm meat. He removed the organs, set them aside and cleaned the bum-gut. He split open the stomach and ate the undigested vegetation. Using a length of babiche, he wrapped the meat in the hide to sled back to camp. Then he dug a hole in the snow and cached the rest.

Busy with his work, Angunatchiuk hadn't noticed the dark line of clouds forming on the horizon to the north. A torrent of wind and blinding snow slammed into him, catching him off guard. In a minute he couldn't see his hand in front of his face. The elders had mentioned conditions like this. Their warning, "Wait it out," rang in his ears. He dropped his work and groped toward a large snowdrift in a clump of trees. He put on his gloves and hollowed out a tunnel with his snowshoe. Once inside he sealed the entrance and lay in the dark, catching his breath and listening to the wind's howl. Then, saying a prayer for the end of his difficulties, he fell asleep.

As he slept, Angunatchiuk's body heat raised the temperature in the cave to a tolerable level, and his clothing kept him warm. After he woke, listening as the wind rattled the frozen willows, he knew the storm was still raging. He cut strips of frozen meat and ate them. There was nothing more to do but shift his weight once in a while and make an air hole, which lengthened as the snow deepened.

Days later, he awoke. Everything was silent. The wind had stopped. He kicked a hole through the snow and crawled out. The sun was rising, and the sky was clear. A cloud of warm air followed him out of the cave and hung over the willows. He inhaled deeply and nearly doubled over in pain; the cold burned his lungs and his face and hands stung with frostbite.

"This is very cold," he said out loud. "This isn't good."

Angunatchiuk had half a mind to step back into his shelter but he knew his family would be worrying about him. With the wind down, he was confident he could make it home. He strapped on the snow-shoes and moved down the valley. He crossed a frozen creek, climbed the far bank and headed across the tundra. He quickly realized that he'd underestimated the situation. The cold had him shivering. After three days in the shelter, his clothes were damp and insulated him less.

Looking around he saw a single strand of warm air rise above the ground about twenty feet in front of him. The wisp floated up, lit by the pale sun, and then dissipated into the air. Angunatchiuk knew what the warm air was: a bear hibernating in a den.

He removed his snowshoes and crept to the air hole. He smelled the bear a few yards below. It was a grizzly; black bears smelled like dogs. Carefully he chipped open the entrance and slid headfirst down to where the bear lay. The animal's back faced the tunnel, and its bulk was nestled into a space that it had carved out with its powerful claws. Angunatchiuk moved closer, confident that it wouldn't awaken, and closed his eyes as exhausted sleep overcame him.

In a split second he was wide awake, fear racing down his spine. The urge to flee strained every fibre of his body, but his mind slowly took control.

He heard whimpering. The bear cubs weren't hibernating. They lay with their mother, suckling and waiting for spring. A cub was making its way over its mother's body toward Angunatchiuk. It crawled with the unsteady bumping motion of the young, and its breath smelled of sour milk. The cub ran its cold nose over Angunatchiuk's face, bumping his eye, and then latched its toothless gums onto his nose. It began to suckle.

He turned his head slowly from side to side, trying to detach the cub. The animal growled and hung on, placing both paws over Angunatchiuk's eyelids to maintain its grip. Angunatchiuk stopped resisting, and when the cub sensed this, it began flexing its claws in contentment. The pain of having his frostbitten nose suckled and five needles poked rhythmically into each eyelid was overwhelming. Angunatchiuk grasped the cub by its fat stomach and pulled it from his face. The cub detached without protest, probably because it was at a dry station, and climbed back over its mother to join its sibling. Angunatchiuk closed his eyes and fell asleep.

He dreamed that he had crawled out of the den and was standing on the tundra. The sky was robin's egg blue, and the sun shone brightly. The Blackstone River valley and the plains below the mountains glowed with light. There was not a sound. He looked to his left, then to his right. The bear stood upright beside him, but Angunatchiuk wasn't afraid. The bear looked around, and its nostrils moved as it sniffed the air. It lifted its right foreleg with paw outstretched and claws exposed. The claws were the colours of a rainbow—red, orange, yellow, green and blue—and sparkled in the sunlight. Angunatchiuk realized that it was a shaman's spirit bear. Then the bear dropped to all fours and headed back into the den.

Angunatchiuk woke with a start. Everything was as it had been when he entered, and the bear had not moved. The cubs whined. He could tell from the smell of the den that the outside temperature had risen. The bear stirred, groaned, shifted its weight and settled again. Angunatchiuk crawled out. The sky was clear, and the sun blazed as it had in his dream. Angunatchiuk covered the entrance behind him so the cubs would not catch cold, then said a prayer of thanks and headed in the direction the dream bear had pointed.

When he arrived back in camp, his family and friends greeted him. Some grasped his arms and gave them a friendly rub. "Good to see you, Angunatchiuk!"

Ayauniq and his children embraced him. His wife had tears in her eyes. "Where were you? I was worried."

His in-laws gathered around, and their relief and happiness puzzled him. "Why the long faces?" he asked. "I was gone only four days. Surely you knew the storm would hold me back."

Everyone began to speak at once. "There was no storm! You've been gone nine days!"

Suyuk stood apart with his arms folded, looking away, barely able to contain himself while waiting for his chance to voice his opinion. "See! I told you not to go. Look at all the trouble you've caused. I should have sent Malak with you. And where is the caribou you promised Alak?"

The crowd around Angunatchiuk went silent. Ayauniq shot Suyuk a glance and took her husband by his arm, herding him toward their tent. "You must be hungry. Let's go now, and I will make food for you."

Angunatchiuk tried to answer Suyuk over his shoulder, but Ayauniq pushed him harder.

Learning how long he'd been away troubled Angunatchiuk, so he sought out Yugunvaq, who said, "Tell no one of this adventure, especially Suyuk and Malak. They burn with jealousy and go cold with hate. We will talk later."

A week later Angunatchiuk was awakened by Yugunvaq shaking his shoulder. Yugunvaq gestured to him to follow him up the hill to his tent. Alak slept peacefully in the corner, and a small fire burned. Yugunvaq dropped a handful of spruce pitch onto it and the smoke cleared their lungs as they inhaled deeply. Yugunvaq leaned forward peering intently at Angunatchiuk.

"Something has made me curious," Yugunvaq said. "How did those needle holes come to be about your eyes?"

Angunatchiuk told the story, beginning with the day he left to hunt caribou. When he described the suckling bear cub, Yugunvaq laughed so hard he fell over onto his side and woke Alak. He told her the story, and their peals of laughter flowed down to the camp, where those who were still awake left their tents and stood out in the cold looking up in curiosity, asking each other, "What is so funny?" They wanted to know what had happened.

Yugunvaq listened intently, and his eyebrows shot up when Angunatchiuk told about his dream. He nodded, smiling. "This was a good thing. You have been given much, but much will be expected of you in your care for your people."

Yugunvaq reached into the corner of his tent and pulled out a small bundle wrapped in bearskin. It contained a tattoo kit, a pouch of soot that he mixed in a bowl with a little water and grease.

"This story is important, so I will tattoo it on your skin. It will be with you forever."

Beginning at Angunatchiuk's right shoulder, Yugunvaq drew the outline of a standing bear. As he worked, he told his son-in-law what the bear meant. "Grizzly spirit is powerful. Few men acquire it, for fear they would be unable to control it. Few shamans have it. But you, Angunatchiuk, were given it. The bear in your dream was your grizzly spirit."

Yugunvaq deftly pierced Angunatchiuk's skin with a sharpened grouse bone, working in the soot until the drawing was complete.

"The only spirit greater than bear is mammoth, but I have never heard of a man taking on a mammoth spirit. An old shaman from the Old Crow flats told me, 'The mammoth spirit should not be taken on, because one day all mammoth will disappear. If you have its spirit, you and all your people will disappear with it. I heard of a squat, heavy-browed people who disappeared with the mammoth in a faraway place.'"

The next day Angunatchiuk told everyone why he and Yugunvaq had been laughing, and people lined up to see the cub's pinhole scars. Those who were far-sighted looked closely and burst into laughter; some buried their heads in his chest until they composed themselves. Suyuk and Malak didn't ask to see the pinholes and discouraged others from asking. "If you want to hear a real hunting story, come and see us. We have many good ones to tell, better than this." Angunatchiuk took all this in stride and was glad his experience had brought so much mirth to his family and friends. The story of Angunatchiuk and the bear would be told far and wide, long after he finished his days on this earth.

In the late summer Yugunvaq's clan met with Angunatchiuk's father and people—as they'd planned a year earlier—at a camp called Moosehide below the junction of the Thron-diukic and Yuqana rivers. It was called Moosehide because from a distance the many tents covering the ground looked like one big moosehide. Every year the two groups met there to hunt and fish; then they would dry the meat and salmon on long lines of elevated racks. Everyone looked forward to this meeting. Eligible men and women of marrying age were particularly excited.

Camp was set up on the east bank of the Yuqana. When the Tetlit arrived, the Tukudh were preparing willow baskets to catch fish. They greeted one another with hugs and handshakes. Families were together again. Parents greeted sons, and grandchildren were proudly shown off. Old friends found each other, and old rivalries were re-established with a glance and silence. Drummers took the skin wrappings from their painted drums, warmed them over a fire and welcomed each other with song and dance. People made speeches of greeting, said prayers, composed songs and sang them on the spot. Storytelling began, and Angunatchiuk's story claimed the greatest interest. Once again he endured the examination of his scars and more uncontrollable laughter.

The young people eyed each other. The girls walked in groups, clinging to one another for support, laughing and holding their hands over their faces. The boys stood with their chests expanding a little farther than usual.

Their parents discussed arrangements; some decisions had been made years ago when the youths were children. Applause from the tent signalled final agreements. Most knew of the selection beforehand, and most were agreeable. One young woman stomped her feet, wept and refused. A refusal would be tolerated, but there were only so many potential spouses, and the elders had done their best.

Malak's new wife's parents were bribed with gifts provided by Suyuk, who later berated his son for costing him so much and being such an embarrassment. "If you had cleaned yourself up and been more presentable, we could have chosen better for less." Malak's new wife overheard this and cried to her parents. The daughter had been a problem to her mother and father, so they told Malak and Suyuk, "She is your concern now." People laughed behind their hands, asking, "Who got the better of that marriage?"

A party gathered to hunt the Thron-diukic River valley. It was a good place to hunt; the hunters would raft game down the creek to the Thron-diukic, then to the Yuqana and downriver to camp. Yugunvaq, Angunatchiuk, Suyuk, Malak, Ukuk, Manikaaq and Iqilan met early one morning by the riverbank.

The brothers Ukuk, Manikaaq and Iqilan were full of merriment. Ukuk was a great storyteller, and his brothers' job in life was to further embellish any story he told. If a large salmon swallowed a fisherman, then it became ten salmon that swallowed ten fishermen; if a man was born from an eagle's egg, the story became a mountain goat born from an eagle's egg. The brothers were comedians and well-liked; people always sought their company.

The hunters hiked the short distance up the Thron-diukic and rafted over to Rabbit Creek. The creek got its name from the shiny yellow stones that littered the bottom and collected in layers on the exposed banks; they were as numerous as rabbit droppings. People sometimes made fishing weights from the soft metal, which they could heat and bend into shape. It was too soft for arrow tips or knives, so it was of little other use. The duller yellow metal that turned green was better. Copper was found in the White River area, home of the Northern Tutchone, who traded the nuggets for dried salmon and caribou.

The men walked single file through thick bush to seek the easiest route up the steep-walled valley. Signs of moose were everywhere. Willows and thick shrubs along the creek provided an abundance of food. That night they camped in a clearing next to the stream. It was a perfect site, and the remains of earlier fires and cut brush testified to its popularity. They lit a smudge fire to keep down blackflies while they prepared and ate food. The men took out spears, knotted babiche into moose snares, strung bows and inspected their arrows. They looked forward to the hunt and agreed that Suyuk should lead them.

"I want the most experienced up front. Angunatchiuk, you follow behind Malak at the end."

Angunatchiuk's face burned at the insult, but Yugunvaq caught his eye and signalled with a wave of his hand not to challenge Suyuk's decision.

As they left camp, the hunters set moose snares as Suyuk instructed. If the moose moved away from them, Suyuk decided, he would strip naked and run one down. Moose don't sweat as humans do, and after hours of running, exhausted animals become easy game.

There were fresh signs of a herd nearby, and mixed among them were fresher signs of a mammoth. In places it had pulled out willows by the roots and scraped the ground with its powerful tusks. The hunters stopped to decide what to do if they encountered the mammoth.

Suyuk said, "The mammoth is old."

He could tell by the marks its tusks left where it dug. The older the mammoth, the closer the tusks grew together at the tips. These tusks touched at the tips. An older mammoth was more likely to present a problem. He advised, "Best to avoid him." Everyone else agreed.

The mammoth caught their scent and moved up the valley. It was old and worn from a hundred years of life, but its memory was long, and the arrowhead lodged in its hip was an aggravation.

The group hiked all morning. Then Suyuk froze in his tracks. Raising his fist, he motioned for the others to stop. Suyuk stood to full height to see ahead into the thick brush. Suddenly he wheeled and ran. The hunters heard a sound like a rock avalanche. The willows parted in front of them, and the enraged mammoth charged out, its trunk held high and a deafening roar coming from deep within its throat. Everyone reacted at once, but it was too late for Malak. The mammoth scooped him up, held him down and stomped once with its foot. The others shouted and cursed as they scrambled out of the way, fitting arrows into bows. They shot into the mammoth's face, which caused it to charge even more and bellow in pain.

Yugunvaq dove into the surrounding brush and fired an arrow. As he turned to loose another, he caught a glimpse of Angunatchiuk, who had been last in line. He wasn't moving out of the way, but had jammed the butt of his spear into the rocky ground. Grasping the shaft close to his body, he crouched low, letting the mammoth bear down on him. Yugunvaq had seen this before; he knew everything would seem perfectly clear to Angunatchiuk. Time would stand still, and he would hear nothing. Yugunvaq watched the spear disappear into the heavy chest of the mammoth. Its shaft shuddered as it sliced through flesh, bone and cartilage before reaching the heart. Angunatchiuk looked toward the hill, and Yugunvaq was sure his son-in-law saw the ancestors beckoning to him. Then he was gone. The beast crashed to the earth, enveloping him. Together they slid down the bank into a pool in the creek and sank to its depths.

A light snow began to fall.

Yugunvaq picked himself up and walked out of the bush. The air was filled with screams and sobbing. Malak lay on his back, his chest crushed. Blood ran from his ears and nose, and frothy pink bubbles flowed from his mouth. He tried to sit up, but Yugunvaq held him down. Malak struggled, but then his eyes dimmed and he was gone. Yugunvaq moved to Ukuk. His leg was twisted at an impossible angle, and he shook uncontrollably, biting his hand to distract him from the pain. Manikaaq tried to straighten his leg, causing Ukuk to faint and go limp. Yugunvaq took advantage of his unconsciousness and expertly set the leg and bound it.

The other men staggered about, all injured and in shock. They returned to camp, then went back for Malak's body and made a litter. Iqilan, Suyuk and Yugunvaq carried Malak up a hill that overlooked the valley. There they built a platform and wrapped the body in a tent hide. They placed him on it, then raised their hands to the heavens and laid their plaintive sorrow at the Creator's feet. Suyuk walked away weeping, and though the men tried to comfort him, he waved them off and would speak to no one.

Yugunvaq returned to where Angunatchiuk had disappeared. He threw himself on the ground and pleaded for strength to tell the families the horrible news. Worst of all, he couldn't recover the body. Angunatchiuk had been his friend and successor, and Yugunvaq had cared deeply for him.

He took off a looped ivory carving that he wore around his neck and placed it on the hill above where his son-in-law had disappeared. The carving represented a storm spirit. Angunatchiuk had been spiritually born in a storm and had died in another storm. Yugunvaq then chanted a prayer that someday Angunatchiuk would be buried with honour.

Back at their camp the men had made a fire and were trying to rest. Yugunvaq sat down, too tired to talk. Finally he said, "Angunatchiuk was the bravest of us all. He carried the grizzly spirit and proved his worth. We all owe him our lives."

The others nodded in agreement.

Suyuk sat with his head down and would not meet Yugunvaq's eyes.

"We all owe him our lives," Yugunvaq repeated, speaking directly to Suyuk.

Suyuk looked up with a face full of rage. "He didn't save everyone."

"If your son had been at the end of the line where he belonged, he would be alive today," Yugunvaq said angrily. He stood up and disappeared into the thick willows. Moments later there was a rustling of wings and a hawk flew from the bush, circled into the sky and headed off in the direction of Moosehide.

Talking at the Woodpile

Wilfred Durant and William Pringle were good friends—had been for years. William usually visited Wilfred bringing newspapers and jars of preserves that his sister Dot put up.

Toward the end of 1931 William arrived with the usual bundle under his arm. "Howdy, Wilfred, brought you some papers flown in this morning and hot off the press. They're only about two weeks old."

"I didn't think the airplane could land in that fog," Wilfred said. "I heard them go over early this morning—must have circled around to Mayo and come back. Reminds me of Lindbergh flying blind over the Atlantic. Have a seat, and I'll make coffee."

William sat at the kitchen table reading while Wilfred served strawberry jam and thick slices of freshly baked whole-wheat bread that was still hot from the oven. They washed this down with brimming mugs of freshly ground coffee, thickened with cream and laced with mounds of sugar.

"I can stand my spoon in it," William complained about the strength of the brew.

"There's no such thing as strong coffee, only weak men," Wilfred reminded him as they settled in to read.

The two of them passed their time as bachelors, having little responsibility for anyone but themselves. William worked seasonally for the Klondike Valley Gold Consortium, which operated dredges on Hunker and Bonanza creeks. Wilfred, an independent placer miner, had claims on both creeks. He was a tall, thin, dark man with a bushy moustache and a bad temper. William had the same moustache and the same temper, but he was of average height, stocky and fair.

Wilfred was from back east, from Rhode Island. He didn't volunteer information about himself, so the people of Dawson City knew little about him. What they did know they'd learned from Markham, the postmaster, who took information from the envelopes and parcels that moved through his hands. He had no reservations about passing this on. In a town that was cut off from the rest of the world for six months of the year, you had to make your own news.

Nearly everyone knew that Wilfred was a Harvard alumnus and his family had money. One cousin regularly sent him books and parcels.

Wilfred had travelled extensively before ending up in Dawson. He camped with Berbers in North Africa, swam the Tigris and Euphrates rivers, walked the Great Wall of China and strode through the halls of Oxford and Cambridge with men such as T.E. Lawrence and Edward G. Browne, both famed orientalists.

William, on the other hand, had lived in Dawson almost all his life. His parents were among the first gold seekers to struggle over the Chilkoot Pass in the summer of 1896. They hadn't worked the goldfields but had made their fortune by building and operating sawmills and the Occidental Hotel. William went "outside" to McGill University, where he married and divorced, and now, like Wilfred, was content to live a bachelor's life. He'd served in the army during the Great War, where he had been wounded and had witnessed unimaginable horror as callous men pushed others into battles that they themselves could not face.

Dawson City was William's home—his sanctuary.

Dawson people craved entertainment during the long winters, and as well-travelled scholars, Wilfred and William were sought-after dinner guests and public speakers. Friends and families valued their congenial company and their stories about their world adventures. Wilfred was in the habit of taking some artifact with him to entertain the children; an old musket from northern Persia was his favourite. People respected William and Wilfred, two well-educated men in a land far distant from centres of learning. But at heart they were both sourdoughs.

In late January of 1932, during a long, deep cold spell—the kind when sourdoughs thrive, cheechakos wilt and trips to the woodpile are quick—William emerged from his cabin and trudged up the street to visit Wilfred. Under his arm he carried a stack of month-old newspapers.

Wilfred greeted him warmly. He hadn't had a visitor for more than a week because of the cold. Soon they were sitting back in their chairs, drinking coffee and filling their pipes full of aromatic tobacco, each completely absorbed in every printed word in the papers.

Time passed in pleasant silence. Wilfred refreshed the coffee pot, and Dot's fresh-baked raisin scones disappeared by the plateful. The late afternoon sun faded into twilight, and once again winter darkness set in. Tossing his paper onto the floor, Wilfred rocked forward in his chair and leaped to his feet. "Time to get the wood in," he announced.

"I'll help," William said.

"No need, I'm okay."

"I insist." William stood and followed Wilfred.

Once outside, they paused to study the inky, moonlit sky, watching for signs of a break in the weather. Seeing none, they moved quickly to the backyard woodpile.

Next door, Taffy Bowen stood at his kitchen sink, having a last sip of tea before turning in for the night. By the light of his kitchen lamp, he could see Wilfred and William heading across the backyard. Taffy set down his cup and walked the few steps to his bed, loosening his suspenders on the way and dropping his pants to the floor. Standing there in his one-piece Stanfield's, he wound the Big Ben alarm clock. He climbed in between the stack of woollen coverings and pulled up the colourful Hudson's Bay blanket on top.

William and Wilfred had barely begun to load wood when William casually asked, "Do you think we can trust these physicists not to turn atomic power into a weapon?" He'd just read in a scientific article about splitting the atom. Wilfred froze. His eyebrows arched and his ears tingled, not only from the cold but from the question. William realized in an instant what he had done—he had unthinkingly started to play the woodpile game with his friend and fellow sourdough, testing who could bear the cold longer—and looked horrified and apologetic.

But Wilfred's pride and anger surfaced quickly and emerged in an answer dripping with sarcasm. "I'd expect someone with a scientific education to have a better opinion of his colleagues."

William regained his composure and answered in an equally curt fashion. "Is that so! It was scientists who invented the mustard gas that killed thousands in the Great War. Why do you think I'd trust them not to blow us all up?"

And the battle—a battle that should never have been—was on.

It was about an hour after he went to bed that Taffy, having drunk too much tea, got up and by chance looked out his kitchen window. There stood Wilfred and William, two feet apart and shivering uncontrollably. Thick ice had formed from their breath and covered their moustaches. Each man had his arms clasped around his chest and was dancing foot to foot. Taffy knew in an instant what had happened. Throwing on his parka, hat, gloves and boots, he leaped over the fence, and without speaking to either of them, pushed the men back into Wilfred's cabin. Neither resisted.

The men's ward at the Dawson City General Hospital was a cavernous affair that smelled of antiseptic; beds were lined up on each side beneath its towering frost-covered windows. You could always tell when the janitor loaded the wood furnace, because a puff of smoke wafted genie-like from the basement and up through the floor grates and hung around the ceiling before disappearing. Catholic nursing sisters and a decent doctor attended to both Wilfred and William. They were alone in the ward except for a young man who had suffered a gunshot wound to the buttocks for becoming too familiar with another person's belongings.

"I was only going to make myself a loan of his gold, for Lord's sake. I would have paid him back. I did leave a signed IOU," he said.

No one listened to him. They knew he'd stolen the gold and lost it all at blackjack.

"Let the magistrate decide if you were wrong or not. I'm sure you will get your due reward or punishment," said the eldest nun as she scurried off to tend to more innocent patients.

Wilfred spent his days convalescing and playing cards with the young man. The tips of Wilfred's ears turned black, as did the tips of two of his fingers. His toes were all right because he'd slipped on his boots to go out. William wasn't so lucky. Having lost a fingertip to frostbite on a prior occasion, he would lose two more this time. The men ignored each other and suffered in silence. Their only visitor during their week-long stay was Dot, who stood over her prone brother William and tearfully scolded him so much that the nuns had to caution her.

"And you ... an educated man! What will the neighbours think?" Dot sobbed, running her hands through her dark hair, then crossing her arms to hold onto her thin shoulders to stop them from shaking. Her husband Nat had come in with her but turned his lanky frame around and fled as the berating started. "I have to go feed my dog."

"Education had nothing to do with it. You're being too emotional," William snapped back. Not wanting to rile her more, he rolled over, turning his back on her, and muttered, "Yeah, yeah, yeah ..." The last word faded to a long, weary sigh.

Winter passed, and spring arrived along with the first riverboat, the SS *Casca*, which brought fresh supplies and passengers. The hot sun melted the snow, which ran in rivulets down wheel ruts in the muddy streets, streaming toward the river where every drop would become part of the whole. Everything that was frozen—rocks, water, trees, metal and earth—thawed in response to the warmth.

Wilfred sat in his cabin with the door wide open, enjoying the sun that streamed in, bringing with it heat and light and chasing out the winter memories and the cold. A robin ran along the top of the fence, snatching insects off the weathered, unpainted wood. He watched it intently. It cheered his heart. Then there were footsteps on the porch ... then a shadow ... then a light knock.

"Can I come in?" It was William. He had a load of papers under his arm.

Wilfred didn't hesitate. "Sure, I'll put the coffee on."

Without a word both settled in, just like old times, as if nothing had happened between them. The papers were up once more, and fresh coffee steamed in the cups. Smoke wafted from their pipes, curled above their heads and was drawn out the door. After about an hour of silence, William spoke from behind his paper. "I didn't mean to do that ..."

"I know," Wilfred replied without looking up.

William folded the newspaper, placing it on the table. Then, standing up to leave, he approached Wilfred and offered his hand. Wilfred reached out and shook it.

"You have a bit of anger in you, Wilfred." William's voice held a touch of annoyance, but he looked the other man straight in the eye.

"And you, a bit of pride," Wilfred responded with a tinge of sadness.

And with that they nodded agreement and unclasped their hands.

William saw himself out the door. On the porch he adjusted his scarf and breathed a long sigh of relief. It wasn't easy settling this, but now it was done. A misunderstanding had gotten out of hand. That's all it had been. He was just thankful Wilfred wasn't the type to hold a grudge. Their friendship was still intact, maybe even better than before. He drew in a large breath of cool air and headed home.

Taffy was washing dishes in his kitchen and saw William leave. He was glad the two of them had made friends; the town didn't need another feud. And Taffy understood cold. It was like a crisis: you had to accept it, manage it; otherwise it would overwhelm you. At that moment the glass Taffy was washing slipped from his grasp and shattered on the floor.

He leaned over to pick up the pieces, and cursed the missing fingers on his right hand.

Yukon Justice

Wilfred Durant would never have expected his well-stocked, neatly stacked woodpile to become the target of a thief. He took pride in his home. The small log cabin was clean and in good repair. The snow hardly had time to settle on the boardwalk that led to the street and the back lane before he had it shovelled and swept clean. Thievery was an affront to his pride and his property.

"How could anyone do this?" Wilfred asked his neighbour Taffy over their common fence. "And to an old-timer like me? There's no respect."

"They're idiots!" said Taffy, who always waxed philosophical. "How did you find out?"

"After that heavy snowfall I noticed an area at the back of the pile near the fence had been disturbed. I thought it was my imagination— I must have taken the wood and forgotten about it," Wilfred said. "But a week later I noticed more wood was missing from the same spot. I knew then someone was stealing my wood."

Wilfred decided not to do anything about it. After all, what could he do? He'd tried to stay awake and keep an eye on things, but being quick to fall asleep, it simply didn't work. Besides, falling asleep in a high-backed kitchen chair and waking up when your head smacked the table was uncomfortable and tiring. After spilling the sugar bowl twice, he decided enough was enough and quit his watch.

The stealing continued.

One Friday mid-afternoon Wilfred joined the crowd in the post office lobby. Most of the town turned out on mail days, Monday and Friday. He checked his box, then herded William, Nat and Taffy into a corner to ask their advice.

"Call the cops," Taffy said.

"The cops are busy."

"I've got a beaver trap," William said.

"Too dangerous. I could catch a kid."

"Move your wood closer to the house," Nat said.

"Too much work."

The suggestions ran dry, and the men left one at a time, wishing Wilfred good luck.

Wilfred made one more attempt to catch the thief. He borrowed Nat and Dot's dog Piedoe and tied him to an old doghouse at the back of the yard. The temperature was sub-zero, Arctic cold, so Wilfred strung an extension cord out to Piedoe's new house and fixed a sixty-watt bulb inside for heat. Nat came over with a bale of hay for the dog to bed on and asked Wilfred, "What's up with the light?"

"Piedoe's reading," Wilfred said.

He fed Piedoe pancakes in the morning, and whatever he ate for dinner, he fed the dog the same.

"A dog that size will eat you out of house and home," Nat said.

Nat's boys Iggy and Ziggy were excited about the prospect of their dog apprehending a thief. "Is Piedoe a detective dog, Dad?"

"If Sherlock Holmes had a dog, it would be Piedoe," their father said.

"Wow, wait until the guys at school hear about this," Ziggy said, but Nat cautioned them not to say anything unless Wilfred caught the thief.

After four days at Wilfred's house, Piedoe was becoming attached to the extra rations of food from both Wilfred and Ziggy. Since he spent more time in the house than in the yard, he also throve on the attention Wilfred gave him. On the fifth night, there was a loud commotion by the woodpile. Piedoe had surprised someone and was baying like a whistle blast on a riverboat. The air was thick with yells and curses from someone obviously surprised out of his wits.

Wilfred had been prepared, like a fireman, and quickly jumped into his clothes and slippers. He grabbed his whacking stick from beside the kitchen door and sailed out into the yard. In the moonlight, Piedoe was leaping in the air on his tether as a shadowy figure pushed a sleigh loaded with wood down the lane.

Wilfred ran down the back boardwalk, but halfway to the lane he stubbed his foot on a loose board. It brought him to a limping halt. Back in the cabin he examined the bloody nail on his big toe; it was torn and bent back.

There was a knock at the door, and Nat and Dot came in wearing parkas over their nightclothes.

"What's the commotion? Did you see him?" Nat asked.

"No, no, I saw nothing at all," Wilfred groaned, holding his foot across his knee and rocking back and forth. He didn't want to look at the wound again.

Dot took one look at his toe and reached for the first-aid kit by the sink.

"This is war, Nat." Wilfred spat the words between his teeth.

The following day William came over, and Wilfred hobbled around the kitchen on the heel of his foot to make the coffee. The dressing on his toe seemed bigger than necessary.

"Looks like my sister wrapped that toe to save you from ever bumping it, Wilf," William said with a laugh.

"I'm in no mood for jokes, William," Wilfred snapped.

"Well, you're going to have to find your own solution to this problem. You have a good imagination, so I'm sure you can catch the rat."

"You're right about that, William. I've got this guy in my sights and I never miss."

That evening Wilfred took his toolbox from the shed and set up in the warmth of his kitchen. He spread newspapers on his table to protect the oilcloth. Then he broke open the tops of eight 12-gauge shotgun shells with a pair of pliers. Discarding the shot, he formed four equal conical piles of gunpowder. He then cut neat squares from an old plaid shirt, wrapped each pile in a tidy bundle and tied it with grocer's string.

Selecting the correct size of log was important; it had to be small enough to fit into a stove without being split. If it were split, the bundles would fall out and ruin the surprise.

He clamped a two-foot log onto the table and drilled a hole almost down its length with a brace and auger bit. He tamped in each package between plugs of sawdust. There was no reason to have them all go off at once. A carved dowel stopper made an invisible finish. Wilfred marked the surprise with an axe, so he wouldn't accidentally burn it himself. Then he set the log back on the pile in a convenient place for the thief to steal.

For the next week Wilfred checked the woodpile every morning to see if the thief had come back. No such luck. He was beginning to give up hope, thinking that Piedoe had scared him off forever. Then, on a quiet Sunday morning, wood was missing—including the bomb.

Wilfred wrote a note to William and sealed it in an envelope. It read, "Wait and see." His toe was still sore, so he called over Ziggy and had him deliver it for a nickel.

It was now a waiting game. No one knew the time or the place. If it had been legal, Wilfred would have sold tickets as people did for the annual Yukon River ice breakup contest.

A few days later, up on the hillside at the far end of town, Neil O'Neill's well-stoked stove leaped six inches off the worn linoleum of his crowded one-room cabin. With the first deafening roar, the force snapped the stovepipe midway between stove and ceiling.

O'Neill awoke with his short ginger hair standing on end, screaming, "Armageddon!"

Billowing black smoke soon made it impossible to see even inches in front of his pale, freckled face. The second blast opened the firebox door, spewing firebrands and driving the stove into the middle of the floor. O'Neill gathered his wits, and ignoring the spreading fire, ran across the dark room toward the door, only to ram both bony knees into the displaced stove. Staggering away, he ran flat into the wall, driving a dowel coat hanger squarely between his eyes. Stunned, he fell backward and sat down hard, and numerous burning coals adhered to his bottom. Instantly he wished he'd kept the back hatch of his pure-wool long johns buttoned up.

O'Neill made it to the door just as a third blast propelled his tall, skinny frame—with arms flailing like windmills—into a snow bank. The snow soothed his cinder burns, and he groaned in relief. He was covered in soot, his hair a haystack. He half realized what had happened and wished it weren't true. At that very moment, the final charge went off, blowing out the only window and causing flames to shoot ten feet out of the disconnected stovepipe.

When the first blast echoed across the river valley, it caught the attention of Dawson City residents. By the second blast, they were on their porches looking up at the hillside. Wilfred watched, amused, and thought maybe one shell per package would have done it. By the third blast, the Dawson City Fire Department was mobilized, and as the fourth package detonated, they were well on their way.

But it was all too little too late. Flames shot thirty feet into the air, and the whole cabin went up in a blaze and a roar. A few .22-calibre shells went off, causing firemen to duck behind their truck. Apart from unhitching O'Neill's dogs from their backyard tethers, there was nothing anyone could do. The firemen stood downing mugs of hot tea and eating biscuits—these always seemed to turn up on such occasions—while watching the log walls cave in upon themselves, sending a cloud of sparks and ash flying skyward. When it was over, firemen sprayed down the embers, loaded the truck and, with sirens blaring, headed back victorious to the fire hall.

The crowd dispersed shortly thereafter. O'Neill's dogs wandered around, not understanding what had happened. O'Neill, with a blanket draped over his shoulders, made his way to a friend's house for the night.

"Whoever did this is going to pay," he said. "You just can't go around blowing a man's home up. I'm talking to the RCMP first thing I get settled. There will be hell to pay."

Three days later a most unusual conversation took place at the Royal Canadian Mounted Police detachment near Saint Mary's Hospital.

"I want to report a bombing and destruction of my property." O'Neill sat confidently with his knees crossed and his hat in hand.

Sitting across the table from him taking his statement was Sergeant Selnes, who had seen everything from cannibalism to murder, thievery and kidnapping in his thirty years in the Klondike. He didn't tolerate nonsense.

The sergeant wet the end of his pencil stub. "Is that so, Mr. O'Neill? And just how did this explosion come about?" He had a bit of an accent, having been born in Saskatchewan of immigrant Norwegian parents.

Over the last few days he'd heard the story many times and couldn't imagine how O'Neill had the nerve to show up on the detachment's porch with this cockamamie tale. But in the interest of justice, he was willing to listen to all sides.

"I borrowed firewood from a Mr. Wilfred Durant, whose address we all know, and he had secretly and deviously disagreed with my borrowing that wood and hid dynamite in it."

The sergeant didn't look up but continued to take notes. "And why would Mr. Durant do such a thing, Mr. O'Neill?"

"Because I borrowed the wood late at night, disturbing his sleep, and he greatly resented his sleep being disturbed. And I heard that he did a personal injury to himself, which he blamed on me."

"And what might that injury be?"

"He stubbed his toe."

The sergeant involuntarily jerked his shoulders at this answer. "And how many times did you borrow wood from Mr. Durant?"

"Three or four times, and one time he set his dog on me."

"And what did you pay Mr. Durant for this wood?"

"We have yet to discuss that end of the bargain."

At that moment Sergeant Selnes lost his temper and thrust his meaty hand across the table, grabbing O'Neill by his shirt collar, and demonstrated why he had the complete respect of every miner in the Yukon.

Bringing their faces together, he snarled between clenched teeth, "Listen here, you thieving runt, I wish enough powder had been packed in that firewood so the only question was what landed first on the other side of the river, you or the stove!"

O'Neill went limp. The sergeant released his grip and pushed him back in his chair. He then stood, tugged at the bottom of his tunic, twirled each side of his moustache and growled, "We will see you in court, Mr. O'Neill."

Months later, on a sunny spring day, the high-ceilinged courthouse hallways and the courtroom itself were packed shoulder to shoulder with people straining to see and hear every word of the proceedings. The smell of wet wool, stale tobacco and woodsmoke was soon overpowering, and a few people shouted, "Open the windows!" The court clerk quickly complied, much to everyone's relief.

O'Neill sat at a table facing the witness stand and tried unsuccessfully not to look sheepish. His face and balding head bore patches of freshly healed skin, and around his eyes were faded, yellow, raccoon rings of old shiners. He didn't look at the crowd. He only leaned over to ask the time from Sergeant Selnes seated on his right. The sergeant ignored him.

Without notice, a door swung open at the front of the room, and those in the courtroom rose and fell swiftly silent. Magistrate Arthur Goodman took his seat and signalled with his brow for the room to do the same. They did so without a word. Elevated above the masses in his black robe, Goodman struck an imposing figure with his handsome face and silver hair. The clear crack of his gavel began the proceedings. He scanned the room, left to right. Few dared return his gaze. Among men he stood higher because of his impeccable judgment and fearlessness. Arthur Goodman and his kind had brought law and order to a land that would otherwise have dissolved into lawlessness.

"I will not tolerate comments of any sort, at any time, in my courtroom. If you are wearing a hat, remove it. No smoking. No spitting. And no outbursts, or I will have you thrown in jail." He meant it. A few of the men nodded in acknowledgment. If a pin had dropped, they would have heard it.

There were three cases on the docket, one of stealing gold from a claim, a second of theft under one hundred dollars and a third of destruction of private property. Arthur Goodman quickly dispatched the first two. The claim thief had suffered enough; the gunshot wound to his buttocks drew him a lighter sentence. O'Neill was fined twenty-five dollars and thirty days of cutting wood for the RCMP woodpile. The claim thief elbowed his way out of the courtroom, but rather than following him and facing the crowd, O'Neill took a seat at the front.

The clerk called Wilfred to the stand. He'd trimmed his moustache, and his dark hair was parted in the middle and slicked down. He wore a suit jacket but no tie. His collarless striped shirt was buttoned at the neck, and his waistcoat sported a gold-nugget watch and a chain that hung just below the fifth button. He held his hat in front of him.

Magistrate Goodman demanded, "How do you plead?"

"Guilty as charged, Your Honour," Wilfred said in a clear, loud voice. A true sourdough would never avoid truth or justice.

"Sixty days on the woodpile!" Goodman boomed.

Wilfred dropped his hat.

Then the magistrate paused and his blue eyes surveyed the hushed crowd. He bellowed, "Suspended!" and crashed his gavel on the desk, breaking the head off the handle. It flew across the room, just missing Wilfred as he stooped over to pick up his hat.

The crowd was uncontrollable. The roar of approval was deafening, the windows shook, papers were launched into the air and people hugged each other. Wilfred made his way out through the crowd and had his shoulders slapped every step of the way. The din followed him out of the courthouse and down the street.

In the empty, silent courtroom, O'Neill sat alone with his head in his hands, contemplating what had happened. His stomach sank when the door opened behind him. Arthur Goodman, having exited when the celebration started, re-entered to leave by the front door. Without a glance at O'Neill, he spoke sharply. "Son, let this be a lesson to you. There is no toleration for a thief. There is no honour in thievery." Then the magistrate strode out of his courtroom. Neil stood in his place until Arthur was out of sight down the hall.

As for Wilfred ... well ... he didn't have to buy himself coffee or lunch for the next year.

Piedoe

On Eighth Avenue, where the flats of Dawson City slope up toward the Dome Hill, lived William Pringle's sister Dorothy Duffy and her husband Nathan. People called them Dot and Nat.

Ziggy, their eldest son, born in 1921, was proudly named after Dot's great-great-grandfather Ziegfeld, who had served the King of Prussia as keeper of the royal treasure and had been disgraced for borrowing "a few minor jewels." After Ziegfeld wore out his welcome in New York, he moved to Seattle. Ziegfeld's daughter Zola married Clarence Pringle, who swept her off her feet and into the great Klondike gold rush of 1896. Dot was born in a tent on the shore of Bennett Lake five days after her parents climbed the Chilkoot Pass. She was the first gold rush child, and men and women stopped their mad stampede for a moment to wish her parents and Dot well.

Iggy, the number-two son, bore the fire-breathing Irish name Ignatius after his father's great-uncle, who'd joined the Catholic uprising in Ulster against the injustice of the Brits and their bloodthirsty Black and Tans. Ignatius was hanged for throwing a grenade at a parade of soldiers, though Nat insisted on his great-uncle's innocence. Most people called Nat's son Eggy.

Nat's boon companion was a friendly black husky named Piedoe. Nat, on a trip to Whitehorse, picked Piedoe from a litter when the pup waddled over and peed on his boot. He was eight weeks old, barely old enough to leave his mother and seven brothers and sisters. His mother Boo was a silver Siberian husky; his father was a black husky named Shara, which means "little bear" in the Tutchone language.

Nat, Dot, Ziggy, Iggy, Piedoe and Dot's cat Po lived in a rambling gold-rush-era house with a faded green metal roof. The outside of the building needed painting. It had decayed far beyond what was acceptable even by Dawson City standards. The scaffolding leaning against its walls, the rusting cans of paint with paper labels weathered off and the rock-hard paintbrushes attested to Nat's good intentions of completing this job.

"The road to hell is paved with good intentions," Dot cheerfully reminded him, but she didn't push him to get the job done.

The horizontal shiplap siding on the house had warped in waves from the uncontrollable random lifting of permafrost. The floors were noticeably uneven. Anyone entering the porch walked downhill, then started uphill again in the kitchen. Stacks of mismatched cribbing timbers leaned precariously under the house, evidence of jacking up to try to level the floor beams. Piedoe found this crawlspace warm in winter and in summer a good place to escape the hordes of mosquitoes and blackflies.

Nat took Piedoe everywhere. The dog rode in the box of his battered 1928 Ford pickup, but in very cold weather, he was allowed to wedge between Nat and Dot in the cramped cab. Piedoe sat taller than both of them. Nat tried to teach him not to use his booming voice in the vehicle. More than once, Nat brought the truck to a screeching halt in the middle of the street, jumped out with both hands over his ears, and yelled back into the cab, "Don't do that, you crazy mutt!" Because both Piedoe and Dot were in the truck, people mistakenly thought that Nat was yelling at Dot. In a small town, you don't want to make that kind of mistake. Tongues will wag.

Sometimes when this happened, Nat would throw Piedoe out and make him walk home, no matter how far from town they were. A tired Piedoe would drag in late at night, then mope around the house with his feelings hurt. Finally he would rest his head in Nat's lap, and Nat would pat his head and tell him that he was a good boy and it was okay. But then, barely able to contain his annoyance, he would end up yelling, "And don't bark in the truck again!"

Piedoe had a good life. He watched the house, trotted after Nat wherever he went and was well-fed and loved. Once in a while Nat would harness him to a sled, and Dot would put Ziggy and Iggy in it and walk around town doing her shopping and picking up the mail.

Piedoe's nose and forehead had hairless white scars showing through the fur; these were scars from fights. One dog that Piedoe repeatedly fought was Howard Bungle's Sunny, a handsome yellow husky. They attacked the moment they spotted each other. Nat and others would grab tails and pull the dogs apart. The fur-flying, ferocious battles were loud and vicious but over in seconds. The dogs' thick coats prevented injury; the most damage done was a bloody lip.

When Nat drove through Sunny's part of town, Sunny would run leaping at Piedoe in the back of the truck. The ruckus would move down the road until Sunny was satisfied that he'd driven off the enemy. The dogs' dislike for each other was more obvious than the dislike that developed between Nat and Howard.

Piedoe was friendly, but if he didn't like someone, that person should stay clear. Late one Friday afternoon, Piedoe was sitting in the back of Nat's truck parked in front of the Dawson City General Store. The usual crowd had gathered to pick up groceries and engage in chit-chat. Neil O'Neill—a thief despised by man and beast, a pariah in a community of unlocked doors and unguarded woodpiles—strode along the boardwalk and stopped beside the truck. O'Neill made the mistake of grabbing Piedoe's head with both hands and giving it a vigorous, friendly shake. In the blink of an eye, Piedoe snapped at his face. O'Neill instinctively pulled back, but it was too late. Piedoe's sharp white teeth nipped the end off his nose. O'Neill recoiled, clutched his face in horror and screamed unintelligible curses through his bloody fingers. Then he ran across the street to seek aid in the Sunrise Restaurant and Hotel.

Everyone who witnessed it waited until O'Neill was out of earshot and then broke into guffaws of laughter. Some bent over, hands on knees, before they straightened and looked at each other, exchanged "Oows!" and broke into laughter again. A tale was born that day, one that would be told for decades to come. Soon afterward, someone went into the store and bought Piedoe a meaty soup bone.

Nat was having a busy Saturday. He was getting back to painting the house and he had plans to clean up the yard. He fixed himself a cup of coffee by running hot water from the sink into the half-filled cup from the night before. As he stood in his striped pajamas looking out the window, Dot called from the dining room, "Breakfast time, sweetheart." Nat sat in the captain's chair at the head of the table, and Dot slid a heaping plateful of poached eggs on toast with bacon and fried potatoes in front of him. A fresh cup of coffee followed with plenty of sugar and milk. Nat adored Dot. He adored everything she did for him, and he was full of praise for her. "Well now … how did you make this?"

"It was nothing, and you know it," Dot said, laughing and smacking him on his shoulder. She cleaned up and left to do her shopping.

Nat had barely climbed the scaffolding with his paintbrush when Piedoe, who was lying below on the lawn, stood up and growled. He looked back at Nat for support, then let out a whimper.

Three figures were coming up the street. Sunny walked in front of Howard Bungle and Neil O'Neill, whose face was still heavily bandaged, and his eyes were riveted on Piedoe. He raised his body and started forward in a stiff-legged gait. Piedoe responded with a bark, just seconds before his powerful legs pushed into the ground and launched him toward Sunny.

Nat was only halfway down the ladder when Piedoe and Sunny collided in mid-air in mid-street. Their chests thudded together heavily, and both fell back onto their haunches, only to recover and attack more ferociously than the first time. Their wide-open jaws slashed back and forth, slinging strings of saliva as they searched for a vulnerable place to clamp down and tear.

Howard and O'Neill stood back, but Nat rushed in. Winston Higgens, Nat's neighbour, was stacking his woodpile nearby. He ran through the gate in his fence to help out. Nat and Winston grabbed tails and pulled.

"Let them fight!" Howard yelled.

O'Neill said nothing and didn't help; he seemed to be enjoying the trouble. He had a short rope in his hand, and he coiled and uncoiled it as he watched.

Howard finally grabbed Sunny by the neck, taking him from Nat. Winston held Piedoe by his collar and pulled him toward the house.

"Why don't you keep your dog home?" Nat asked.

Howard laughed in Nat's face, which infuriated Nat.

O'Neill spoke in a nasal voice from the bandages covering his face. "You go to hell, Nat. I've come to take that dog. He is being put down for what he did to my nose."

It was Nat's turn to laugh. He gave out a snort before he leaped at O'Neill and punched him so hard on the side of the head that his eyes rolled back and he crumpled to the street.

Winston let Piedoe go and ran over, put his knee on O'Neill's chest and raised his bony arm and fist menacingly. "Stay down!"

O'Neill was too dizzy to get up, and Winston was too small and skinny to keep him down. But Winston knew the fighting wasn't over and he was trying to stop a donnybrook.

Nat and Howard circled each other.

Nat spat into his hands and moved his raised fists in a windmill motion.

"So you thought you were going to take my dog, did you?" Nat said.

"That dog bit my friend," Howard said.

"You're not taking my dog," Nat said. He jabbed a left, then caught Howard squarely in the middle of the face with a powerful right.

Pat Henderson, a former boxer and retired bartender, knew without looking up from his garden work what the distinctive smack of fist hitting cartilage and flesh meant. He had heard the commotion but paid little attention. Now he walked into the street to get a better look.

Howard staggered backward surprised, worried now that Nat could box. Blood streamed from his nose and onto the front of his checkered shirt. His eyes watered from the pain, and red bubbles formed and popped in his nostrils. He shouted at Nat, "What did you do that for, you jerk?" Howard smeared blood across his face with his sleeve and lunged forward, threw both arms around Nat's head and pushed him violently to the ground. There he pummelled him with his right fist. Nat was quick. He dodged the blows and wrapped one arm around Howard's head to flip him over onto his back. Both men grunted and breathed heavily. Curses peppered Pat's attempts to pull them apart by their shirt collars, but his efforts only popped their buttons. Sunny was confused. He whined and jumped forward and backward, legs together, as if waiting for a chance to join in the play.

The two men locked in an angry embrace. They squeezed each other as hard as they could and, at the same time, tried to jerk free. Nat felt Howard's teeth clamp down on top of his ear, and in one excruciatingly painful bite, Howard tore off the top of his ear. Screaming in pain and charged with adrenalin, Nat threw off Howard, stood up and kicked him as many times as he could before Pat pulled him back.

Howard rolled over onto all fours and pulled himself to his feet, dazed. His breath came in rapid gasps. He got his bearings, looked Nat in the eye and spat the piece of ear at his feet. Pat strengthened his grip on Nat's shirt and yanked him back a step.

Now both men's arms hung limply at their sides, and their legs had no strength left. Nat waved one arm flaccidly in the air as if to say, "It's over!" Winston let O'Neill up, and the men turned and staggered away in opposite directions.

"I'll get you for this," were O'Neill's parting words. He held his hand over the lump on his head.

"No, you won't," Pat Henderson said, "and if I ever see your ugly face in this part of town again, I'll do the beating." He smacked his hoe on the ground for emphasis.

O'Neill knew better than to argue with Pat. He walked away waving a hand behind him, heading home. Nat shook off Winston's help and staggered up to his house. Blood pumped from his ear and soaked his shoulder. Slurring his words, Howard called Sunny, who bounded out of a field of tall grass. Both of them headed down the street.

In his kitchen, Nat collapsed onto a chair at the table. He took off his shirt and sat in his undershirt. He rested his head on his forearms, feeling depressed that such a fine day had turned so bad. His runny nose mixed with blood and his head pounded.

The truck pulled into the driveway, and when Nat heard Dot's voice calling him, he raised his head. Dot followed the trail of blood along the porch and into the kitchen. "What happened to you?" she gasped, putting down her groceries.

"That fool O'Neill and Howard Bungle came for Piedoe. They thought he should be shot for biting O'Neill. They even had a rope. It was luckier than hell that I was home, or they would have taken him for sure."

Dot removed her hatpin, then her hat, and set it on the sideboard. She dipped a towel in warm water and dabbed his wounds. She scrutinized the ear and visibly quivered. "You will have to go see the doctor."

Iggy and Ziggy had come in and wanted to go after Howard and O'Neill.

"Let's go, Iggy. We have to fight back," Ziggy said.

Nat tried not to laugh—his ribs hurt—but he scolded them, "You stay out of this. It doesn't concern you."

But it did concern them, and because Dawson City was what it was, it would concern generations of Duffys to come.

"Let's go to the hospital," Dot said. This time she drove, and the boys sat in the middle. At the hospital Sunny lay on the front step sunning himself; oblivious to the commotion, he barely looked up as Nat walked past. In the emergency room, the doctor was removing pieces of Howard's broken teeth.

"So this is the other half," he said, holding a piece of tooth in forceps up to the light for a better look. "I didn't think Howard beat himself up."

The men glared at each other through swollen eyes. The doctor sensed that the fight had gone out of them, but as a precaution he asked, "Am I going to have to call the boys in scarlet?" The RCMP detachment was next door, and if need be, one of the nurses could easily walk over to fetch an officer.

Neither man answered. The doctor waited a moment and then spoke again, louder for emphasis, before continuing his work. "I will take your silence to be an answer in the negative."

Winston had retrieved the piece of Nat's ear and had given it to Dot. She had washed it in the kitchen sink, wrapped it in a damp cloth and put it in a teacup. But it wasn't going back on. The doctor froze the wound and cut the bite mark straight, so Nat wouldn't have to wake up to the outline of Howard's teeth every morning.

Nat's wound healed, but he would always be resentful of how Howard Bungle had disfigured him. Frequently, particularly when his glasses slipped off, he would curse under his breath, sometimes loud enough for Dot to hear. Then she would gently admonish him. Howard was always resentful that he lived the rest of his life with a missing front tooth. O'Neill understood the consequences if he bothered Piedoe again and stayed away, but Nat was always cautious that no harm should come to his dog. The Duffys and the Bungles never spoke again.

Piedoe and Sunny met on several occasions. They growled and postured, but didn't fight; they seemed to sense that enough was enough. Piedoe and Sunny lived out their lives as good and faithful dogs to their owners.

When Piedoe died at the age of twelve, Nat was heartbroken. He swore he would never have another dog. He buried Piedoe under the poplars at the top of his backyard. For days afterward, neighbourhood kids put fresh flowers on the grave, and when Nat went out at night, he placed flowers of his own.

About two months after Piedoe died, Nat was in the darkened kitchen tidying up before going off to bed. By the silver light of the autumn moon, he could clearly see the backyard, and there was Sunny, stretched out asleep on top of Piedoe's grave.

By morning Sunny was gone.

Victor the Gypsy

Being blown up by his own actions changed Neil O'Neill's life. After his stove full of stolen firewood exploded, he started to attend church regularly and got married.

Neil and his wife Faith could be seen Sunday mornings, rain or shine, headed to St. Paul's Church with Bible in hand. Faith was the youngest of seven sisters born and raised in Carmacks, a hundred miles north of Whitehorse. Her father, an accountant, managed the British Yukon Navigation Company office there and in 1933 was transferred to Dawson City. As the girls came of age, their strict mother scrutinized a steady stream of suitors at the front door. Just two months after Faith finished high school, she married Neil, who was ten years her senior.

The newlyweds moved in a few doors down from Wilfred Durant, the creator of the exploding firewood. Victor the Gypsy moved into the neighbourhood about the same time.

Wilfred was a forgiving, Christian type of guy, so it was not surprising that Neil became his friend. It also helped that Faith was keenly diplomatic and regularly took baking over to Wilfred. Some were not so forgiving and never trusted Neil for being a one-time thief. In fact Neil still pretty much stole everything he could get his hands on.

Faith knew his habits, and because the houses were close together, neighbours could hear her shouting, "You're going to get caught, you dumb ass. Then what? Will our house get blown up again and kill us both? Wait and see, Mr. Go-to-church-man, we'll all be blown to Hades." She never said Hell, just Hades, as if she didn't want to offend anyone.

Faith wasn't much of a puncher but she was a crusher. She would force Neil up against the wall with her ample body, then lean in and squeeze the breath out of him like an anaconda wrapped around a bug-eyed Amazonian creature. When Neil was released, he would collapse out of breath with indentations in his back from whatever he was pressed against. The light switches and wall tacks hurt the most. After the squeezing, Faith would stomp out of the room, slamming doors and refusing to cook or sleep with him.

Victor Caldararu, who had bought the house between the O'Neills and Taffy Bowen, got busy moving in. He didn't hear what his new neighbours were talking about. If he had heard, he wouldn't have given it much attention. Gypsies have learned to ignore the whisperings of others.

"What the hell is a gypsy doing in the Klondike anyway? That's what I'd like to know," Taffy said to Neil and Faith. "Maybe he's here to get more gold for his teeth."

"He's probably stolen everything he could at the mine in Elsa, and now he's here to do the same," said Neil, who had slung his arm around Faith's rounded shoulder and leaned on her.

Faith stepped away from Neil, and he almost lost his balance. She shot him a glance, and his face went red. Neil had made his own midnight raids on the mining town, prowling streets and back alleys in his battered pickup truck, looking for whatever he could steal.

"Well, he shouldn't be here in the first place. This is no place for a gypsy. They don't belong here," Taffy said. "They belong with their caravans in Bulgaria or someplace like that." He pounded his walking stick into the ground to make his point and walked back into his cabin muttering to himself.

Taffy thought there were too many thieves moving into the neighbourhood. First you had O'Neill, who purported to be a reformed thief, but Taffy doubted that. Now a gypsy moved in. He was going to have to lock things up, and the inconvenience made him angry.

Victor had just completed five years at the Elsa underground silver mine, where he made more bonus money than any other worker before him. He saved his money, paid cash for the house and was making plans for his future.

"Maybe I send for wife," he said to Wilfred one day.

Victor was handsome, thin and muscular, with a heavy black moustache and a gold front tooth that flashed when he smiled. "Gold from Upper Bonanza Creek," he was proud to say. "All gypsies have gold tooth. My grandmother looked like jewellery store when she laughed."

"He looks a little like Rudolph Valentino," Faith said to her neighbour Dot Duffy.

Victor was born in the Southern Balkans. His people had come to Europe from India by way of Egypt a long time ago. He was Romani and proud of it. His family was related to the Baro Shero, or the "big head" of his wandering people.

O'Neill had no problem with a gypsy living next door; in fact he liked it. "It will take the heat off, having a neighbour like that. If anything goes missing, they won't come looking for me so fast."

Faith, being a friendly neighbour, baked a pie for Victor. She and Neil went over and introduced themselves.

"This is very kind of you to do this. Please come in, sit and have tea with me," Victor said. He was happy to have company and showed Faith and Neil every courtesy. He spoke clearly and slowly so that his heavy accent wouldn't interfere with what he had to say.

"Thank you," Faith said and led the way into Victor's kitchen.

She surveyed the empty and sparsely furnished rooms. A jar used for a drinking glass sat on the kitchen table along with an empty kipper tin full of knick-knacks, a deck of worn playing cards and a cribbage board with matchsticks for markers. A bookshelf hung on one wall, and a collection of well-worn hardcover books leaned to one side. A quick glance told Faith, to her surprise, that Victor read Shakespeare and Kipling.

"*Wee Willie Winkie*," she said pointing to the books.

"Yes, Vee Villie," Victor said.

Packing boxes and suitcases lay on the floor throughout the house. Some lay open, and Victor had apparently tried to find places for their contents. Although he said he planned to stay, Faith guessed his gypsy spirit would not let him move in completely.

Victor removed clothing from a kitchen chair and pulled another one from the living room, wiping it clean with his hand. "Please sit down. I make tea." He filled the kettle with water from the tap and placed it on the electric hotplate.

"So where do you keep the chickens you steal?" Neil asked with a grin.

Victor was standing at the counter with his back turned and didn't answer right away. When he turned to face Neil his eyes were narrowed to slits and his body was tense. "Steal chickens? What do you mean, steal chickens?"

Faith went red in the face, and Neil realized his joke wasn't very funny. Victor looked angry.

Trying to get off the hook, Neil shrugged his shoulders and stammered, "I mean, you are gypsy, aren't you? I was joking."

Faith rolled her eyes. Even she knew the importance of first impressions. Neil didn't seem to care, because he didn't have a reputation that he wanted to impress anyone with.

Victor tried unsuccessfully not to glare at Neil. He didn't like this man. He looked at his cigarette, which he held between his thumb and forefinger, and decided to give Neil a little benefit of the doubt. He said with a smile, "Chickens? Store has them. I buy them there." He waved his hand in the air and laughed a soft laugh.

"But come now, let's not talk chickens. Let's drink tea and visit," he said. "Tell me, how long you been living here?"

Neil breathed a sigh of relief and took a sip of the tea.

Victor knew that the slight had sealed their relationship. From now on Neil would be someone to disrespect and insult. Gypsy insults had been honed for centuries and were always delivered with a smile.

They visited for a while longer. Faith got up first, and when she was out of earshot, Victor politely bowed to Neil and said, "You have nice house, nice wife, you are very lucky man. Too bad people have no trust in you."

Neil's eyes went wide as saucers, and he started to respond. Thinking better of it, he said nothing but scurried across the yard to catch up to Faith.

"What an ass, that man," Victor said to himself as he watched them walk out the gate and around the fence toward their own home. "Why do I have neighbour like that all the time?"

Fuming, Neil went down to Cooper's Grocery and Hardware Store and bought two keyed-alike locks. He placed them on the counter and told Richard Cooper, "Got new neighbours, got new locks."

Richard didn't like Neil because he had probably stolen from the store. He'd never caught him red-handed, but after fifty years in the business, he had a sense about the people who walked in the door. Richard was nobody's fool. He put two and two together with the locks and the new neighbour.

"Need some new security, do you?" Richard asked.

Neil couldn't have answered any faster than he did. "You could say that—if your new neighbour happens to be a gypsy!"

Richard had delivered supplies over to the Elsa Mine for many years. He had met Victor and liked him. Richard was also too old to hold his tongue, so as he opened the ancient cash register and handed Neil his change, he said, "Seems like the kettle is calling the pot black these days, ever since some firewood exploded."

Neil absolutely hated being reminded of that event. Even more he hated anyone challenging his opinion. He slammed the door behind him when he left the store.

Soon afterward, Richard Cooper hired Victor to make his deliveries and gave him a five percent discount at the store, where Victor immediately bought material for his new home.

Taffy saw Victor carrying cans of paint into his house, and with a wave of his hand, Victor invited him over to see what he'd done so far. He proudly walked Taffy through the three small rooms painted in purples, greens and blues.

"Damn gypsy has the place looking like a rainbow," Taffy reported later to Wilfred. "I thought I was inside a Ukrainian Easter egg."

When he'd completed the interior, Victor painted the exterior to match. He also removed the warped and weather-worn fascia boards and with his coping saw scrolled new boards with elaborate detailed scenes of people, animals and symbols.

"Legend and stories of my people. The moon, the stars and the sun," he said.

"Finest scrollwork I've ever seen," Pat Henderson, the owner of the Flora Dora Café, told William Pringle. "Very detailed."

Victor loved his home and lavished care on it. The neighbours took some time to get used to it.

"It will grow on you," said William, Wilfred's friend and sometime business partner.

Taffy scoffed. "Who does he think he is, bringing that junk onto my street? Looks like a circus, it does. The only things missing are a giant Ferris wheel and fireworks."

As much as Taffy was concerned about Victor being a thief, he was more concerned about Neil being a proven thief, and a wood thief at that. He told Wilfred, "That Neil, I'm sure he's up to his old tricks. I can't leave anything out without it going missing. I'm going to catch that rat red-handed one of these days. Then you're going to see action, I tell you."

On sunny days Victor liked to work in the garden, but on rainy Saturdays he sat inside the doorway sipping tea and smoking aromatic pipe tobacco rolled in Zig-Zag cigarette papers. He had an old gramophone and played scratchy records of Django Reinhardt, the famed jazz guitarist. In the dim room, where light struggled through the drawn curtains, he would drift off to another place in another time. After a while he would sit up and say, "This is true gypsy music by a true gypsy," and pretend to strum a guitar.

Victor liked Faith. She was smart and kind, but more than that, he liked her because she beat up Neil.

"You're good woman, Faith. Neil is very lucky man to have you for his wife."

Sitting on his porch, they talked for hours.

"I started work in Elsa Mine as slop man," Victor explained. "I carried buckets of toilet slop out of the mine all day every day. Then they let me be driller's helper, then I become a driller. If I had not been gypsy, I would be top boss manager. I would sit in office, drink coffee, sleep with feet on table and have nice secretary." He traced the outline of a shapely woman with his hands.

Faith wasn't convinced he would have made "top boss manager," but he had the ability to pull more tonnage out of the mine than any other single person in its history. Banking a small fortune even after paying for his house, he was able to live simply but comfortably.

Victor met Faith's sister and took an interest in her. "Lily is not gypsy woman but she is good person. I think she likes me."

"I'm sure she does, Victor," Faith said.

"I think I take her to baseball game this Saturday. She told me, 'I like good sports.'"

Faith tried to explain what Lily meant, but Victor didn't seem to understand. Finally she said, "That would be nice."

Victor did date Lily for the better part of the summer, but come fall, she took up with the new dredge master at Bear Creek. He was widowed and needed a mother for his four children. Lily wasn't really keen on becoming a mother overnight, but the status of being a dredge master's wife was too attractive. They had a whirlwind romance, and quicker than you could say "Bonanza Creek," Lily and the dredge master were married.

"That okay," Victor said, "I never like her anyway. She lied. I took her to baseball game and tennis game, but she didn't like, she told me so."

Late one night, about two o'clock in the morning, Victor was awakened by scraping and clinking sounds in the back of his house. He sat up and waited to hear more. Sure enough, something was out back in the shed attached to his house.

"Could be bear," he said as he pulled on his pants and slipped his feet into his slippers.

Through the kitchen window he could see a person bent over his tool bench. Victor went out the front door, picked up a piece of scrap copper plumbing pipe that he'd left on the porch and silently walked around back.

Neil O'Neill was too busy pocketing tools to notice Victor coming up behind him. Victor stuck the copper pipe in the nape of Neil's neck and said, "Don't move, gangster, or your brains make spaghetti." Neil froze, raised his hands and dropped the tools clattering back onto the bench. He was dressed in his bathrobe, pyjamas and slippers. His thievery was so casual that he didn't even dress for the occasion.

"Bend over bench," Victor commanded.

Neil hesitated, so Victor said, "Or your head get one big hole for chicken to fly through."

Neil bent over the bench.

"Drop pants," Victor snarled, jabbing the pipe more forcefully into Neil's neck.

Neil let out a shrill, girlish scream, but hooked a thumb on each side of his pyjamas and pushed them down below his buttocks.

"Don't move," Victor said, then tipped the lid off a paint can that held brushes soaking in turpentine. He selected the biggest one, and with one swift movement, painted Neil's backside.

"Now run like hell before your ass burn off," he said.

Neil covered the distance to his house in record-breaking time. Victor heard him yelling for Faith and watched as the lights in the rooms came on one by one.

The best the nurse at the hospital could do was to wash the area thoroughly with warm soapy water; it did help to ease the sting. Faith then applied liberal layers of white ointment.

"It's costing us one tube of ointment every time we cover your skinny behind," she said, lathering it on.

Neil hung his head. Even in pain, there was no peace for him from this woman.

The next day the town was abuzz with the news that Neil had met Yukon justice once again. A parade of well-wishers turned up at Victor's house, and when he went uptown, everyone wanted to shake his hand—but no one offered to take him to lunch.

Taffy was the first to congratulate him and the happiest. "What a good neighbour I have, the best there ever was." He then invited Victor over to his house for the first time.

Amongst the crowd of visitors was RCMP Constable Smithers, who'd been sent to arrest Victor for assault.

"Assault with turps?" Wilfred scoffed, and he and Taffy tried to talk the officer out of it.

The officer said, "Charges have been laid, so now it's up to the magistrate to decide."

Faith went around the neighbourhood apologizing profusely for her husband's thievery. "I don't know what I'm going to do with him. He just won't stop."

"Don't you worry, dear, this has nothing to do with you," Dot told her.

"But yes it does, Dot," Faith said tearfully. "This is the most embarrassing thing I've ever had to face in my life."

To make amends, Faith hauled out a trunk of contraband that Neil had been storing and dumped it onto the boardwalk outside her house for all to pick through.

"There's my damn garden shears," Taffy said. "I wondered where the hell they'd walked off to."

"And look here," said Wilfred. "If it isn't my brace and bit."

The rest of the street went through the pile, and people took what was theirs. Some even took what wasn't theirs in compensation for something they'd lost.

When his court day arrived, Neil still couldn't sit comfortably on his turpentine burn and squirmed in his place. Faith sat behind him wiping the tears from her eyes with a pink handkerchief. Neil turned and said, "Don't sob so loudly."

"Shut up," Faith snapped back.

The courtroom was packed to capacity. It was a typical day: a few assaults, one drunk and disorderly and a few break and enters.

When it came Neil's turn to state his case, he hummed and stuttered for so long that he was hardly understood. He had brought the pastor from his church to speak for him, but even the pastor had a difficult time finding enough positive things to say about Neil. The pastor's unenthusiastic presentation did more harm than good. Neil was a thief through and through, and nothing was going to change that, not even religion.

Magistrate Arthur Goodman looked exasperated. O'Neill was back in his court, accused of almost exactly the same thing as he had been after Wilfred Durant put gunpowder in his firewood.

"I'm not happy with you, Mr. O'Neill, not happy at all," Arthur said as he looked over O'Neill's papers. "Caught stealing again, and Mr. Caldararu took matters into his own hands to punish you. I see here by the report that your buttocks are somewhat the worse for wear."

There was a titter of laughter in the courtroom, but after one sharp glance from Arthur, everything went silent again.

"This is becoming a habit, a bad habit. I'm fining you a hundred dollars for thievery, and when your burned butt is up to it, you can go spend thirty days on the RCMP woodpile cutting cordwood."

Neil shook his head in disagreement. He hated the woodpile. Everyone in town could see you working on it, and that was embarrassing. He turned and whined to Faith, "I've been punished enough. This isn't fair."

Faith ignored him, but she couldn't conceal her look of disgust.

"As for you, Mr. Victor Caldararu, you are to spend thirty days in the RCMP jail for common assault."

Everyone in the courtroom sat in silence, holding their breath, waiting for the gavel to come crashing down and the word "suspended" to roar out for all to hear. But it never came. Magistrate Goodman stood, turned and walked through the door at the back, with the court clerk following quickly behind him. The room sat in stunned silence. The drama had not played out as they had expected.

"Those gypsies, always causing trouble," the clerk said as he helped Arthur off with his robe.

"Gypsy or anyone else has nothing to do with it," Arthur said. "I'm tired of people taking the law into their own hands. Let this be a lesson to all of them."

Victor was handcuffed by the officer and led away to jail. Faith stopped him in the hall and said, "Don't worry, I will take care of your place."

Later that day Wilfred and William made sure Victor's house was closed up. They met Neil coming down the boardwalk and warned him, "If we see you even come near Victor's house, you will get a beating so you can't walk. We mean it."

Neil looked away and didn't say anything.

That night Faith could be heard giving Neil the dressing-down of his life. In the morning he was still asleep on the old couch on the front porch. People laughed out loud as they wished him good morning on their way to work. Neil pretended not to hear them, and as soon as Faith unlocked the door, he picked up his blanket and ran inside to the warmth of the kitchen.

Faith baked and cooked for Victor every day he was in jail. She also made enough food for the young RCMP officers tending the cells, who couldn't hide their pleasure at getting decent cooking. They were not allowed to marry until they completed five years of service, and were on their own as far as housekeeping went.

"If I have to eat one more of Sergeant Selnes's moose pot pies, I think I will desert," Constable Smithers told Faith as he took a second helping. Dipping slices of thick rye bread into a plate of steaming pork and beans, he dryly added, "I will be sorry when Victor's time is up." He asked Victor, "Could you do something else, like throw a rock through a store window or something?"

"No, no," Victor said, waving his index finger in the air. "Once I go, I'm gone and never come back." He seemed to lose his appetite and put down his plate. Quietly he trudged back to his cell, pulled the door closed behind him, lay down on the bunk and drew the blanket over his head.

"You hardly ate anything again," Faith shouted so Victor could hear, but he didn't respond. She gathered up the dishes and left.

After thirty days the lights came back on in Victor's place, and the neighbours dropped by to see if he needed anything. Faith called on Wilfred, and together they went over to see how Victor was.

"I think he might need some cheering up," she said.

There was no response to the knock on the door, so they let themselves in. Victor stood by the kitchen table, where a Bible lay open. A grey blanket was draped over his shoulders, and he held a small, worn book in one hand. The other clutched the folds of the blanket to his chest.

He put up his hand to silence them. "Listen to this. Tell me if Shakespeare is true," he said. In his strong accent he read slowly, "Hath not a Jew eyes? Hath not a Jew hands, organs, dimensions, senses, affections, passions: fed with the same food, hurt with the same weapons ... " He paused there.

Wilfred knew the passage well and recited the last line with him.

"Poor Jew. I'm very glad I'm not Jew," Victor said. "They have terrible life. No justice, fairness or anything. When God made man, he made the Jew last. I feel badly for them. I've met them, they are good people. If you don't like Jews, you don't hurt because you don't like. If a Jew comes to Dawson, we should welcome him, make him feel at home, not steal from him, not make him feel alone. Not put him in prison. That's what I hope for Jew." By the end of this, Victor was passionately thrusting out his arms as if begging for understanding.

No one said anything. They were too surprised.

"Never mind," Victor said, waving an arm in the air. "It's just words from long ago, it means nothing." He put the book on the shelf, took off the blanket and draped it over the back of a chair. "Come and sit down. I'll make tea. We celebrate and never speak of these things again."

Soon the three of them were sipping hot tea, enjoying each other's company. Wilfred told of his mammoth find on Bonanza Creek a few years ago, and when he described how they'd been scared out of their wits, they all had a good laugh. Next door, Taffy looked out his window at the sounds of conversation and laughter coming from the brightly lit kitchen.

The gypsy must be having one of those parties they have, he thought. Then he went out and made sure his sheds were locked up.

Buford's Tooth

Born and raised in Mayo, the brothers Buford and Craven Clutterbuck followed their father and laboured in the Elsa underground silver mine. They worked as a team of blasters.

"That nitroglycerine is good for your heart but it gives you bad headaches," Craven said, reaching for the bottle of aspirin in his locker before he walked home from work.

After twenty years the headaches got to them. They were offered jobs as catskinners hauling the silver ore from the mine to the riverboats and barges at Mayo Landing, but they wanted to follow their bosom buddy Victor the Gypsy to Dawson, so they quit.

"Too bad we weren't here when that stealing went on. We would have stood by you, Victor," Buford said over a cup of tea the day they arrived.

Buford was named after the first British sailor to be devoured by a great white shark off the coast of Australia in 1770. Apparently, after so many months at sea, young Buford Gateman spotted some near-naked aboriginal girls on the beach, jumped ship and tried to swim to shore. The great white bit him neatly in two, leaving the upper torso and head floating in the water. The captain's log recorded that the shark must have known Buford had no brains, since he took the best part.

"That is the funniest thing I ever heard," Orville Clutterbuck said.

Craven was named after the brand of cigarettes his mother, Claris Clutterbuck, enjoyed. She was a farmer's daughter from Saskatchewan who'd smoked Craven A since she was sixteen years old and died of lung cancer at fifty-six.

"I have to have my cigs and coffee," she said.

"I'm just thankful she didn't add the A and name me after the place they were made. I could have been called Craven A Jamaica."

Claris, who had ignored her children all her life, tried to apologize on her deathbed. Craven and Buford weren't buying it.

"Sometimes 'better late than never' is crap," Buford said.

"We had no mom," Craven said.

Craven was over six feet tall and had not an ounce of fat on him. His veins were like road maps on his arms and legs. His hands and feet were long and thin, a sprout of uncombed red hair topped his narrow head and wire-rimmed glasses sat crookedly on his broken nose. He personally didn't care how he looked; fashion to him was a new pair of green GWG work pants and matching shirt. He had an inquisitive nature about crime and justice, and when people got to know him, they started to think that if Sherlock Holmes had a father, it might be Craven. When someone mentioned this, he admitted that he really was the father of Sherlock Holmes. Not knowing a lot about Arthur Conan Doyle, some people believed him. Years later, when he died, his friends wanted to write "Here Lies the Father of Sherlock Holmes" on his headstone, but his wife stopped them in time.

"It's funny how rumours start and grow," Buford said.

Parents would point out Craven to their children. "Look, there goes the father of Sherlock Holmes, the famous detective." They thought Sherlock was a real person.

Buford, the younger sibling, was the opposite of Craven. He was a man of girth at three hundred pounds, bald as a billiard ball—he played billiards with great skill—and a thick beard that hid the bottom half of his face and ended at the top of his ears. For such a big man, he had dainty hands and feet. Buford was determined to do as little as possible in life, and if he could have been anything at all, he would have been a famous writer and poet.

That is why they pooled their savings and bought a bungalow with white bevelled siding next door to Pat Henderson and down the street from Robert Service's home on Eighth Avenue.

"Maybe the spirit of Robert will rub off on me and end the writer's block I've had for the past ten years. Then I'll become famous," Buford said.

"I doubt it," Craven said. "You hardly wrote anything before."

Buford had the most childish of faults—craving to become the centre of attention—but he rarely succeeded. "It's because his mom never paid attention to him," Craven bemoaned. It was by chance that Buford found attention. Over the years his teeth had either been knocked out of his head or fallen out through neglect.

"Maybe it would have been wise to have brushed every day, as father told me, and listened more than spoken in those bar fights," Buford said to Craven and Victor as they drank coffee and repaired a bicycle chain at the kitchen table.

"That's why God gave you two ears and one mouth," Craven said.

Victor agreed with Craven. "Yes, very true what Craven said. Two ears, one mouth, God very wise."

Finally Buford had only one tooth in his head and that was a top front one. He became obsessively possessive about this last tooth and determined to keep it. He quit playing hockey. The players who had been boarded by his bulk were thankful.

Buford had a beaming smile, so the tooth gave his face the appearance of a large, round jack-o'-lantern carved out for Halloween. The tooth began to garner Buford more attention than he'd ever had, and he loved it.

"It's only a tooth, but I'm famous," he said. "That's all it takes, a tooth."

"You must be desperate," Craven said.

Buford brushed three times a day and flossed the tooth with a shoelace as though he were pulling a rope around a hitching post. He had the tooth capped with gold and admired it every morning in the mirror.

"That lovely tooth, you make gypsy proud," Victor said.

"Let me pull that damn thing out," Craven demanded. "It's the ugliest thing I ever saw. Just let me get the pliers." He would run out to the shed and rummage through piles of rusty tools in their beaten-up storage boxes.

The men moved in their sparse furniture and had a housewarming party. Buford cooked and baked all day while Craven tidied the already cluttered house. They had a bad habit of bringing in mechanical things, mostly bicycles, to be worked on. The kitchen looked like a workshop, with tools strewn about and a sawhorse in the corner. They used the sink to wash greasy parts, and it was paint-stained from washing brushes.

"We need a woman's touch. You should get married, Buford," Craven said.

"Not on your life, Craven. If anyone had a chance to march down the aisle, it would be you, the more handsome of us."

Craven never knew if Buford was kidding or not.

Neil, Faith, Taffy, Wilfred, Nat, Dot and their boys plus others showed up and brought small gifts for the house.

Dot brought tea towels and wrinkled her nose at the kitchen. "Don't use these for grease rags," she said, opening the sink door and hanging them on the towel bar inside.

Faith baked a pie. Wilfred brought a Home Sweet Home wall hanging, and Victor had carved a plaque of the moon, stars and sun, which Craven hung over the front door.

"Bring you lots of luck, this gypsy thing. Keep bad people out," Victor said. When he said "bad people," he looked at Neil.

Neil got up immediately, grabbed his coat and dragged Faith out the door. Craven watched him walk down the street, still dragging Faith and waving his arm in the air, obviously upset, and said, "It's so easy to set O'Neill off on another tirade."

Victor's eyes narrowed, and he took a draw on his cigarette as he looked out the window at their departure.

Buford didn't agree with what Victor did, but they didn't say anything. After all, it was just a friendly housewarming, and Faith's pie was delicious.

"I don't like being hard on Faith, but Neil—that's okay," Victor said, shrugging his shoulders and waving his arm.

The men settled in and became part of the community. Buford worked as a cook at the Flora Dora Café, where a sirloin steak with all the trimmings cost sixty-five cents. With Buford's culinary skills, business picked up, and the tables and booths were packed with diners appreciating every mouthful.

"Best damn cook I ever had, that Buford," said Pat Henderson, the owner, as he shuffled about taking orders and waiting on tables.

Craven worked part-time at the library and became a man about town who did odd jobs. He guarded at the jail, helped out at Cooper's store, cleared snow for the city and substituted for absent teachers at the school. He was never without work.

Buford liked being around people, which gave him more of a chance to show off his tooth. He would often leave his grill to visit the tables. Wiping his hands on his apron, he would ask the patrons how their meal was, joking and sharing news all the while. "Caught those salmon this morning right out front here," he would say, pointing out the window to the river. "Dove right in and caught them, slippery beggars they were."

If Victor was in the restaurant, he would pipe up, "It's truth. I see Buford catch fish with tooth. Looked like great whale getting dinner."

Building on his celebrity status, Buford made a point of greeting tourists as they descended from their riverboat journey and soon had them thinking he was a gold miner off the creeks.

"My God, you have the most interesting tooth, and to think you helped discover gold on Bonanza Creek with Mr. Carmack and Mr. Skookum," Victor heard an English tourist exclaim. The man took a picture of Buford standing at his grill with spatula in hand, flipping eggs and laughing for the folks back home.

"You should be on a postcard," the tourist's wife said as she stood on her toes and peered into Buford's mouth for a better look. She wanted to tug at the tooth, but Buford wouldn't let her.

After work one evening Buford lay on the couch, barely able to peer over his ample stomach, polishing his tooth.

Craven stood by the sink, having pushed parts of a bicycle aside, scooping the last bits of a plate of stew into his mouth with a knife. Gravy dripped onto his shirt. He found Dot's tea towel buried in a pocket of his overalls and wiped his face and hands clean.

"Mighty delicious, that stew!" he shouted.

They had no reason to shout—they could hear each other clearly—but it was a bad habit from their days as blasters in the Elsa mine.

Then, as if he'd just had a second thought, he said, "I'll give you a poke of gold if you let me pull that tooth."

"Where in hell are you going to get that kind of money?" Buford asked.

"I don't have that kind of money right now, but I will get it. That tooth is such an embarrassment to our family, I don't see how you can keep it. How are you ever going to get married with that damn tooth sticking out? You'll scare the girls away!"

"First of all, take a good look in the mirror and see who is an embarrassment to the family, and second, I ain't getting married no time, no place, no how! And furthermore, you're hurting my feelings, Craven."

It was true. Buford had soft feelings, and they were hurt easily. But Craven couldn't keep his mouth shut, the tooth bothered him so much.

Summer left with the last riverboat, and an early winter howled across the land, bringing deep snow and metal-snapping cold. The drafty house held little heat, and not having brought in winter wood, the brothers tore down the backyard shed to feed the hungry stove.

As they crowbarred boards from the walls, their teeth chattered, and they hunched their shoulders to draw their arms close to their bodies. Craven couldn't look at Buford. The tooth was moving up and down like a needle on a sewing machine and beating out a staccato rhythm on the bottom gum.

"Why don't you send Morse code greetings to all our friends in Elsa while you're at it?" Craven yelled.

Buford stood for a moment with his arms piled high with wood and his nose running. Then he threw the boards at Craven's feet and stomped off to the house, yelling over his shoulder, "Go to hell! Pack the wood yourself."

In the next few days their driveway piled high with snow, and the battery froze solid in their battered blue Ford Model T truck. By early January the cold and dark were straining relationships throughout the Yukon.

One night, Craven woke from a restless sleep. He thought he'd heard someone calling his name. He looked across the room. Buford lay on his back with his mouth wide open, snoring noisily. The gold cap flickered in the oil lamp's light like a one-ounce nugget. Craven knew the tooth had called him.

"I'm coming," he whispered and reached under his bed for his tool box.

Silently Craven rummaged until he found an ancient pair of pliers. He walked across the room on his toes in his sleeping robe, poised himself over Buford and brought the pliers closer to the tooth. Just as the metal jaws were about to snap shut, the tassel on his nightcap brushed Buford's face and woke him. Buford opened his eyes and screamed horrifically. Craven jumped up and ran madly around the room in circles.

"You monster!" Buford yelled. "If Pa was here, he would kick your ass, you idiot."

"If Pa was here, he would smack you until that tooth dropped out," Craven shouted back, waving the pliers at him.

"Don't ever try to murder Mabeleine again," Buford cried. He pulled the pillow tightly over his head and rolled over muttering to himself.

Craven was puzzled. Mabeleine? She must be an old girlfriend he'd never known about.

At breakfast the next morning, Craven lied, "I did that because I had a vision in my dreams. I've found that poke of gold to pay you for your tooth."

Buford was skeptical. "A vision? A poke of gold? You tried to rip a tooth out of my head. Make no excuses."

"I did have a vision," Craven said, "and it told me that this year's Yukon River ice breakup is going to be exactly as it was thirty-eight years ago in 1896, on May 19 at 2:35 in the afternoon."

Buford shook his head and snorted a laugh. "This is all too crazy," he said. "You're crazy."

"Furthermore, with this information we're not only going to win the gold, but you, my brother, are going to be remembered forever and go down in Dawson's history. People will never forget how your tooth was pulled, and you will have all the attention you want."

"How's that?" Buford asked.

"You know how the tripod on the river ice is wired to a clock? When the ice breaks up, it trips the time. Well, because we know the time, we'll attach your tooth to the tripod with fishing line. When the river goes out, so does your tooth. It's a sure thing. Remember, I had a vision. You have to do this for history and the gold, Buford," Craven said, pointing his finger in Buford's face.

Buford wanted to grab it and break the end of it off. *Vision smishion*, he thought. But he said, "I'll think about it. But the thing is, once the tooth is pulled, it's gone."

"But the story will live forever," Craven said.

"I don't know." Buford shook his head.

Life around the cabin deteriorated after that. Buford was extra protective of his tooth and went to bed wearing an old baseball catcher's mask that hardly fit his large, round face. Craven didn't help matters by carrying the pliers around and snapping them open and closed. The sound sent chills up Buford's spine, and he feared for his Mabeleine.

At the dinner table one evening, Craven and Buford were peeling fruit for dessert.

"Did you really have a vision, Craven?" Buford asked quietly as he reached for an apple.

"Yep," Craven said.

"And do you think the river will pull my tooth and we will win the gold?"

"Yep," Craven said again.

"Do you really think me and my tooth will be famous?"

"Are you thinking of doing this?" Craven asked.

"I'm thinking," Buford said, and bit into an apple. He always wolfed his food, and in one gulp he swallowed most of the apple.

Craven stared in amazement. Where the tooth had once stood, there was nothing but an empty field. Buford hadn't noticed that anything had changed. He got up from the table and went to nap on the couch.

That night Craven woke with a great weight on his chest. Buford was perched on him like a gargoyle on a flying buttress with a pair of pliers clamped firmly onto his front tooth. Buford leaned closer, looking crazier than Craven had ever seen anyone looking before, and quietly said, "I too had a vision, Craven. It said, an eye for an eye and a tooth for a tooth." For one second Craven was distracted and wondered when Buford had gotten religious. Then Buford gave a solid tug, and the tooth came out like a sink plug on a chain.

He waved the tooth in front of Craven's face. Craven went white and his eyes bulged. He screamed in pain, threw Buford off and ran with his hand over his mouth to find water and a towel. The pliers had axle grease on them and tasted terrible.

"You idiot!" Craven screamed, spitting blood. "You crazy, out-of-your-mind idiot!"

Neither of them slept for the rest of the night, each now being afraid of the other, and in the morning they silently turned their backs. They maintained monastic silence for months, which they both admitted was difficult in the small house. Craven didn't even try to explain; he knew Buford believed with all his heart that he had somehow stolen Mabeleine.

"Where is she?" he would ask in the dark of the night, causing Craven to rise up on one elbow and squint to see that his brother was still in bed. He wasn't sure if Buford was awake or talking in his sleep. It gave him reason to be afraid.

When the river ice broke up, the relationship thawed. Even Victor could see Buford was becoming depressed. One day Craven said, "I can't see us going on like this, Buford. Either we settle this or we should sell and get separate cabins."

Buford didn't respond for a few days, but then he agreed. "I can forgive you for losing us the poke of gold, since now we can't pull my tooth on the trip wire, but I cannot forgive you for taking my tooth. Not just now, anyway."

"I didn't touch your damn tooth. You ate it," Craven said.

Buford got tears in his eyes and turned his head away. "Yeah, sure," he said.

Craven could see that he had to make up with Buford even though he was not guilty.

"You should get new tooth for Buford," Victor said. "His tooth was like friend, made him happy. People liked Buford with tooth."

Dr. Gillis was back for the summer, so Craven had him make a front-tooth bridge and encouraged Buford to get a full set of dentures.

"I hate dentists," Buford said, but he eventually gave in to Victor and Craven's encouragement and had the work done. Once it was done, though, he refused to smile. "Makes me look like an idiot," he said.

A week after the dental work was finished, Craven noticed that teeth were disappearing from Buford's head. He mentioned it to Victor.

"Just wait," Victor said with a wink. "I know what Buford is doing. Not happy."

Months later there was only one tooth left, and Mabeleine was back in her spot. Buford looked like his old self; people wanted to see the tooth, and his happy celebrity status returned.

"I would like to go see Dr. Gillis again," he said.

Craven made an appointment.

"You're lucky you caught me," Dr. Gillis said. "I'm leaving tomorrow, going back to Seattle. You're the last patient this summer."

When Buford emerged four hours later from the dentist's office, he had a gold-capped tooth with a diamond insert. He was so happy he couldn't stop smiling, and everyone got a good look at the new Buford. He walked around the restaurant like a peacock in love.

He called the tooth Gertie after a gold-rush dance hall girl and kept a picture of her in his wallet.

Townspeople called him Diamond Tooth Buford, or Diamond for short.

"I love my name and I love my tooth and I love my brother who got me Gertie to replace Mabeleine," Buford told everybody.

After all the trouble, Craven now left Buford's tooth alone and never found fault with him for anything ever again. Well, not for a while, anyway. He realized that a person's happiness is much more important than a person's appearance and that a quest for fame has to run its course.

"And that's a law of the Yukon, Victor," he said.

"That's good law, very good law," Victor said. "I like it."

Mimosa Nightingale

Craven Clutterbuck was superstitious beyond anything that could be considered normal. "I'm sure bad things will befall me if I don't complete my rituals," he said. "I'm a fearful man."

He had a full inventory of standard superstitions: black cats, walking under ladders and putting new shoes on a table. He was much more imaginative in the ones he invented for himself. In the morning he got out of bed, walked backward to the door, turned the door handle five times each way then hopped on one foot out of the room. He avoided crossing any street until he had recited the alphabet. If he got a haircut, he tipped the barber exactly seven cents in pennies, and he always said "sis-boom-bah" as he hammered a nail. All these actions and more he recorded in thick pencil in a lined scribbler. He made his entries daily.

His brother Buford and Victor the Gypsy watched Craven heading to work down Eighth Avenue. Every couple of steps he would hop.

"It's like he lives in a world of his own," Buford said.

"I like it very much," Victor said.

Neil and Faith were walking behind Craven on their way uptown.

"He and that gypsy are nutcases," Neil said.

"You're the nut," Faith said. "People had to blow you up just to keep you in order."

Craven had organized and chaired the Dawson City Spiritualists' Fellowship. Young, blond Hudson Godwit was the secretary-treasurer. The group had no problem recruiting members; Dawson was full of people interested in spiritual things. Craven had more of a problem finding a place to meet, because proprietors were wary of such a group. But the Carnegie library had just recently been remodelled into a Freemasons' Hall, and the group rented a basement meeting room once a month.

Craven was sincere, but fake conversations with the departed and levitations unfortunately led the fellowship astray.

"See if you can contact my dead partner and ask him where he stashed that deed for our gold mine on Brewer Creek," one old sourdough member asked.

"They're just a bunch of spook chasers," Miss Mimosa Nightingale said to Mr. Cooper as she picked up groceries from his store.

"You got that right," Mr. Cooper said, "but half the town will turn up for their meetings."

"I tend to deal with reality, not half-baked ideas that have no foundation," Mimosa said, handing her money to him with a henna-tattooed hand.

"I go to church," Mr. Cooper said, and at that the conversation ended.

The DCSF sometimes met at Buford and Craven's house. Buford would have nothing to do with it. He left before the fellowship members arrived and returned home only after they left. On winter nights he would sit in the permafrost-tilted Occidental Hotel bar while they met, and in the summer he would walk the hills behind the house. He would make a joke when he came in the door by spinning around three times, bowing, whistling "Jimmy Crack Corn" and hopping on one foot around the kitchen table so that his great weight caused the dishes to rattle in the cupboards.

Craven was infuriated by Buford's disrespect. "Don't make fun of the spirits," he warned.

Buford snickered and went off to polish his tooth.

Mimosa, an attractive middle-aged lady with dark hair and dark eyes, lived at the north end of Dawson City next door to Chief Daniel and his extended family. It was rumoured that she was to be married once at Mayo Landing, but the groom had jilted her. Grieving, she hadn't taken off her wedding dress for a week. The people in Dawson didn't know who he was, but someone had heard that he was dark and handsome and looked something like Victor the Gypsy.

Mimosa lived alone on an inheritance left by her father, who'd made a fortune on a claim twenty-seven above the Discovery claim. Robert Nightingale had been one of the lucky ones who'd lived and mined at Forty Mile, fifty miles downstream from Dawson, where George Carmack registered the Bonanza Creek discovery claim on August 21, 1896. The news of the gold strike had spread like wildfire, and like many others, he'd dropped everything and sped to the creek in time to make his claim. Once he got wealthy, Robert sent to Seattle for his bride, Mary. A year after her arrival, Mimosa, their only child, was born in a tent on the creek with a Chinese cook and a Norwegian schoolteacher acting as midwives.

"I never delivered baby before," Changchang said.

"Ya, me neither, but I heard my neighbour in Fredrikstad explain it once," Frieda said.

The baby was delivered without a problem. When news of the birth spread up and down the creeks, the homesick miners showered Mary with gifts.

Robert was handsome, and Mary was strikingly beautiful. Mimosa grew up a beautiful woman. She was also highly intuitive. She read cards, palms, tea leaves and whatever else a person might want. These were all props, but she used them to make it easier for people to understand her readings. She only had to hold someone's hand for a moment to understand that person. Sometimes even that wasn't necessary.

"I have to humour people with the cards, otherwise they won't believe I can do it," she told Craven once. "I think I can be of help to people, but at times I hate my intuition. It tells me too many things."

Craven was very interested in Mimosa. "Beautiful and an oracle," he sighed.

Mimosa liked Craven. He was honest and her friend, but she didn't agree with his spiritualism.

"Those table levitations, trumpet blasts from the other world and fortune telling aren't real, Craven. Don't be taken in by that nonsense," she said, "especially if you are asked to pay money for it."

Some people didn't like Mimosa; they thought she dabbled in dark subjects. Others were drawn to her and sought advice. Chief Daniel and his family visited her often. They had a secret that Mimosa had asked Chief Daniel never to tell anyone. The secret was that Mimosa could heal; she had healed the Daniel grandchildren when they were ill with the influenza.

"Everyone will be at my door if they find out, and I will be a spectacle," Mimosa said. "Besides, it drains my energy. I can only handle a few healings in as many days."

Chief Daniel and his wife Martha knew healers well and kept the information between themselves. If a healing was necessary, they asked Mimosa first and kept their pledge of secrecy.

"That woman is evil, I just know it," Neil O'Neill said. "Anyone that can read the future in tea leaves has to have held hands with the devil."

"You are the devil," Faith said. "You lie and steal."

One Monday midmorning Hudson Godwit's long legs sped him up the middle of Second Avenue toward Mimosa's house. He was carrying a still-warm pancake wrapped in a tea towel. As he went by Cooper's Grocery and Hardware Store, Mr. Cooper was sweeping the boardwalk and called out to him, "What have you got there, young man? Looks like you're being chased by a fire."

"You won't believe this, Mr. Cooper, but what I've seen in this pancake that my mother cooked me this morning is amazing." He pulled back the tea towel to show the markings on the cake. "See, it's a message, and I'm taking it up to Mimosa to read."

"You'd better get going before the ravens try to take it off you. Hey, if she tells you who will win this year's Stanley Cup, let me know." Mr. Cooper laughed and went back to his sweeping.

Mimosa was waiting at the door when Hudson arrived. "I've been expecting you," she said.

Hudson laid the pancake down and started to explain.

Mimosa signalled with a finger for him to be quiet. She glanced at the pancake and then, for theatrical effect, ran her hand over it as if it were a burning flame. It was the only way she could get him to believe, but pancake or no pancake, there was something she had to tell him.

Hudson was entranced.

Mimosa closed her eyes, bent her head back and hummed a few bars of a tune she'd heard earlier on the radio. Then she sat bolt upright, her eyes wide open as if she had returned from another world, and spoke in a calm voice. "This is only for the present, Hudson. You are going to be given an opportunity to become something you always wished for. Your life will change for the better forever."

"Wow," Hudson said. "That is significant. I've always wanted to be a writer and reporter."

"Of course," Mimosa said, leaning back in her chair.

The light from the window shone on her, and Hudson thought how attractive she was. If only he were older.

Mimosa was looking out the window at the Daniel kids playing in their yard next door, and without looking away, she said, "There are plenty of fish in the sea, Hudson."

"I have to go, thank you," Hudson said and went to pick up the pancake.

"Leave that here," Mimosa said, placing a finger on the pancake. Hudson obeyed and opened the door to leave.

"Tell Mr. Cooper to put his money on the Montreal Maroons."

"Yes ma'am, I will," Hudson said, then did a double take. He hadn't mentioned hockey.

When he was gone Mimosa fed the pancake to her little black dog Weasel.

Later that week Hudson received a letter in the mail from the publisher of the *Whitehorse Star* newspaper, asking if he wanted to be a reporter for Dawson City. Hudson was overjoyed and responded with an emphatic "yes."

Hudson told Craven the good news and of his meeting with Mimosa.

"Did you return a gift to Mimosa? You must always give something, not as payment but to complete the circle of giving."

The next day, Hudson personally delivered a package of candy wrapped in white and tied with a bow.

"Why thank you, Hudson, how very thoughtful and sweet of you," Mimosa said as she patted his cheek.

I'm in love, Hudson thought.

Buford had little respect for fortune tellers, but he had a ton of curiosity. He sat in the truck on Second Avenue outside City Hall as Craven went in to pick up his cheque for repairing the town's boardwalks. He watched Mimosa in her colourful flowing skirt, hands bedecked with jewellery and long hair flowing, as she walked home with a package under her arm. *She looks like a gypsy*, he thought.

At that moment a raven swooped, and Mimosa called to it. The bird landed in front of her and waddled ahead, leading the way. It kept this up for the next block, when it cawed and flew off.

Strange, thought Buford.

At that moment Buford decided to see what she was all about and to ask her for a reading. He hopped out of the truck and followed her up the sloping street, past the Palace Grand Theater and Lucky Inn Restaurant, to her home.

Buford knocked on the weather-worn door, out of breath. The place needed repair and paint. He thought that this woman needed a man.

The door swung open, and Mimosa stared Buford coldly in the eyes.

"What do you want?" she asked through her teeth.

He was caught off guard and stammered, "I've come about a reading."

She smiled a wicked smile and asked, "Are you sure?"

Suddenly Buford was very much aware that something he considered ridiculous could be serious. Furthermore, now that he was up close, her beauty and directness intimidated him.

"Or are you here because I need a man?" she asked.

Buford had to think fast, so he lied. "I've been thinking about this for a long time. My brother Craven said I should do this."

She knew it was a lie. "Oh, now it's your brother who sent you. That's strange, because I know Craven quite well, and he never mentioned this to me."

They stood in the doorway for another awkward moment. Then she moved aside and said, "Come into the parlour. I'll read your cards."

Buford felt trapped and heard the unspoken words "said the spider to the fly."

Mimosa looked at him and smiled again. He was now totally unnerved.

As he squeezed into an overstuffed chair, Mimosa reached up to a shelf for a deck of tarot cards wrapped in velvet.

A cloth with numbered spaces trimmed in gold covered the table. She handed the cards to Buford and said, "Shuffle." He obediently shuffled the deck and handed it back to her.

She spread out the cards like a fan. "Pick ten, take your time, and lay them on the spaces face down. Do you have a question for the cards? If you do, don't tell me. I'll answer at the end."

For the next hour Mimosa read the cards, telling Buford where he was in the present, what lay above his head in life, his immediate difficulties, what stood in the way of his goals, what others knew about him that he didn't know and what the next six months of his life held.

Buford had nothing to say when the reading was finished. He thanked Mimosa and got up to leave.

Mimosa was putting the cards away and, without looking up, she said, "The answer to your question is absolutely no chance whatsoever."

Buford knew he shouldn't have been thinking those thoughts about her.

"What a pile of crap that was," he told the early afternoon barflies lined up on stools at the Occidental Hotel. Shaking his head and muttering under his breath, he took another long drink of beer and said, "That's one lonely woman up there. She thinks she can read a deck of cards and tell you things about yourself that you didn't even know. Crap, that's all it is … crap."

Buford was a little drunk when Craven found him. "I thought you were going to wait in the truck. I've looked all over for you."

As they drove home, Buford bad-mouthed Mimosa. Craven slammed on the brakes and came to a sliding stop on the side of the road.

"Get out of this truck right now," he yelled. He raised his foot and kicked Buford out of the door.

Buford rolled down the shoulder into the ditch. He was getting up and dusting himself off when Craven came around the side of the truck yelling. "You idiot! You had your cards read and now you're criticizing Mimosa. Do you want to bring bad luck down upon us, you imbecile? Why are you talking this way about such a nice person anyway?"

Buford shrugged his shoulders.

Craven said, "You can walk home." He got in the truck and showered Buford with gravel and dust as he sped away.

Craven didn't speak to Buford for the next two days but insisted he meet with the DCSF at their next scheduled meeting. Buford reluctantly agreed.

The club members sat around the table and encouraged Buford to relate absolutely every single detail of his meeting with Mimosa.

"This is very serious and critical," Hudson said.

"Yes, very serious, Buford," said Victor. "In my village, big trouble for people who speak like you."

Buford was intimidated by Victor. As instructed, he repeated the derogatory comments he'd made about her being a pot-stirring witch and a broom-riding crazy woman. The room went cold.

"You have to make amends, Buford, and take Mimosa a gift and stop bad-mouthing her," Hudson said. "Even if you don't believe, even if you are blind to the forces around us, you must make amends."

Buford wasn't going to make amends at all. In his mind he had done nothing wrong and this was just hocus-pocus. "All of you go to hell. I'm not a believer and I'm not going to do it."

The members tried to prevent him from leaving the room by standing in his way, but he used his girth and elbowed his way through them to make his exit.

That night Buford had terrible dreams and tossed and turned in his sleep. He sensed that something was in the room with him, and sat up. A silver-grey apparition stood before him at the end of the bed. It seemed to have its own luminous source and was dressed in a wide-brimmed hat, tattered shirt and trousers held up by suspenders. Rubber boots came to its knees. It held a gold pan in one hand and a shovel in the other. It looked weary and stressed; its face was furrowed with lines and its beard was unkempt.

Buford rubbed his eyes and said out loud, "Who are you?"

The apparition set the gold pan down on the bed and tucked the shovel under one arm. It brushed dust off its sleeve, took a pouch of tobacco from its shirt pocket, rolled a cigarette with one hand, lit it, pulled the string on the pouch shut with its teeth and put the tobacco back in its pocket. Only then did it speak. Coughing and blowing clouds of smoke, it said, "Buford, I have been sent here by the Legion of Wayward Gold Miners to issue this one simple warning: Make amends! You've been given another chance!" Its voice sounded like it came from under a washtub.

The ghostly miner stood for a moment, then started to move backward, fading out. Buford watched it become smaller. Then, to his surprise, it got bigger again and came back into the room. "Forgot my gold pan. And, oh yes, beware the raven." It then left in a flash, never to return.

Smoke hung in the air.

Buford rubbed his eyes. "What the heck was that?" He spent the rest of the night awake.

In the morning he staggered about the house, not knowing if the apparition had been his imagination or a warning from the beyond.

Craven noticed his uneasiness and asked, "What's up, Buford?"

Buford tried to explain but gave up.

Weeks went by. Buford didn't heed the miner's warning, and the fact that nothing had changed emboldened him. He wasn't afraid and continued to make slight of Mimosa, Craven and the DCSF.

A raven flew to the house one morning. The bird's claws could be heard scampering up and down the tin roof and hopping along the eavestrough. The raven cawed loudly. Buford heard it and looked up from his bowl of cereal. As he prepared for work, he couldn't find his wallet, although he tore the house apart searching high and low.

On the second day, the raven's scampering and cawing woke him an hour earlier than he was used to. After breakfast he had to walk to the Flora Dora because the truck keys were nowhere to be found. He burned the chickens for the lunch menu.

On the third day the raven woke him two hours ahead of his alarm clock. Exhausted, he got out of bed but didn't eat breakfast—his stomach was upset—and spent an hour looking for his glasses. He never found them. At the Flora Dora, his kitchen help quit.

On the fourth day the raven kept him awake by sitting over his bedroom window, cawing into the darkness. This was unusual; ravens never caw at night. The raven then woke Buford two hours before the sun rose. He couldn't find his left shoe and staggered to work in an old pair of sneakers. The power had gone off in the Flora Dora the night before, and the freezer was thawing.

On the fifth day his favourite Swiss Army knife that his dad had given him was gone, and the raven cawed on. Life had become perplexing and painful for Buford. He stayed home from work and Pat Henderson had to close the Flora Dora Café for the day.

In tears he went to his brother, blubbering, "Craven, you have to help me. I believe Mimosa put a spell on me and sent a raven. All my things have gone missing."

Craven started laughing. "Sent a raven? Now that is a new one. But I thought this was all superstition and crap. Isn't that what you said?"

"Yes, but now I've changed my mind. I can't stand this any longer. I know I've had the curse of the raven. And the ghostly gold panner visited me."

"There are no such things as a curse of the raven and a ghostly gold panner. You're imagining things," Craven said emphatically. "But you do look like hell, so I will see what I can do."

It was true. Buford had dark circles under both eyes. He looked and acted drunk from not sleeping and he'd lost weight in five days.

Craven advised Buford to do repairs for Mimosa, who had told him, "My house needs fixing. The roof leaks, and a little tar would help. It doesn't need much."

Buford showed up the next Saturday on Mimosa's doorstep with a can of tar and his tool box in hand.

Mimosa opened the door and smiled. "Why, Buford, what a pleasant surprise. It's so nice of you to drop by again," she said.

Buford set his tools and the can down and removed his hat. "I come for more than a visit, Miss Mimosa. I noticed last time there was a bit of work that needed doing around the place, don't you think?"

"Why, yes, I do. I think it needs a man."

Buford blushed and went to work.

He spent the day tightening and adjusting the door and hinges and making repairs to the roof. Sitting near the peak with the sun warming his broad back, he scooped and spread tar where he thought a leak might be. A large raven circled overhead and landed noisily, its feet scraping the tin, a few feet from where he sat. Buford stayed perfectly still, and he and the raven eyed each other. In a few bold hops, the raven landed on Buford's leg. Its sharp claws dug into his flesh. The raven's big black beak was inches from his face. Buford was afraid it would poke his eye out. The raven cocked its head to the left and right, and shuffling closer, looked down and reached into Buford's shirt pocket. It pulled out a carpenter's pencil with its beak and gouged Buford's leg again when it pushed off. It swiftly flew away.

Buford was surprised and amused at what had happened. All this raven stuff was too much for him. He sighed and went back to work.

Mimosa made a lunch of sandwiches and tea, which he ate hungrily. He didn't mention the raven.

"That's a very interesting tooth you have there, Buford. It gives you character," she said.

Buford was so happy at the compliment that his eyes went misty. *I'm in love*, he thought.

Mimosa sighed. *Men are so simple*, she thought.

By day's end Buford had finished the repairs and packed up. As he thanked Mimosa for lunch and coffee—for the third time—she handed him a paper bag and said, "I believe these are yours. Sometimes healing comes in different ways, Buford. Sometimes it all hinges on belief."

Buford drove down the road, pulled the truck over and opened the bag. Inside were his wallet, keys, glasses, shoe, knife, and strangest of all, a pouch of tobacco and his pencil.

"That is so weird," he said out loud. "I'm not even telling Craven about this."

Time of Change

My name is Tobias Gandhi Godwit. I was born in 1949, and all things considered, my life has been just about perfect. Like my father, Hudson Godwit, I became a news reporter, writer and Yukon historian.

My mother, Rebecca, had travelled by train, plane and car from New England to visit her Uncle Wilfred. My father spotted her having lunch at the Flora Dora Café with Wilfred and knew in an instant he had to have an introduction. They fell in love, and my mother never went back home.

The next spring, the crew of the riverboat SS *Casca* unceremoniously dumped wooden crates of her belongings on the dock. A terse note arrived in the mail shortly afterward announcing that the family had disowned her for marrying down and without their permission. She sat in Wilfred's cabin with my father's arm around her shoulder, wiping tears from her eyes as he read the letter.

"This is exactly why I'm here and not back east. I had to get away from that interfering family," Wilfred said.

"It's all money," Rebecca said. "My brother Cecil had a hand in this. I know he influenced Mother and Father. This was his idea."

My mother never got over the hurt the family caused her.

When I was three, my mother would take me to the *Dawson Daily News* building on Second Avenue, where she worked five afternoons a week. I sat near the office and watched as the deadline-driven staff hurried to get the paper out. The smell of ink, molten lead and newsprint, combined with the rhythmic clatter and smooth swoosh of the printing press, fascinated me. By the time I was five, I knew I wanted to be a newspaperman.

I used to make my own newspapers by cutting foolscap into pages, punching holes in their edges and tying them together with pieces of brightly coloured knitting wool. I still have some of them today. One front-page headline blared "Man Bites Dog," and inside, a full story related this tragic event. The details included the punishment meted out by the Royal Canadian Mounted Police and the dog's convalescence in the Dawson City Animal Shelter. I also had a *Letters to the Editor* column; I made up comments and names for it. These imaginary writers were just as outraged as the editor when the dog was bitten.

I made up ads and coloured them brightly with crayons to advertise fresh produce with prices way below anything the Dawson City merchants would offer. I did this for my mother's sake and pointed these out to her as she complained about the high prices at the grocery store.

My father was tall and wiry. His thin arms bulged at the biceps, and he cinched his belt tightly to the last hole to hold up his pants. He worked part-time as a reporter for the *Whitehorse Star* and at the Bear Creek Machine Shop as a machinist, repairing and rebuilding gold dredges. He was a talented writer and an expert at the metal lathe, turning out pieces that would otherwise have taken months to ship in. I remember the sweet smell of oil and grease when he came home after work and picked me up.

His temper surfaced when he drank, but he reserved it for fights outside the Occidental Hotel, never fighting inside an establishment because "that would be unmannerly." He would call out his opponent, and over the years there were a number of them. The bar crowd came to expect and appreciate them. Some became legend, like the Friday payday when the Swedish Arvid twins, Olof and Harald, both strapping six-footers, went out one after the other and my dad dispatched each of them with one punch. They soon made up—no hard feelings—and my dad got so drunk that night that Olof and Harald carried him home through the town, singing "The Maple Leaf Forever" and bringing lights on in every home along the way.

That Saturday morning he slept on the living room couch, where he had fallen the night before, his knuckles red and sore-looking. Buford proudly told me, "I never saw your father lose a fight, and some lasted barely a minute." Buford used to be a well-known scrapper, so I took that as a compliment.

My parents were lovers and friends. My father would sit in a kitchen chair and sweep his arm around my mother's waist as she went by. He would look up and say something charming; she would become soft and delicate in his arms and place her hands on his shoulders. Even as they grew older, she still blushed when this happened. I loved them both dearly.

Later, when I started to write a history of the Klondike, I realized that for decades Dawson seemed to have been frozen in time. It was as if the end of the gold rush of 1896 had traumatized whole generations into complacency and apathy. The glory days would never return. The Great Depression of 1929 to 1939 had little effect on the Yukon; it survived better than most other places. The Territory was situated in a remote corner of the world, which insulated it from the influences of a troubled global economy. In most cases people were unaware of the turmoil outside.

My friends and I loved the CBC news reports. It was surreal to sit on my bed twisting dials on the brown Bakelite radio and hearing the news of the world come over the airwaves. We were so far from the stories that it seemed we might be on another planet. People didn't know about us, but we knew about them; the radio told us.

World War II was different. Its darkness had influenced even the fairest regions of the planet. I interviewed Wilfred, Taffy and William extensively, and they provided reams of information and corroborated each other's stories.

In 1940 twelve young men were conscripted into the army, and Dot and Nat's eldest son Ziggy left, never to return. He was blown up in a bombardment near Bastogne, and his body was unrecognizable. His grave in France says "Known unto God." Years later Nat and Dot visited the cemetery and brought back a picture of one of the graves with that inscription on it.

"It was hard not knowing where he really was buried," Dot said, her face red and tear-streaked, "but it was some comfort to be there."

Buford and Craven, who were like uncles to me, organized a service on behalf of Ziggy's parents, who were overcome with grief and bore the burden of their loss the rest of their days.

William Pringle cursed when he heard the news. "I've seen this before. The young always pay the price," William said. "If I had my life to live over, I would never have gone to war. It was such a horror, I might have even left for South America." He turned out to the service with his medals pinned on his uniform and saluted smartly when Mr. Cooper, a veteran himself, lifted his bugle and played the last post.

William spent his life as a businessman and passed away in 1975. His old war wounds gave him trouble till the end, becoming red and sore in the middle of winter if he didn't take enough vitamin C. I was a pallbearer at his funeral; it was the first time I had done such a thing. I stood in for Uncle Wilfred, who was too frail to carry a coffin.

Neil O'Neill had answered the call to arms by volunteering as a seaman. He took a boat to Whitehorse, and my dad told me he'd stood on the dock next to Faith, who clutched two small children, one at her breast, and waved a tearful goodbye to the boat disappearing around the bend. They wouldn't see each other for four years.

Neil caught the next train to Skaguay, then a boat to Vancouver, arriving there in late June 1940. From there he was shipped to the east coast, where he was trained and assigned to a destroyer escorting convoys of supply ships across the North Atlantic. He saw action against German U-boats and rose in rank by proving himself as an able seaman. He wrote home as often as he could, professing his undying love for Faith and the children.

"Looks like something changed him, because he was never this responsible before," Faith said. "I wonder if he met another woman."

"No, don't you worry," Uncle Wilfred said, "the navy has made a man out of him."

Neil came home after the war as a decorated hero. The town was proud of him, and he worked hard and became a town councillor. He was thinking of running for mayor in 1962 when he was arrested for graft. It had something to do with the city's purchase of a tractor and road grader. He resigned from city council and the charges were dropped. After that he started to drink heavily.

"I risked my life. I'm a veteran, a decorated veteran, damn it. I should be treated with respect," I heard him say drunkenly as he sprawled on the couch on his front porch.

Faith kicked him out of the house anyway. "Go live in the Sunrise Hotel with the rest of the bums," she said.

"I wish you knew my life, Faith," he said and packed his bags, never to return.

Their marriage breakup and the thought of Neil taking up residence in the hotel deeply saddened me. Their eldest child Rob was my friend all through school and became a lawyer who defended the downtrodden throughout the North. He was appointed a judge in Iqaluit on Baffin Island in 2001.

Victor tried to enlist, my dad told me. "I go shoot those damn Germans, teach them a lesson they don't believe." But our army didn't trust gypsies any more than the Germans did. Victor was deferred and told to contribute by going back to Elsa and working in the essential mining service. Instead he worked on the gold dredges in the Klondike River Valley.

One bright spring morning, Victor had the first and only epiphany of his life. He put on his suit, picked a bunch of flowers, walked up to Mimosa's house, knocked on the door and invited her to have coffee with him at the Flora Dora Café. They married three months later. Their boy Adam looked like Mimosa, and their girl Shawna looked like Victor.

My parents and I attended the wedding, a wild happy event, with summer flowers and gypsy music and dancing.

"I've never been so happy," Victor said.

"Neither have I," Mimosa said.

My mom asked, "Was that you who left Mimosa at the altar years back?"

"You cannot unlove," was all Victor said.

Buford and Craven were both in their fifties when they got hitched. I attended both weddings. Craven married Faith's divorced mother Harriet. She was a stern, humourless woman who pulled her hair too tight in a bun. Her former husband Robert, a good man by all accounts, had taken the boat to Whitehorse for business and kept on going. The last they'd heard of him was a postcard from Vancouver instructing Harriet on which lawyer she should contact.

"Good riddance to that fool," she said, with more anger than one man could have ever borne.

Harriet didn't grieve too long. She married Craven within a year.

Craven's marriage was a small private affair with my dad as a witness and Buford as best man. Buford, overcome with happiness, cried through the whole ceremony. His girlfriend Beth kept tugging at his arm and telling him, "Shut up, you big baby." Harriet cast him a dirty look.

From the start Harriet badgered and controlled Craven relentlessly. Craven was inexperienced with women and buckled to her demands. Even I could see that he went from a talkative, happy man to a whipped husband and grew old and grey. He thought this was all part of marriage, so he didn't complain and always answered, "Yes, dear."

"Sad," Victor told me. "Marriage should not be this way. Fifty-fifty, not one person telling all the time."

Harriet brought out melancholy in Craven, and I avoided her whenever possible.

Buford's wedding was a big public affair. It was uneventful until a drunk miner asked his new wife Beth for a dance too many times, and Buford decided to teach him some manners. Before doing that, he removed his tooth and told me to "hold this while I take care of business." Buford waded into the crowd. There was a smack, then a dog-pile. My father helped pull them apart.

Beth was a cousin of Chief Daniel and was as round as Buford and half his age. She already had four children from a previous marriage and she didn't want any more. "I'm too old to have more kids. If Buford wants them, he can have them himself."

In 1968 Buford, having put on weight from Beth's biscuits and gravy, died of a heart attack while hauling a hindquarter of moose that Beth had shot out of the bush to a truck waiting on the Dempster Highway. Craven was crushed. "Best damn brother anyone ever had," he cried.

I helped Craven and Victor make an impressive wooden monument for his grave with the moon, the sun, stars and one tooth carved and scrolled on the top.

"We all shine on," Victor told me.

Craven carefully lettered in black paint, "Here lies Diamond Tooth Buford, the best brother anyone could hope for." It didn't quite rhyme, but it was the best Craven could do under the distressing circumstances.

The funeral was a surprisingly happy affair, due in part to the many friends who came to see Buford off and the potlatch that Beth organized. "He is my husband. He gets a potlatch," she told her family, and everyone agreed. Even the fellow Buford punched out at his wedding was there and praised "the big guy with the big heart."

Uncle Wilfred grew more dignified and respected with age. He took to wearing a suit and tie everywhere he went and seemed to walk straighter.

In 1964 a black 1958 Lincoln Continental Mark III with suicide doors—back doors that swung open toward the rear of the car—drove across Canada and headed north on the Alaska Highway. The car turned right outside of Whitehorse and completed the 333 dusty miles to Dawson City in two long days. After a night at the Stewart Crossing Lodge, its occupants arrived in the early morning when the grass was thick with dew, and stopped at Hughie Ford's Chevrolet Automotive Garage for directions. They arrived unannounced and woke Wilfred from his sleep. It took him a moment to realize who they were. Overcome with emotion, he cried as he welcomed them in.

"Surprise!" said his sister Joyce. "We just had to come and see for ourselves where you've been hiding all these years."

They hauled in their many suitcases, delighted at the idea of camping out in Wilfred's cramped cabin.

Taking a draw on his ever-present pipe, Jacob said, "Very enjoyable, this roughing it in the Klondike."

They acted like two kids at summer camp.

No one had ever seen such a luxury car in Dawson before, and it was the buzz of the town. School kids went out of their way to see it and were late for class. "What a beauty," they said.

I was introduced to my relatives and missed school for the entire day.

Wilfred's sister Joyce and her husband Jacob Wertheimer, a Wall Street financier, had come to make amends, saying their part of the family hadn't treated my dad or mom the way they should have. Jacob, as the executor of his niece Rebecca's parents' estate, had brought a bundle of legal papers for her to sign. "With your parents' passing, you were entitled to some of the property and moneys, but it has been a battle. Cecil fought your inheritance every inch of the way, the dirty bastard."

Joyce looked shocked. "Why, Jacob, in all our forty years I've never known you to use such language."

Jacob's cheeks went red as if he were a schoolboy caught smoking. "Well, maybe it's about time and the right occasion," he said.

Regardless of the small inheritance, Jacob and Joyce's visit took a burden off my mother's shoulders, and I will always be grateful to the Wertheimers for that. Sometimes I thought that my sadness as a boy was the result of my mother's treatment by her family, which I know gave her great sorrow.

Wilfred and I spent the next week shuttling Jacob and Joyce around town and the goldfields to show them the people and the sights. They were a wonderful couple, and I learned to love them dearly. I also developed an affinity for yacht-sized classic cars and owned many in my lifetime.

Joyce would hug me, call me her angel and tell me, "You must come and stay with us. We'll visit the museums, take a carriage ride in Central Park and visit the opera. Would you like that, Tobias?"

I would like it, I told her, and I kept her invitation close to my heart. It was years later that I discovered it was Chanel perfume she was wearing.

Wilfred entranced Jacob and Joyce with the many stories of his life.

"My good God, Wilfred, I should write all this down," Jacob said. "It would make a fabulous book, don't you think, Joyce, darling?"

I told him, "I have already written a lot of this, Uncle Jacob."

"Then send it to me, my boy, and we will publish a book together," he said.

The thought of being a published author really interested me, and I started writing history in earnest. I sent copies off to Uncle Jacob, but apart from a thank-you note, nothing ever came of it.

We would sit at a booth in the Flora Dora Café, Joyce in her fox stole and Jacob in his ascot, receiving the many well-wishers who came by the table. I introduced them, having known practically everyone in town since my birth. In a way Joyce and Jacob were something like royalty, thanks to the Lincoln. I was so proud of them.

On an afternoon when Wilfred stayed home, Craven, Buford, Victor and I piled into the back seat, with Buford taking up half the room. We drove around town with Buford and Victor at the windows waving for everyone to see.

"How much you want for this beautiful car?" Victor asked. He lit a cigarette and blew the smoke out the window. "One thousand? Maybe two thousand? How much? Five? I pay you cash money on the barrel, no worry."

Jacob looked in the rear-view mirror at Victor, who wasn't looking his way. "How would we get home?" Jacob asked.

"You fly big plane," Victor said.

"I don't think so. We drove here because Joyce can't fly. She gets nervous and airsick."

"Aww, too bad. I love this car," Victor said, rubbing the red leather armrest and waving to more people passing on the street.

Victor could very well have bought the car and paid cash, since he'd made a small fortune working at the Elsa Mine years ago, but I don't think Uncle Jacob took him seriously. He probably thought a gypsy wouldn't have money.

Joyce got gold fever panning Wilfred's claim on Bonanza Creek. She found a few colours in the bottom of her pan and couldn't stop digging. As she crouched on the side of the creek, the nose of her stole dipped into the water so the fox seemed to be thirsty and gratefully drinking. The bottom of her dress, bought at Saks on Fifth Avenue, floated on the surface.

I said, "Aunty, your dress is getting wet," but in her excitement she didn't hear me.

"Come along, sis, it's getting dark," Wilfred said. "The gold will still be here tomorrow when we come back."

"The bottom of my dress is wet," she said as she got into the car.

Jacob was an admirer of Robert Service, and he and I visited the poet's cabin a number of times. He stood in front of the porch looking up at the door as if Robert would walk out and greet him. He found it fascinating that Wilfred lived a stone's throw from the cabin.

"Greatest poet that ever lived, Tobias. This man is a hundred times more romantic than Byron and a million times more adventuresome than Tennyson. And Keats, ha! Keats doesn't hold a candle to any of them, never mind Robert Service. If I lived here, I would visit this shrine every day," Jacob said.

Wilfred introduced Jacob to an ancient Norwegian, Roald, who'd known Robert well.

"My God, Robert Service actually cashed this old guy's cheques when he worked at the Canadian Bank of Commerce on Front Street," Jacob exclaimed. "Just wait until I tell the boys at the firm about this."

He went out and took pictures of the bank, Roald and Robert's house.

Victor and Jacob were becoming friends. They visited the cabin, where Victor recited "The Cremation of Sam McGee" flawlessly in his heavy accent.

"Well, that was an unusual rendition," Jacob said as we sat at the dinner table that evening.

Joyce told me that Jacob borrowed a pair of Wilfred's woollen one-piece long johns and took to wearing them and a bush hat around the cabin. He was an early riser. One morning he was standing by the sink, making coffee and flipping flapjacks, when Wilfred walked in from the bedroom donning his bathrobe.

"Is that where you made the bomb?" Jacob asked, pointing to the table.

"The very spot," Wilfred said, yawning.

"I had a curious dream about Mr. Service last night, Wilfred," he said. "He was sitting on his porch in his suit and tie, spats on and all that, and he said, 'This was the only home I was ever truly happy in.'"

"Interesting," said Wilfred.

"I think I can understand what he meant," Jacob said.

Joyce had woken up and was listening in on the conversation. She had the heavy covers over her head—the wood stove had gone out in the night—and she pulled them down to show her tousled blonde curls.

"Bring me a cup of that, please, Jacob dear," she said, yawning.

Jacob crossed the room and gave her a cup. She took a sip. "Ah, just how I like it," she said. Joyce and Jacob seemed to be very affectionate, like my parents, and I was sorry they didn't have children.

"Wilfred, I just remembered—we brought your diploma with us." Waving a hand, she instructed Jacob, "Get it out of the suitcase, darling."

Jacob dug through the clothing and pulled out a framed sheepskin certificate. In Latin written in scrawling calligraphy, Harvard had bestowed upon Wilfred David Durant an *Artium Magister*, a Master of Arts degree, in 1912.

When I saw it that afternoon, I couldn't take my eyes off it. "Wow, Uncle Wilfred, you really went to Harvard. Wait until the kids at school hear about this."

Wilfred held it at arm's length and studied it for a moment. "Funny, I thought this was so important at one time, but my life went in a completely different direction. I'm not sorry. You have only one life to live and you have to make your own choices and be true to yourself." He then hung it on the wall. "Wait until Taffy sees this. I don't think he ever believed I had it."

Two days later my mom and dad, Wilfred, Joyce, Jacob and I had a weepy farewell. Even Taffy, who'd only met our visitors briefly at the Flora Dora Café, came out and got teary-eyed.

"You must come and live with us in the Hamptons," Joyce said. "You'll love it there. But I can see why you live here. You have so many friends, and this is your home. It's a lovely country. I hope we have made some amends for the family trouble."

Taffy thought the invitation included him and said with a sigh, "I'll try to make it, but on my pension, I'll probably only get as far as Winnipeg."

My mother gave Joyce a long hug and told her, "Don't ever think of the family trouble again. That is all done with. We appreciate everything you and Jacob have done for us."

We all waved until the Lincoln was out of sight. I went home and sat in my room and cried a little as I listened to the radio. My mother called me for dinner. I hoped my eyes weren't red, but both my parents glanced at my face, and by the slight pause of scrutiny, I knew they'd noticed. They said nothing.

I grieved when Wilfred passed on in 1977. Windy Sale attended the graveside service, and because he was becoming forgetful and forgot he was at a funeral, he went into a long explanation of the mammoth discovery on Bonanza Creek some forty-five years earlier. Sitting in his wheelchair, he ended his narrative with, "Damn civil servants. They should have minded their own damn business!" The service went on longer than expected, but it was interesting, and no one seemed to mind. I loved it, because it was just more fodder for my writing and convinced me all the more of the uniqueness of this land and its people.

I wrote a two-column description of the event, and it made the front page of the *Whitehorse Star* under the banner "Harvard Sourdough Who Discovered Mammoth Dies."

Dot and Nat continued to live in Dawson. In 1973 they bought Cooper's Grocery and Hardware Store, and together with Iggy and his wife Petulia, built it into a commercial success. The upstairs was a large sprawling apartment where they all lived happily with the half-dozen grandchildren who came along.

Taffy never got over his distrust of Victor or Neil, and his anxiety probably led him to an early grave. He left a long detailed will that didn't make sense, because he hardly had anything; his bank account sat at zero. He willed Neil his family Bible and Victor his well-worn hymn book.

"What I want to sing this stuff for, Tobias?" Victor asked, turning the book over in his hand.

"Taffy is sending a message from the beyond that he wants you to go to church and sing and listen to the sermon," I said.

"Yes, I know he think I need it, but why listen to crazy old man?"

Nat and Iggy told me the story of Piedoe. After all those years, Nat still hung his head and choked up when talking about their dog.

After his dust-up with Nat and Piedoe, Howard Bungle had gone to work for the British Yukon Navigation Company as a dockworker, unloading freight and delivering it to the miners on the creeks. He'd been laid off when the SS *Klondike* made the last commercial riverboat journey in 1955. He needn't have worried, because he and many others went to work improving the last section of the Klondike Highway into Dawson City. The boats, no longer needed, were mothballed in Whitehorse until a fire destroyed all but one of them. Truckers became the new riverboat captains.

Victor and Mimosa's son Adam studied engineering and managed the Bear Creek machine shop where the dredges were repaired. He dismantled and moved a cabin from Hunker Creek to Bear Creek and lived there with his young family until the price of gold forced the closure of the entire gold dredging operation in 1966. With the money he'd saved, Adam bought the Flora Dora Café when Pat Henderson retired. With the help of his parents, he ran it for many years.

In 1970 Parks Canada funded a multi-million dollar plan to restore Dawson City to its former glory. Offices were set up in Saint Mary's, the old hospital, new staff moved in and workers raised and stabilized buildings. The post office and the beached SS *Keno* riverboat had construction funds poured into them.

An era had passed, the present was fleeting and the future held hope for Dawson City. I felt like I was in the right place at the right time and all I had to do was pay attention and record it all. It was something I was happy to do. The old-timers would be around for decades to come, but life in the Klondike was never going to be the same. It was the start of a time of change.

The Rock Creek Boys

I was nineteen years old in 1968 when a migration of new people arrived in the Klondike. How they learned about Dawson City, I don't know. Perhaps the spirit of the Yukon and the call of the wild beckoned them.

My mother warned me, "Tobias Gandhi Godwit, I don't want you associating with the likes of those hippies. They're scruffy and without morals. If I see you with them, your father will hear about it."

My father could care less. After many years of working for the *Whitehorse Star,* he and the editor passed the reporting job on to me. I loved it and saw stories everywhere.

A caravan of assorted vehicles and makeshift campers constructed precariously on top of ancient truck frames arrived in town. I wrote a feature story about these cabins on wheels and took pictures, and the *Star* ran everything on page two of a Friday paper. Part of the story was about an ancient, rusting, one-ton Dodge truck that drove through town with a stovepipe streaming smoke. The driver curtly answered my question about the stove's safety. "How the heck else am I going to keep the family and dogs in the back warm?" Then the door of the camper opened, and a big mountain momma with a bandana flashed a gap-toothed smile and threw water from a wash basin onto the ground.

"Isn't she beautiful?" he said.

I politely agreed, "It's a fine-looking camper."

"I meant my wife," he said.

"Her too," I quickly replied.

I learned their names were Marty and Judy, and they had six children, all under the age of ten and all named alphabetically starting with Attila and ending with Flipper. Yes, named after the dolphin.

"Dolphins are almost human," Judy informed me. "They evolved from the lost citizens of Atlantis, and Attila was a saint of sorts who only destroyed what was necessary. You know, when they wouldn't surrender to him."

"We wanted kids to match the whole twenty-six letters," Marty said, "but I don't think the old girl can do it."

"That would be hard on any woman," I said.

"I'm talking about the room in the camper," Marty said.

They made their own goat's cheese and kept the goat inside the camper for its comfort.

"A happy goat produces more milk. We treat it like one of the children," Marty said earnestly.

Who was I to argue? They seemed to have plenty of dairy products.

Marty looked like a young Jethro Tull with his wiry blond hair and blue eyes. Judy was dark with brown hair, and kept the shelves of the camper packed with books.

"She's seeking enlightenment," Marty said, pointing to the books with a nod of his head. "Judy wants the truth, reality or whatever you call it."

I read a few of the spines: Lobsang Rampa, Kahlil Gibran and Adelle Davis. Judy was searching high and low.

When the camper's door opened, Galahad the goat would jump out wearing a red bandana and trailing clumps of hay.

One afternoon I took Sunny Moon Delight herbal tea with them, and between the bleats and the noisy kids we had a pleasant conversation about reality. The cheese and multi-grain bread was tasty, but somehow it's disconcerting when the supplier sits looking you in the face. Goats are ugly. Something about their eyes bothers me; they're too far back on the side of their heads.

Days later the smell of goat still clung to my clothes. Holding my jacket over the washing machine, my mother wrinkled her nose and asked, "Tobias, where have you been, in a barn?"

"No, Mom, I was in a camper," I said.

"Are you hanging out with those hippies again?" she asked.

"Just doing my job, Ma," I said.

"Wait until I tell your father," she said, slamming the washer lid down.

The new Klondike citizens reminded us of the gold-rush era; they brought a lifestyle that made the people of Dawson City uneasy. I, on the other hand, was pleased to meet them and made a point of introducing myself to as many as possible. Soon I became an unofficial Klondike historian and guide. These people were colourful, and in no time I was filling notebooks with the stories of their lives and their daily antics.

The Dawson folk prodded me for information. One day, when I stepped into the Dawson City General Store, a crowd deep in discussion turned and surrounded me.

"We hear there's a commune of them camping up on Hunker Creek, and they have a herd of forty goats and are selling goat cheese for a living," said Walter Rather, the owner of the store, as he wiped his hands on his striped apron.

"Nothing of the sort is happening," I assured them.

"And we hear they are all going skinny-dipping together at the Bear Creek swimming hole," Walter said.

I knew that much was true, because I had been invited to dip with them but declined. My mother would have killed me.

"I don't know what to say, Walter. I guess it takes all kinds," I said. "Why don't you go out and take a look for yourself instead of listening to everyone else's opinion? That would be the fair thing to do. And while you're at it, you could go skinny-dipping with them."

The thought of seeing old, wrinkled Walter cannonballing into the tailing pond was a frightening thing.

Walter didn't like that last comment. He shot me a look and muttered under his breath, "I knew it. Damn hippies."

I figured that by the end of the day Walter's rumour mill would be spinning at full speed.

That evening Diamond Tooth Gertie's Gambling and Dance Hall opened for the season. It didn't help public opinion when a horseback rider in buckskins and a Kit Carson goatee rode through the hall, scattering dancing girls and roulette wheels.

The RCMP arrived with sirens and lights blazing, and Kit galloped off, leading a merry chase into the never-setting midnight sun.

The next day, picking up a quart of milk, I bumped into Walter. He gave me a look and shook his head as he slipped past in the aisle. "Tobias," he said accusingly.

"What do you mean, 'Tobias'?" I asked angrily. "It's not my fault!"

"You hang out with them," Walter said, shaking his finger angrily as he continued down the aisle, sweeping a broom in front of him.

What an ass, I thought.

"Look, Walter, like I said before, find out the facts for yourself before you start making judgments about people."

About the same time as this migration, Parks Canada transferred in all kinds of staff people and made their offices in the old hospital building on Front Street. Jobs and money were pumped into the town. Parks laid claim to a vast amount of property and was soon collecting countless artifacts and repairing and stabilizing buildings and the SS *Keno*.

Summer deepened, and the universe continued to unfold with the arrival of the Halloo family. These people were to influence my life in many ways for years to come. Before I met them, I'd heard of a bunch of ill-mannered no-goods living at Rock Creek. People were calling them the Rock Creek boys.

On a pleasant sunny afternoon, I walked into Cooper's Grocery and Hardware Store and straight into a storm. Richard, the ancient owner, stood behind the counter holding off three of the biggest men I had ever seen. They were like a herd of elephants milling around a watering hole. Two of them looked identical, and these twins bookended the third man. They glared at me, then snapped their attention back to Richard.

"What the hell do you mean, we can't have any more credit?" the largest one was saying. He leaned over the counter pointing a finger in Richard's face. The other two stood to one side with their meaty arms folded across their chests.

Mrs. Byrd, the pastor's wife, clutched her coat collar and took my arrival as her opportunity to scurry out the door. She rolled her eyes as she passed me.

But no one was going to intimidate Richard. All five feet of him stood up on his toes, and glaring through his wire-rimmed glasses, he gave it right back to them.

"You don't get any more credit because you haven't paid your damn bill. How can I be any more clear? Do you want it in writing?" Richard's voice grew louder as he spoke.

The big man, realizing Richard wasn't going to back down, sighed and stepped back. He motioned with a jerk of his arm for the others to come over. They put their heads together and had a quick mumble. Meanwhile Richard ignored them. He grabbed the end of the wrapping twine from the dispenser above his head, pulled off a few feet and finished tying a parcel of cheese wrapped in brown paper. The big one turned back to Richard, reached into his overall pocket and pulled out a wad of bills.

"We were just trying to stretch out our funds on your credit until we found work, but we'll pay up and get going," he said. "We always pay our bills, Mr. Cooper, maybe not on time but we do pay them."

He laid out the money on the counter, and Richard scooped it up and counted it into the cash register.

"Okay, boys, your credit is good. Buy what you want," Richard said, not looking up but flipping his hand at them. "I'll trust ya. If that's your word, then I'll trust ya."

Richard did trust people. All you had to do was pay up, and it was business as usual.

The three men gathered armfuls of groceries and supplies and signed for them. The odd one, the one who wasn't a twin, winked at me as they shoved out through the door and piled into their old pickup truck.

Mrs. Byrd was still on the boardwalk outside the store waiting for her ride, and as he walked by, one of the men leaned over and went "Boo!" in her face, making her jump. I'm sure Pastor Byrd would put something in his next Sunday sermon about the evils of frightening people.

So finally I had met the Rock Creek boys, and despite what I had just seen, I liked them. They might have tried to twist Richard's arm for more credit, but they seemed genuine to me. Also, I wasn't one to take other people's opinions seriously. I was born with an insatiable curiosity and desire to know the truth, so I didn't let gossip distract me. The Halloos had my curiosity, and after meeting them, I wanted more information. The opportunity came when I got the assignment of interviewing newcomers to the Klondike for the *Whitehorse Star*. The editor was mostly interested in the new Historical Sites staff, but I broadened the story to include the Rock Creek boys. I phoned them up, and they invited me out.

The one who wasn't a twin met me in the driveway. "We saw you in the store that day, didn't we?"

"Yes," I said, "you were asking Mr. Cooper for more credit."

"Asking, nothing," he said. "Winch here was ready to stick the place up if the old geezer didn't give in. The only thing that stopped us was you coming in the door." He winked at the others.

I half believed them.

They introduced themselves. I had never heard of names like Winch, Clutch and OP.

OP spat a wad of tobacco chew at my feet as I entered the house and invited me to sit at the kitchen table, which was covered with pots, dishes and newspapers. Once they got over their suspicion of who I was and what I was there for, they were polite and helpful. I was beginning to realize that they were not what they appeared to be and were more intelligent and better mannered than they let on.

The interview went well, and this was the beginning of a symbiotic relationship. The boys accepted me because I was unthreatening, and their vanity allowed me to record the stories of their lives. Their strong sense of family made them interesting, and if you got past their toughness, they were genuinely good people.

They started by telling me they had moved from a farm near Fort Saskatchewan north of Edmonton.

"We'd had enough of those phony Klondike Days in Edmonton," Winch said. "We wanted to come to the real North."

"Yeah, we homesteaded where land was cheap," Clutch said.

"Our prairie neighbours weren't sorry to see us go, and I think some of our new Rock Creek neighbours are sorry to see us arrive," OP said with a laugh.

Clutch chuckled. "Our reputation must have preceded us."

It sounded a little sinister to me, but they all smiled with big toothy grins, so I decided they were pulling my leg.

As I got to know them better, I could see they accepted themselves and didn't try to hide their shortcomings. This honesty was disarming and endearing. No thought of changing their behaviour ever crossed their minds. They liked themselves just the way they were.

The three brothers started life on the right foot, not with a silver spoon, but with good opportunities all the same. Their parents were well-educated professionals who taught them well and had given them solid names—names full of hope and expectation—names they changed to car parts.

Clutch was the youngest and the smallest, weighing 310 pounds. I discovered he caused no end of trouble with his ambitions. His greatest aim was to become a Member of Parliament.

Winch and OP were the older twins and together weighed seven hundred pounds, though the amount wasn't equally divided. Winch was the leader. He was a bit of a bully and he ran things his way. Most of the family troubles resulted from his pride and anger. If the RCMP came to the house, it was Winch they were looking for.

I was there once when the police called.

"Honestly, officer, I was only defending my honour. That man had no business calling my malamute, Stalin, a mongrel," he said.

OP was a yes-man, forthright and a perfect gentleman but sometimes a fool. OP was short for Oil Pan, though some Dawson folk thought it was short for "other people's," the brand of cigarettes he liked to smoke.

The brothers had handsome features; their wavy brown hair grew as far down their backs as their beards grew down their chests, just to the top of their GWG bib overalls. Their wives thought they were the best-looking men they had ever seen and loved them dearly.

When they were together, it was difficult to be in the same room with them, but if they were alone they were totally different. Sizing them up, I thought, *Let's see what the Yukon makes of the Halloos.*

The extended family—brothers, sisters, aunts, uncles and cousins—had purchased a sprawling, rundown house that sat above the flood mark on the banks of the Klondike River near its confluence with Rock Creek. They eventually added onto the hipped-roof log building from the gold-rush era as they needed space. The original skilfully scribed logs had aged to a silvery grey, but the new, framed additions were amateurishly built and poorly maintained. Rain and snow water ran off the metal roof, staining the walls and rotting the boards. Numerous rusty nails left dark comet-like tails on the unpainted siding. The wood on the porch was rotting, and the screen door hung listlessly from one hinge. Fat dogs lounged outside on sun-faded couches that had lost their stuffing. Scruffy, self-absorbed cats sashayed in and out of the open door along with insects.

The buildings had a charm of their own. The mismatched levels made it impossible for people not to bump their heads when moving from room to room. It was a fine example of bush architecture that provided warmth and shelter for an ever-growing family.

On my visits I discovered the Halloos were accomplished musicians and graceful dancers. They took out violins and guitars and played and danced in the spacious kitchen. For such big men they were amazingly light on their feet. At a town dance I watched them waltz with their wives to the "Blue Danube" under the moonlight and patio lanterns. It was inspiring.

The wives complemented their husbands in size, appearance and character. Three sisters—Lulu, Olive and Stella—were married to the three brothers. The women wore simple homemade frocks of bright paisley cotton. They'd made the men's shirts of the same material. On my birthday they presented me with a shirt the same size as their men's; it was huge on me, but I wore it anyway, all tucked in. The women never stopped complimenting me on how good I looked in that shirt. Whatever the season, the women wore practical red-soled rubber boots with thick grey woollen socks pulled up to their knees. The boys dressed like their dads, the girls dressed like their moms, and their clothes were spotlessly clean.

It wasn't completely by chance that in a universe of diversity and in a small town like Dawson City, the Rock Creek family chose someone to collectively dislike. No dinner conversation or daily small talk was complete without a vile or slanderous reference to their chosen victim, Joshua Shackelton. The talk was vicious, and they missed no chance to make his life miserable. Any attempt of mine to mitigate this derision met with blank stares.

"We hates who we hates, Tobias, and we hates things that are not true," Clutch said.

"Sure," I said. "But look at it this way—what could Joshua possibly have done to deserve this?"

"He didn't fight when his country asked him; he dodged the draft," OP said. "That's what we heard. What's an American doing here, anyway?"

"He is a yellow-bellied sapsucker, that's what he is," Clutch chimed in.

Winch looked at me across the table while he cut a piece from an apple with a knife too large for the job. "You heard what my brothers said, we hates who we hates, and that's the end of the story—unless you want to join Joshua in Halloo hell?" He looked down his nose at me as he ate the apple off the knife and laughed.

I didn't answer and turned my head away. Of course I didn't want the Halloos' wrath, but I sure as hell felt sorry for Joshua.

Joshua was the only person I'd ever thought was cool. He tried to be spiritual, and in the Age of Aquarius, he was interested in peace and love. I never saw him angry, and he had the ability to remain calm no matter what the situation. He quoted Kahlil Gibran and listened to Ravi Shankar in a town of Merle Haggard and *Real Romance* magazines. Slight of build and of medium height, he had dark skin and a full head of thick brown hair. In summer he kept himself clean-shaven; in winter he grew a beard. He had "Mystic" embroidered above the pocket of his green GWG work shirt. The number "1548" was tattooed over his heart as a reminder of a special place and time. He worked at Hughie Ford's Chevrolet Automotive Garage pumping 'tane, as he called it.

At the time Dawson City was still locked in a post-gold-rush era of boom and bust. Crooked boardwalks lined the dirt streets, where more houses and buildings were boarded up and abandoned than occupied. It was a slow, seasonal, dusty town with a melancholy aura. Joshua felt at home here and rarely mentioned his past. Until I told him what the Halloos thought, Joshua never knew why they'd chosen him as a target for their anger.

"I didn't dodge the draft, I was 4F. I'm colour-blind," he said, pointing to his eyes. "The draft board said I wouldn't be able to tell the difference between a Viet Cong and an American and I would end up shooting the wrong person. I was glad to get out of the draft, but I was only colour-blind, not blind."

"All draft dodgers are liars," Winch said when I explained Joshua's 4F, "and he's a lying chicken-livered draft dodger."

"Yeah, they're all chicken livers," OP said.

I didn't try to reason with them but told Joshua, "My best advice is to run if you have to." I was confident that Joshua's skinny legs could outdistance those behemoths.

In the hot summer, when winds lifted great columns of dust off the sandbars at the junction of the Klondike and Yukon rivers, old men—relics of another age and adventure—sat outside the Occidental Hotel on well-worn benches, retelling stories and reinventing history. The story of how Piedoe bit off Neil O'Neill's nose never stopped drawing guffaws of laughter. Joshua showed the old men respect, and they allowed him to sit in and contribute; others who were less polite were not welcome. Occasionally the Rock Creek boys would walk past, but the old-timers would go silent until they left, giving them no acknowledgment. This irked Winch the bully to no end, but what was he going to do, beat up a sourdough?

There were two gas pumps within thirty-five miles of Rock Creek. One was at the Dempster Highway corner, and the other was in town at Hughie Ford's Chevrolet Automotive Garage. The next-closest pump was at Stewart Crossing, one hundred miles west. The Halloo men didn't like having to deal with Joshua, so they drove out to the Dempster Corner, but that proved costly and impractical. Their solution was to send the women to fill the truck's gas tank. While the men didn't like Joshua, the women despised him. When they met, they spared him no slight or insult.

"I would rather deal with the men than the women," Joshua told me. "The men are predictable."

One ideally warm afternoon the Rock Creek women drove a one-ton primer-painted International Harvester truck to town, bringing a plume of dust and noise along with it. Winch's wife Lulu was driving, and OP's wife Olive sat on the passenger side. Neatly wedged between them was Clutch's wife Stella, who was the youngest. The three women wore matching bright-orange paisley dresses that together looked like a blanket thrown over the front seat of the pickup.

On Olive's lap was a large brown wicker picnic basket lined with the same cloth as their dresses. Olive unwrapped the waxed paper from thick egg salad sandwiches and distributed them in the cab and through the rear window to the kids in the back. They were out for a pleasant afternoon of driving, eating, shopping and listening to CBC music on the radio. In the box of the pickup sprawled an assortment of kids, dogs, laundry, bales of hay, spare tires and cordwood. Every once in a while, Olive would glance at the side-view mirror and yell a sharp warning at the kids, "Sit down!" Then she would flail her arm backward out the window in a feeble attempt to land a corrective smack.

Drifting around the last corner, Lulu made a beeline for the garage. Joshua stood still at the pumps. He fought the urge to dive for cover, but at the same time was convinced that if Lulu had the chance, she would drive over him, back up and do it again. The truck came to a sliding, screeching, gravel-showering stop. The dogs leaned out and barked in his face while the kids threw clumps of straw that stuck on his hair and clothes. The three women looked back and glared at Joshua. Stella leaned out the window and made the sign of the cross that people used on vampires and other evil beings. She looked at the

"Mystic" embroidered on his shirt, and in her most disdainful voice, ordered, "Fill it up, mistake."

Joshua was amazed at how anyone could be so dumb as to mispronounce such a simple word. He never got used to their insults. Some days he was tempted to refuse them service, but he knew they were waiting for a fight, so he didn't contend. Stella threw money in his direction, and the truck left in the same cloud of dust and gravel it had arrived in.

"Goodbye and good riddance," he said under his breath.

Every year the Dawson City Social Club held three or four dances that were well organized and well attended. The family dinner and dance closest to September 21, the first day of autumn, was a particular highlight. The New Tones, an eight-piece orchestra hired out of Whitehorse, made the 333-mile journey north to Dawson City in their battered van. The bandleader, Hector Badham, swore there wasn't a song they didn't know and couldn't play. Dressed in red-sequined jackets and silver-trimmed pants, they set up their matching music stands and were primed to entertain.

My mom was on the committee that organized the dance.

"Remember, Tobias, don't eat the potato salad," she said. "You remember what happened back in 1964 when Mrs. Robinson's turned, and the whole town got sick."

How could I forget? Mom reminded me so often about the salad that I never eat potato salad at any event. On occasion I even refused to eat Mom's at home.

Men, women and children showed up in their finery and took their seats. Food was piled on tables, and while everyone ate, the band played dinner music. Huge pots of steaming corn on the cob and platters piled with roast beef, moose and fish accompanied potatoes, beets, peas, cabbage and cauliflower—all locally grown, some by my father. All of this was washed down with gallons of tea and coffee and soda for the kids.

The best was saved for last: the three tables groaned under the weight of pumpkin pie served with mounds of whipped cream, apple pie with thick slices of aged cheddar cheese and cream pie with shredded coconut. There was also blueberry, raspberry and rhubarb pie, all served with healthy scoops of vanilla ice cream. The pièce de résistance was the mile-high lemon-meringue pie, which no one could resist; every last slice was devoured. The treats were set out for everyone's dining pleasure, and people indulged themselves to the last slice and scoop.

By half past seven the men pushed themselves away from the tables and casually strolled out the back door for a smoke and a nip from a mickey. The women knew exactly where they were going and what they were doing. They complained among themselves and, trying to feel better, scolded the older children to help with the cleanup. After an hour, when the women had put away the dishes, the clatter and voices from the kitchen died down.

The New Tones were eager to start the dance and did so with a lively arrangement of fast-paced tunes. Hector's baton became a blur. Without the slightest hesitation, the Rock Creek boys, with their wives in tow, sped out onto the dance floor. They and only they commanded the space—but what a show! What graceful elegance they displayed, moving as if on clouds, twirling and waltzing in perfect time. The women wore smiles; the men wore grins. Bow ties matched dresses. Their steps grew lighter. They knew that the Halloos were showing the town.

After the first three dances, the Halloos took their seats to a smattering of applause. Other couples stepped forward onto the dance floor, and my mom and dad were among the first.

"Don't you have a girl you could ask to dance?" my mother called out as she waltzed past where I sat.

"Yeah," I said, "but I think she's married to the actor, Richard Burton."

"Don't get smart with your mother, young man. I was only asking," she said the next time she danced by. My father then led her in another direction.

In the midst of the crowd, Joshua danced with Angel. Angel was pretty, blonde and lithe, and when they danced together it was as though Fred and Ginger had flowed out of a silver-screen movie and taken their place at centre stage. Round and round they went while others stood aside to watch and applaud. They soon grabbed the spotlight. The Halloos were good, but Joshua and Angel were sensational.

The Halloos watched sharply. As if a message had been telegraphed through the autumn evening air, every man, woman and child realized that something was afoot. More than anyone, the Halloos realized it and called an on-the-spot family conference in the back hall to discuss the situation. I quietly joined them to listen in. A great dance-off was shaping up.

"Why don't we just pick a fight with him now? That will be the end of it," Winch said.

"No, no, that would be too obvious," OP said. "We have to beat him on the dance floor. We can't let that jerk show us up. We have to do something, and quickly."

"Let's not panic. We can do this! We're good enough!" Clutch said. "Let's go back in there and pull out all the stops and show this town who can really dance."

I had no doubt whom the town was going to root for—everyone but the Halloos liked Joshua—but I stayed out of it and privately wished both sides good luck.

The Halloos moved back onto the dance floor. This time their lips were pursed and their faces more serious and tense. With complete concentration they twirled, whirled and quick-stepped. Caught up in the intensity of a tango, Stella clasped a celery stick in her mouth. As they dipped, Clutch gently removed it with his teeth and dropped it down the front of his overalls. The onlookers laughed and applauded.

Half an hour later, after giving it their best, they sat exhausted, breathing heavily and sweating. The women made fans out of placemats and wafted them in the faces of the men.

Then Joshua and Angel, fresh as spring flowers and full of energy, got up to a warm round of applause and followed the Halloos' sequence of dances. They executed each step flawlessly with flair and precision and with even more beauty and grace. The Halloos looked on with their mouths gaping, muttering among themselves and probably writing Joshua's epitaph.

But the night belonged to Joshua and Angel. The Halloos knew it, and the appreciative crowd knew it. The New Tones switched rhythms and tunes so that the samba, the mamba, the bomba and the tango, along with the cha-cha-cha and the bossa nova, challenged everyone's abilities. The Halloos grew exhausted and stumbled during the bossa nova. Joshua and Angel demonstrated the dance with such flair that the audience burst into more thunderous applause.

"They're wonderful, those two," my mother said. "And to think those big men were so dainty but such bad sports, booing like that."

Two days later Joshua was back at work. His legs were sore from dancing. Before he heard or saw the truck, the hair on the back of his head stood up. He turned to face his tormentors, but to his surprise, this time Clutch was sitting behind the wheel. Stella sat by the window, and wedged between them was their round and rosy unmarried young niece Missy. Clutch pulled up so that Joshua and he were at eye level.

"Morning, Joshua," everyone in the truck said in unison.

Joshua must have looked a little taken aback, because Stella immediately started introducing Missy. "Joshua, honey, I want you to meet our Missy. Missy, I want you to meet our friend Joshua. Go on, shake his hand."

Missy, who was all smiles, held out a plump, soft hand for Joshua to shake.

"Pleasure to meet you, Joshua," she said breathlessly in her sweetest voice.

Joshua was totally bewildered and stuttered, "Likewise." A stirring filled his body with a strange combination of physical attraction and fear. Was he attracted to Missy? Was this the forbidden fruit he had heard about?

The Halloos sat talking quietly in the cab while Joshua filled the gas tank. The dogs in the back tried to lick his face, and the kids offered him a bite of a chewed, gooey chocolate bar. Joshua politely refused and walked back to the cab, where Stella offered a wad of bills to bring their account up to date. Missy leaned over Stella to reach the window, showing her ample cleavage, and in the same breathless voice told Joshua, "Come up to the house and see me sometime."

As Clutch pulled out, Missy smiled and waved twinkly goodbyes with her chubby red fingers.

Long after they were out of sight, Joshua stood by the pumps deep in thought, unconsciously wiping his hands on a greasy cloth. Slowly he came back to the present. Suddenly he was enjoying the cool morning breeze, the pristine air and the sun's heat on his shoulders.

The Man Who Thought His Wife Was an Alien

Brian and Joshua worked together at Hughie Ford's Chevrolet Automotive Garage in downtown Dawson City. Hughie and his brother Mordechai were more interested in placer mining on Dominion Creek and winters in Florida than running a garage. They left the running of the business to Brian, whom they trusted but supervised closely. People thought Mordechai was a silent business partner, but it was just that he rarely spoke.

"Show Joshua the ropes, Brian. Maybe he'll be a mechanic someday," Hughie yelled as he left the dim garage bay for the morning sunshine. Mordechai followed behind him and gave Brian the nod.

"You don't have to tell me twice," Brian yelled out after them. He turned to Joshua, who wore the same green coveralls as Brian, but two sizes taller. "I hate that nod Mordechai gives after everything Hughie says."

I walked in on the tail end of the conversation, and Brian's anger turned to a cheery, "Good morning, Tobias. How are you doing?"

"I'm doing fine," I said, giving Joshua a nod.

I liked both men. Joshua was level-headed. He had a friendly smile and a calmness about him, but his dealings with the Rock Creek boys had proved he also had a resolve of steel for what was right.

Brian was a helpful, pleasant person—customers and friends agreed on that—but he also believed that aliens lived amongst us. Every day he made a clandestine scrutiny of Joshua's features for any sign of alienness. As they talked, Brian scribbled notes in a grease-covered memo pad that he kept in his left shirt pocket. In his right shirt pocket he kept his memo pad for the garage, but it stayed fairly clean.

When Brian thought he'd discovered an alien, he gave a wink and a nod as an attempt to communicate, but a wink was as good as a nod to a blind horse.

Joshua failed the test.

"You're not an alien," Brian said, stuffing his notebook in his shirt pocket. He was disappointed; he was hoping to work with an alien.

"What?" Joshua asked.

"You're not an alien. Go pump some gas," Brian yelled over his shoulder as he walked into the dark, cluttered tool room to look for parts. Outside, a customer was honking impatiently.

"Okay, okay, thanks for letting me know that," Joshua called after him. He had no clue that he had been struck off the alien list and saved from further annoying scrutiny.

Brian was a writer's dream, since his wild imagination and scientific knowledge gave me fodder for enhancing the Yukon's mystique. He was a great talker, and at times I pulled myself back from the brink of belief in his tales.

"Tobias, there are a few things you have to know about identifying and catching aliens. The first is that they have pointy ears." Having said that, he froze slack-jawed and fixed his gaze on me. Seeing that this priceless bit of information had sunk in, he snapped his mouth shut and continued, "And they have different-coloured eyes, like malamutes, sometimes stutter and prefer colourful hair."

He pointed out that, due to a bureaucratic bungle in their administration, they all had the same cover story of an Aunt Maggie and Uncle Sidney living in New Mexico with their two children, Roberto and Roberta.

I enjoyed covering the news around town for the *Whitehorse Star* by sitting in on city council meetings, political party gatherings and dances organized by the Dawson City Benevolent Fund Raising Society.

They did an excellent job of raising funds for everything from the starving children in Biafra to a new television set for the seniors at the McDonald Lodge. Brian took every opportunity at these occasions to passionately explain that aliens were not people-eating monsters but warm-hearted, intelligent beings seeking a home.

Most people knew Brian, so they shrugged off his antics. To them, he was Brian the alien man, the friendly garage manager who gave them an amusing distraction from the rigours of daily life in the North.

"I wish I had his optimism and conviction for a cause," Mayor Bullard told me after a meeting, though he sometimes got impatient at Brian's appeals to city council. "Next order of business," the mayor would announce, exasperated, banging his gavel on the ancient town hall desk.

Magazines and books of all sorts were stacked haphazardly on shelves around Brian's house, giving off a smell of mildew and creating a fire hazard. He imaginatively researched in this library for what was necessary to support his theory.

Thick manila envelopes crammed with correspondence from like-minded enthusiasts were filed into stacks of wooden fruit crates that leaned precariously as they towered toward the ceiling. Once a stack tipped over onto the kitchen stove while Brian was cooking and almost burned the place down.

"Hot bacon grease and beans splattered everywhere. They burned my hand and ruined supper," he said, showing me his grease-stained bandages in the grocery store the next day.

His largest collection of information had its own battered army-surplus file cabinet and was labelled in bold red ink ROSWELL SITE 51. Roswell was the ultra-secret military base in New Mexico. Brian was convinced that the military studied alien bodies recovered from a crashed spaceship. Despite numerous letters, he never heard back from anyone at Site 51.

"I was hoping they would send me a sample of the metal that the spaceship was made of, but they wouldn't part with any of it. I know they are keeping secrets there, Tobias. If it wasn't for the armed guards, I would take my two-week vacation, and you and I would drive down there, crawl through the cactus and sand dunes and get right in. I'd take Polaroids of the whole operation. Maybe one of those bubble-headed aliens would be walking around. A picture like that would be nice on the front page of the *Star*, don't you think?"

I wouldn't have gone. I knew Roswell was the most secure area on Earth, and we would be shot for sure.

"Do you know why aliens want to be with us, Tobias?" Brian asked.

"They got lost in space and crashed here and won't leave because they like the *Ed Sullivan Show*," I said.

Brian looked at me as if I was trying to be funny. I was, but he was too serious to appreciate it.

"The reason is obvious. They're lonely. In this vast universe, is it not conceivable that someone would be lonely? For heaven's sake, look at the distances out there! That is why aliens have every Roy Orbison record ever made. They're lonely! They want company and they like Earthlings. Is that so very hard to understand? They want to be loved. Is that so bad?"

I was getting gas, and Winch was checking his tires and giving Joshua a hard time in a friendly way.

"A smooth dancer like you should be on Broadway. What are you doing pumping gas in this hick town anyway?" Winch asked.

"Must be my good luck," Joshua deadpanned.

Winch stuttered. Not badly, but "th" sounds tripped him up if he got excited. When Brian heard this, he not only figured that he had an alien but tried to pinpoint exactly where in the galaxy his particular stutter came from.

"Accents happen everywhere," Brian said. "Barcelona, Cape Town, Moscow and outer space."

Brian saw Winch and came out of the garage. He went into a space greeting of bows and genuflections that resembled the courting ritual of the Wood Buffalo National Park whooping crane. Circling around and moving his head like a chicken, Brian smiled pleasantly and offered salutations. "On behalf of the United Nations and all Earthlings, I greet you, I greet you." Then in a soft, singsong voice he sang, "Peace is to you, distant traveller, peace is to you." This sounded very much like Brahms' *Lullaby*.

"I wish he wouldn't do this," Joshua muttered.

I took a picture.

As much as Brian pleaded, Winch would not return the welcome but angrily responded with the vilest of words. This increased his stuttering and convinced Brian that he was indeed dealing with an alien. Winch sped away in an angry cloud of dust. At coffee break Brian announced, "I have determined Winch's origins and hope he will eventually see me as a friend and embrace me as a brother."

"You don't want to embarrass a guy like Winch in front of other people," Joshua said. "He might turn on you."

Why Winch and his brothers did not pound Brian into the ground was a bit of a mystery to Dawson City folks. People speculated that maybe the Halloos really were aliens. It was a joke and a good way to get back at the Rock Creek boys, who were becoming more of a problem each day with their surliness and disregard for the town.

The annual summer solstice celebration on the Dome above Dawson City attracted tourists and townsfolk alike. On the longest day, when the sun is farthest north and communication with outer space is at its best, Brian would join in the festivities. Dressed head to toe in his extraterrestrial costume of tinfoil, with red whip-licorice antennas glued to a silver-sprayed hard hat and his face painted bright blue, he would weave and dance through the crowd, holding his hands shovel-like in front of him. While dancing, he sang an alien-greeting song, which sounded much like the Hawaiian aloha greeting. His quivering voice bleated, "Welcome to you, welcome to you. I paint my face blue to say welcome to you!"

I followed him up the Dome one year, taking pictures and keeping notes. A German film crew took an interest and followed him throughout the night. Brian loved the attention and hammed it up, making up alien poems on the spot. "Saturn has its rings, Mars is red, the aliens are here, let's celebrate."

Brian thought aliens greeted each other by flashing their bright blue faces. It was akin to humans having red faces when embarrassed, but the aliens had more control. He was certain he had picked up blue-face greetings from people in the crowd, but unable to respond in kind, he waved back instead.

What no one knew was that Brian paid equal attention to the winter solstice, the shortest day of the year, around December twenty-first. I drove him up to the Dome one grey and windy afternoon to record the event. Bundled in my parka, I shivered and held his coat as he prepared. His celebration costume was a pair of tie-dyed, one-piece wool Stanfield's long johns with the rear flap sewn shut. Dressing to represent life and growth in the universe, Brian painted his entire body bright red and his hair green, draped a bright yellow flowing cape over his shoulders and wore aviation goggles and knee-high snow boots. The dazzling display of colour was in sharp contrast to the frozen, grey-brown, snow-covered landscape.

"You look really cool," I told him. A lot of the newcomers to Dawson City that I'd befriended liked brightly coloured and tie-dyed clothes too.

"I know," Brian yelled over the howling wind. "Hold on to your hat. If this doesn't bring those aliens in, nothing will."

Then, like the male lead in a bizarre ballet, he held a flashlight in each hand and ran around the top of the Dome, screaming, "M92! M92! M92!" at the top of his lungs. Brian thought our aliens originated in M92, a globular cluster in the constellation Hercules that was billions of years old.

He was a sight to behold and would have continued longer if it wasn't for the cape wrapping around his feet and making him fall repeatedly on the icy rocks. Bruised and covered in snow, he staggered back to the comfort of the truck.

"Wow! That was absolutely incredible, I feel that contact was really made this time. I'm sure of it," Brian said, shivering as we drove back down the steep, icy Dome road.

In fact he'd attracted no one, not a person or an alien or a dog. Even the ravens stayed away, which isn't a good sign, because ravens will attend anything.

I wish other people had seen him; it was an amazing sight. I was glad I took pictures, because no one believed me when I described Brian's performance. Sadly the *Whitehorse Star* turned down the opportunity to print the story and pictures.

"We have our standards," the editor told me. "Try the *Whole Moose Catalogue*. They like stuff like that."

My mom looked at my pictures and said, "That man is not normal. You shouldn't be around him, Tobias. I might have to speak to your father. Don't let that man influence you with all his alien spaceperson talk."

Mom never said spaceman; she was reading up on gender equality. I wondered for a brief moment if my mother was an alien.

People as far east as Keno City and as far south as Carmacks knew Brian and never gave his alien interest a second thought. In the Yukon, the cold and distance defeated formality and the conventional standards of the south. The North is a place where people can be themselves and excel at it, at least until they come to their senses.

Brian was a good worker, always on time and honest, but he was driven to look for aliens among those who filled up at the pumps. Hughie cautioned him, and Mordechai confirmed it with a nod. "I don't want those alien shenanigans on the job. And don't be a blue face either! Just work."

"Winch must have complained," Brian confided to Joshua and me.

None of us could have guessed that his first friendly alien was already heading this way. Brian's destiny was approaching from many thousands of miles away.

I was checking the oil on Mom's Rambler when a dusty Winnebago pulled up. We didn't see many of those in Dawson City this early in the year. The door swung open, and a big woman daintily stepped out. She was wearing hot pink stretch pants, sparkly slippers and a white frilly blouse. Her eyeglasses matched her pants and had wings on them like the fins of a 1956 Cadillac. At her heels jumped a small white poodle with a green head.

Brian looked stunned. He wiped the sweat from his brow with a greasy cloth, smearing black on his forehead. "A sure sign, a sure sign," he muttered excitedly. "Green hair, green hair!"

Then he stared in amazement. The women's ears came to a perfect point. Brian slowly folded to his knees, completely forgetting to dance and sing his alien greeting. He asked, "Are you an alien?"

She thought he had tripped and offered her hands to help him up. Having just left a job that dealt mostly with aliens, illegal or otherwise, she thought he wanted to know if she was from out of country. "Why yes, I am. I just arrived five days ago," she said.

Brian released one of her hands and bit his other forefinger; the pain probably helped him to concentrate. Tears flooded his eyes. "Thank God. You've come. And you're willing to communicate," he said breathlessly. He would have wrapped his arms around her knees but he had on his greasy coveralls.

She dropped his hand and stood there thinking, *surely he doesn't think I'm a space alien?* Never one to beat around the bush, she asked, "Alien? What kind of alien do you think I am, you pencil-necked geek? A Martian?"

The dog barked in support.

Brian snapped back to reality at her forcefulness. He had overstepped his manners and embarrassed himself. If he was going to meet this interesting woman, he had to do better.

"I was just wondering where you came from," he muttered as he got up from his knees.

"Miami! Where the hell do you think I come from, the Belgian Congo or the planet Neptune? Can't you read licence plates?"

Brian apologized furiously, half out of respect for her aggressive demeanour and half out of fear of being fired by the garage owners.

"Okay, okay," she said. "Let's start over. I'm Maude Montgomery from Miami, and this here is my dog Miami."

In ten minutes Maude had a tank of gas and an invitation.

"Let me make it up to you, please. Come for dinner at my place," Brian pleaded.

Cautiously Maude accepted.

I was so surprised that I forgot to take a picture for the *Star*.

Maude was talkative, and as Brian prepared dinner she told him her life story. She was an African American widow who had just cashed in her deceased husband's insurance policy, sold her belongings, bought a second-hand Winnebago and loaded up everything she owned.

"Good riddance to all that," she told Brian, who told me all about it the next day. "I'm sorry that runaway cement truck ran over him, but that man was mean, mean, mean! I put up with him far too long. I took my twenty-year pension and resigned from the Department of Immigration.

"As I drove away, my family and friends stood in my parents' driveway wailing and waving handkerchiefs. None of us had ever moved away from home before.

"But I had to go. Something was calling, maybe the spirit of the Yukon. I never thought it would be the Great White North. Why do they call it the Great White North? Is it because there are no African Americans here?" But she didn't wait for Brian to answer.

"I took Miami, my poodle, whose head I dyed green, and drove off in the direction that my heart told me to follow. A green-headed dog is hard to lose," she said.

Brian seemed friendly enough, Maude told me when I interviewed her a few weeks later, and being twice his size, she could handle him if he got fresh. If worst came to worst, she would sic Miami on him. She had done it before, and the poodle seemed to enjoy sinking her sharp little teeth into a trouser leg and getting whisked around in the air. Maude was a full-figured single woman, and men found her attractive. Why wouldn't she accept a dinner invitation?

Miami yipped in agreement.

It wasn't love at first sight for Maude, but for Brian it was. He was head over heels and worshipped Maude.

"Tobias, usually I hold my cards to my chest when it comes to personal feelings, but I love that women. I love her dearly," he told me.

He knew from the very first moment that she had to be his. She agreed to marry him, but only after settling in her own place and only if she could think it over for the next few months.

"I don't want to make the same mistake twice, Brian. I don't want to have to fight with you like I did my first husband to get any affection out of his cheating heart," she said with anger in her voice.

Finally she agreed to set a date. "You seem like a real nice man, Brian, and I believe we could be happy together. Miami likes you, and her I trust."

Maude went to work for the City of Dawson as the Clerk of Works. Their relationship had captured Brian's complete attention, and he stopped annoying Winch and others with alien accusations. After all, he had a full-time alien with him and he was playing his cards close to his chest.

Maude met the Halloo women during a battle over a building permit, which Maude helped settle in favour of the Halloos. Lulu was grateful that they'd been treated fairly, and because they admired Maude's honesty, she became a favourite of the sisters.

"If anyone ever troubles you, just let us know," Lulu told Maude. This was a sure sign their friendship was sealed.

Maude, who'd grown up in the toughest part of Miami, laughed. Shaking her finger in the air, she said, "No, no, if anyone needs talking to, you just let me know!"

The families visited back and forth, and over time, Winch decided that Brian wasn't totally crazy, just interestingly eccentric, almost like a Halloo. They even became friends.

Then meddling Howard Bungle got wind of the engagement. He called up Maude at the city works office and rudely told her to forget about marrying Brian. Lulu Halloo told me all about it later.

"He is a real nutcase. He thinks people are aliens," Howard told Maude. "He should have been shipped out of here in a straightjacket a long time ago." Then with distracting casualness, he added, "And besides, it's not proper for a white person to marry a black person. It's not done in this town, and you should know better. What about your kids? What colour will they be and how will they fit in?"

Maude was almost struck speechless, but she said, "I can't have kids." Then she came to her senses and said angrily, "You mind your own business, Mr. Bungle. This has nothing to do with you," and slammed down the phone.

The heated conversation drew the attention of the other workers in the office, and when Maude put her head on the desk and cried, they came over to comfort her and ask what had happened.

"I have to go home. I'm not feeling well," she said.

"I never thought I would find such racism in Canada," she said to Brian, "I'm going back home. I need my family."

"Honey baby," Brian said, "Howard Bungle is nothing but trouble. Everyone knows that. Pay no attention to him."

Howard voiced his opinions around town and was doing so in Cooper's store where he was told, "Shut the hell up. Get out and don't come back." Mr. Cooper would have thrown an orange from the crate on the counter, but they were just out of his reach.

As Howard left, he stood at the door and angrily shook a finger back at the people standing by the till. "I remember when it all started," he said. "It was when that damned gypsy Victor married Mimosa. That Mimosa was a beautiful woman. She had no business going with a gypsy."

Lulu heard from Maude about Howard's hurtful words and would have gone after him herself, but Winch and his brothers said, "We'll handle this."

Brian had also put in a phone call to Rock Creek and asked the brothers for their help. The three of them drove into town crammed into the front of the pickup so tightly that Winch couldn't reach the stick shift, and their beards looked like one big hairy blanket. OP, who sat in the middle, shifted the gears on Winch's instruction.

"First gear, OP. Second gear, OP. Third gear, OP."

OP missed them all, though, and the metal ground all the way into town.

The brothers picked up Brian at the garage, put him in the back and went looking for Howard. They found him on his back step, sipping coffee, and all four men walked across the lawn toward him. Winch put one leg up on the step and rested his forearm on it. Brian, OP and Clutch stood behind him, staring Howard down.

Howard looked nervous. He knew this couldn't be good.

"How are you doing, Howard?" Winch asked.

"Fine until you showed up," Howard said.

"You're very perceptive, Mr. Bungle, because no one wants a Halloo visit like this one. We hear you're bad-mouthing Brian and Maude."

"Maybe I am and maybe I'm not," Howard said.

"Yeah, you are," Winch said. "It's all over town."

"Are you going to stop?" Brian asked.

"Maybe I will and maybe I won't," Howard said, trying to save face.

"Wrong answer," Winch growled, moving his face closer to Howard's.

Howard averted his eyes and went pale. His hands shook when he raised his coffee mug.

Winch knew at that moment that their visit had the effect he wanted. He backed off and stood up straight, all the time glaring at Howard. All four men then turned without another word, got in the truck and left. Howard stood up as soon as their backs were turned, stepped into the house and locked the door.

When the brothers dropped off Brian, he shook their hands and thanked them.

"That was a right honourable thing you just did for us. I will never forget it. Imagine sticking up for a man because he wants to marry an alien."

Winch started to explain, but he muttered in frustration and said nothing.

"You're welcome, Brian," Clutch said dryly, and they drove off.

"I'm staying now," Maude said cheerfully. "When I have friends like this, the world is a great place to live."

Brian and Maude decided the date of their marriage and sent out invitations. I took a photo and sent it into the *Whitehorse Star* along with details. Winch had his arm twisted into being the best man. He must have enjoyed the role, because he bought new bib overalls for the occasion, and I heard him telling everyone, "What the hell, I'm just happy for the crazy guy."

Winch also invited more than forty of his family members to attend with him.

"Hmm, I didn't expect that," Maude said. "I'll just have to whip up an extra batch of chicken."

The morning of the wedding, Brian dressed in his finest suit, shoes and hat. I drove him to Maude's doorstep with a bouquet of garden flowers supplied by the Halloos. Maude came to the door, and Lulu and Stella trailed behind her, frantically pinning and making final fittings on her dress. But Maude's face was tear-streaked.

"Oh Brian, Miami is gone. I put her out for a few minutes early this morning, and she disappeared."

Maude hugged Brian, buried her head on his shoulder and sobbed. She said exactly what Brian was thinking. "I hope a fox or coyote didn't grab her."

Maude could barely be consoled, but the Halloo sisters encouraged her and pushed her out the door.

"I can't go through with this, not without my Miami," she cried as Lulu drove the truck up the Dome.

"Yes, you can," Stella said, giving her a hug and sewing a last stitch as the truck bounced over the washboard road. "You have to be brave now."

The sky had turned cloudy, and a stiff cool wind blew from the north.

Everyone was soon aware of the lost dog, and it put a damper on the proceedings.

Brian and Maude and the wedding guests were milling around, trying to get organized, when I heard the rumble of a pickup truck coming up the road. The vehicle came into view, and I saw Howard with Howard Jr. by his side. The truck came to a screeching halt, showering the wedding party with dust and gravel. The passenger door opened, and Miami jumped out, made a beeline for Maude and leapt into her arms. But she wasn't the Miami of a few hours ago. Her head had been dyed black.

As soon as Winch realized what was going on, he called out, "Let's get them, boys," and half a ton of vengeful flesh sprinted toward the truck.

Howard took one look, and before they could reach the truck, sped off down the hill. Maude held Miami in her arms, and the little dog whined happily and licked her face. At that moment the sun broke through the clouds, and the wind died down. The atmosphere completely changed, although feelings smarted from the racial slur the Bungles had crafted.

"It's okay," Maude said, smiling and wiping away the last of her tears. "I have my Miami. Everything is fine now."

The wedding now proceeded as planned. Maude was radiant in her full-length lime green dress, which she'd designed by following a picture of one of Coco Chanel's creations cut out of a fashion magazine. The ceremony included a reference to the bride's relatives, who were unable to attend because of the distance, which Brian perfectly understood to mean light years. He gazed wistfully toward the heavens all during the proceedings, nearly missing his agreement to their vows.

Maude and the Halloo sisters had baked, roasted and fried all week long, making a special Southern meal from recipes that Maude's mother—the granddaughter of an African slave—had taught her.

"Do you eat many of these grits back home?" Brian had asked.

"Why yes, honey flower," Maude said warmly, "we eat them all the time."

Upon hearing that, Brian took an extra helping. "These are M92 finger-licking good."

It took two pickup trucks to carry all the presents back down to Brian's house when the day was over.

The newlyweds settled into domestic bliss. Brian thanked God every day for his wife, whom he cherished. He knew that in time she would reveal her extraterrestrial powers. He had only mentioned it once, reaching across the dinner table to hold her hand. "In your own time, dear, in your own time."

Maude mostly ignored his alien remarks.

"Having your husband think you're an alien is a small price to pay for all the love and affection that man gives me. Brian treats me like the Queen of the Klondike."

"You should do what I do," Lulu said. "Winch loves trucks and cars, so I read up on mechanics, and whenever I mention a carburetor or piston rings he gets all teary-eyed and appreciative. Men are so simple. Just give them a little interest, and they go over the moon."

That week Maude took Lulu's advice and asked Brian at the supper table, "Is it true what I read, that there might be life on Mars?"

Brian got so excited he choked on a mouthful of food and had to run to the sink to spit it out.

"I'll be careful when I talk about space things," she told me later with a laugh.

Brian was so appreciative of her interest that he became twice as doting as a husband.

A month after the wedding, Winch was spending more time with Brian. He also started to look carefully at people's ears and eyes. His stuttering stopped.

I was visiting the Halloos one evening in late August to complete a story on their Uncle Zak's World War II experience. When I looked outside, I was startled to see Brian and Winch down by the barn in the shadows just beyond the light from the house. They were standing shoulder to shoulder silhouetted against the moonlit sky. I could barely make out their voices as they gestured wildly at the vast, starry night.

The women and children sat on the porch, talking noisily as they ate plates of thick chewy chocolate-chip cookies and sipped hot creamy tea laced with sugar. Hours later, having exhausted their conversation with each other and developed kinks in their necks, Brian and Winch walked back toward the house and into the bright light streaming from the kitchen windows. Both wore denim bib overalls. Brian had bright red hair and a blue face. Winch's beard and hair were blue, and his face was red. They looked hideous. A child screamed, and the women shrieked.

Maude's oversized white enamel cup with the red rim bounced with a hollow *bonk* off the supraorbital bone above Brian's eye. Clutching his face with both hands, he dropped to his knees moaning in pain.

"Damn!" he yelled. "That hurt!"

Winch didn't fare much better. Despite his girth, he deftly dodged two strategically thrown cups, one of them filled with hot tea. But a third cup that Lulu threw with full force caught him sharply on the knuckles of his right hand.

"Crazy fools! Idiots! Hare-brained weirdos!" the women yelled angrily. "And don't swear in front of the children!"

Leaping from their chairs, they grabbed their kids by the arms, scooped up their babies and herded into the kitchen, slamming the door behind them with a hinge-busting bang.

Winch heard the latch lock. Turning to Brian, he moaned, "It's the barn tonight."

Brian groaned in response. Winch helped him to his feet and wrapped one arm around his waist to support him. With his other arm he waved defiantly at the faces pressed up against the kitchen window. The men struggled unsteadily to the barn and the yard went dark as the house lights turned off.

Resigned to a night in the barn, Winch pulled the horse blankets down from the loft, and both men made their beds on the hay. Just then the barn door yawned open with a slow horror-movie creak. Like pale space monsters, the moonlit dogs slunk in and bedded down with their masters. Warm and comfortable in the hay, neither man felt inclined to get up and close the door.

"A bear could get in," Brian said.

"Who cares?" Winch said. "The dogs will take care of that."

Brian asked, "Winch, have you ever seen Orson Welles's movie *War of the Worlds*?"

Winch didn't answer, and the question hung in the air between them.

Minutes later, unable to control his need for conversation, Brian asked, "Winch, how long do you think God thought about DNA before he made it? A moment, a month or a million years?"

Winch's tired voice barked out of the darkness, "Shut up, Brian! Go to sleep. You've caused enough trouble for one day."

The dogs growled in agreement.

I slept comfortably in the spare bedroom, and in the morning Stella told me to go down to the barn to call Brian and Winch for breakfast. They staggered out of the barn, stiff and sore from sleeping on the uneven bales. Their faces were now mottled, a grotesque smear of red and blue tempera paint, and in Brian's case also blood, that had mixed into purple. Without night's mask they looked ridiculous. Their own good sense urged them to feel embarrassed as they walked meekly to the house.

Lulu met them on the porch and made no attempt to hide her anger. Without a word she handed each of them a towel, and with a jerk of her head and thumb, motioned toward two porcelain wash basins on the porch table. The basins were full of steaming hot water. As Brian filed by, Lulu took hold of his upper arm and focussed her gaze on the cut above his eye. Scrutinizing it carefully, she half laughed her opinion, "You'll live." Then she released her grip and pushed him to join Winch at the wash bench.

Brian and Winch pulled their chairs up to the breakfast table. I could see they were nervous, though the warmth of the kitchen must have been a welcome relief from the cold barn.

The women and children filed into the kitchen, yawning and wiping sleep from their eyes as they reached for coffee and orange juice. The men appeared shortly after, and soon the room was filled to capacity with people jostling for breakfast and an opportunity to stand next to the large cookstove to soak up its warmth.

Brian's head still hurt and he had a terrible blinding headache. Maude made things worse when she gave him a hug and a kiss right on top of the lump. His eyes watered from the pain. Maude, thinking that soft-hearted Brian was grateful they had made up, gave him another kiss on the same spot. He almost passed out, and it clearly took every ounce of his strength not to groan.

Later that day I caught a ride with Winch when he drove Maude and Brian into town. We dropped Maude off at the house to get ready for work the next day, and the three of us drove down to the river, where we sat on the bank and watched the water flow past. It was a good place to sit and think. After half an hour Brian asked Winch, "Have you ever read Hermann Hesse's book *Siddhartha*? Tobias has. Joshua told me."

I was surprised Brian knew about *Siddhartha*, but Winch knew nothing of Hermann Hesse. He didn't want to know anything about Hermann Hesse. He didn't care about Hermann Hesse. He didn't even answer the question.

Brian let the longest time pass before speaking again. "Siddhartha was looking for enlightenment, so he sat by a river, and through contemplation, discovered the meaning of life."

Winch looked at Brian and gave him his very best I-really-don't-care look.

More silence followed.

Brian left it at that. I guess we both knew that a person has to want to be spiritually enlightened. It's not something you can force on someone.

A lanky, tan puppy ambled over, threw its wagging body onto Winch's lap and at the same time—with that over-the-shoulder move—tried to lick his face. The puppy finally settled down and leaned against Brian, who had put his arm around it, and joined in looking at the river.

I got up and said, "Goodbye."

The two men and the dog sat together, each in his own world: one wanting to know, one not caring to know and a third that could never know. At that moment Howard Bungle drove by, and I said under my breath, "And one who would never think to know."

Joseph Copper and the Small People

I was just enjoying my last pancake, and my mother was folding tea towels to go in the drawer, when she asked, "Tobias, what are your plans for this Saturday morning? I have errands for you."

I said, "'I'm going down to Yasgur's farm, I'm going to join in a rock and roll band, I'm going to camp out on the land, I'm going to get my soul free.'"

She laughed and said, "Don't quote 'Woodstock' to me. I know my music. You're not getting out of helping around here. Besides, you shouldn't be going down to anyone's farm, you should be enrolled in university to study journalism."

I was a bit surprised that she knew about Joni Mitchell and Woodstock but I was learning mothers knew everything. I finished my milk and headed out the door before she could assign the errands.

"The chores will be waiting for you," she yelled after me.

If I told her I was meeting Brian and Winch for an interview about Brian's plans for a convention to discuss aliens, she would grill me for half an hour and say, "I told you I didn't want you getting involved with aliens." I was beginning to think Mom believed in aliens, she worried about them so much.

Winch and Brian sat on the damp gravel levee between the beached riverboat *Keno* and Robert Service's old Bank of Commerce, where a teller had told me some ledgers and receipts still carried the poet's signature.

Neither man spoke as they sat watching the Yukon River. Both were troubled, but their dilemma was of their own making. They had gone too far with this alien thing. They had overstepped boundaries, and the women were united against them and calling them fools. They both hated it.

"I had a sign," Brian said.

"What do you mean by a sign?" Winch demanded irritably. He was angry with Brian for getting them so far into this embarrassing situation.

"A sign from heaven," Brian answered, fidgeting with some pebbles and not looking at Winch.

I could see Winch was wondering whether to ask the obvious question. After a pause he rolled his eyes, sighed and said, "Okay, Brian. What is this sign you saw?"

Brian looked into Winch's eyes and said quietly, "At the corner of Princess and Third streets I saw a three-legged dog chasing a one-legged raven."

Winch's face contorted into a look of pity, then disdain and finally disbelief all in one second. His eyes briefly crossed. He dropped his head onto his knees and covered his ears with his hands.

"I don't want to hear it," he said.

Brian protested, "You have to."

Winch covered his ears with his palms and started to sing "Rock of Ages."

Brian grabbed Winch's forearm and pulled his hand off his ear.

"Don't be such a damn fool! Listen! This is important—it could change our lives. Do you want to get out of this or not?" Brian asked.

Winch stopped singing.

"This is evidence. Alien involvement is written all over it like fingerprints at a crime scene. One-legged or three-legged animals would be of great interest to aliens. They love anomalies. They collect and study them. These animals have been picked up and studied, then released. There is no way on this earth that a three-legged dog and a one-legged raven would end up together in the middle of an intersection. It had to be more than coincidence."

Winch looked at me, "What do you think, Tobias?"

"I'm here only to record the facts," I said without looking up, scribbling every word like mad into my steno pad. I knew it was going to be either a blockbuster story or a complete bust.

It took most of the afternoon for Brian to convince Winch of the significance of what he had seen. By the end of the day Winch didn't believe that a sign had been given but did agree they should continue their alien program to clear their names.

"We need support," Brian said. "We have to invite other alien-believers and have an alien convention. We are going to prove once and for all to everyone in this unbelieving town that aliens live amongst us. We'll rent Gertie's Dance Hall, have a fabulous banquet with speakers, publicity, films, pictures and displays, and Tobias here will record it all, and we'll publish books and movies."

"I'm on board," Winch said.

"How about you, Tobias? Are you with us?"

"I'll be there," I said, trying to sound as committed as I possibly could without joining in completely.

Over the next three months the two men met after work, toiling late into the night and running up postage and phone bills. I joined them as often as I could and helped out with the typing and mailing of invitations.

Maude complained frequently to Brian, "I'm not putting up with any more of this foolishness."

"Just be patient, honey. It's all coming together," Brian said.

Winch had bigger problems with Lulu. One evening I was licking stamps and Winch and Brian were having a tête-à-tête when she barged in, apologized to Maude for doing so and dragged Winch outside for a private talk. She needn't have bothered. The whole neighbourhood could hear.

"Winch, I've had just about as much of this crap as I can take. You're going to have to make a choice. It's me and the kids or the aliens. I'm going home to mother and taking the kids if you don't give us some of your time."

She stood on the lawn, arms crossed, with one foot tapping like Buford's lone tooth on a cold day. Initially Winch was lost for words and stuttered at the onslaught. He was terrified of losing her and the kids. Then he found his voice.

"Lulu, we are almost there. We have this thing in the bag and almost wrapped up. Just a little while longer and bingo, done deal, and I'll never do this again."

Lulu didn't really want to go through the trouble of leaving with the kids; she was having a bad day and wanted Winch to know it. She pursed her lips some more, tapped the other foot and said, "Okay, Winch, but let this be a warning."

She left as quickly as she arrived, and Winch went back to work.

CBC radio got wind of the project and phoned early one morning to interview Brian. Maude was annoyed at being wakened, and thinking the call was collect, shouted threats at Brian to get off the phone. The caller stopped the interview twice, hearing her in the background, and asked, "Is everything all right there?"

The planning continued. Speakers were booked, exhibits built, programs printed and the date set for the weekend of the summer solstice.

Scientists from universities in London, Moscow and Riga in Latvia were invited but politely declined. An excited professor of astrophysics from Moldova responded with an offer to lecture on the subject of Greek mythology and the alien influence. The Russian keepers of the Romanians were such believers in aliens that his passport and visa were issued in two days rather than the usual two years.

Winch's uncle Zak offered to share his World War II experiences. "I'm sure aliens were there and on our side. I took a glancing bullet off the head that put me out for two days, but when I woke, I'm sure I saw spaceships, and they were shooting at those Jerries. Damn good shots they were."

Brian told Zak he was looking forward to hearing the full story at the convention.

As the list of speakers grew, Brian was confident that world-shaking history would be made in Dawson City that summer. The thought of making a contribution to mankind and lifting any notion of weirdness from their shoulders raised Winch and Brian's spirits enormously.

There were doubters in town. Howard Bungle, the most outspoken, yelled at Brian and Winch from across the street as they loaded a sound system into Gertie's.

"You bunch of crazies! What kind of people are you bringing into this town anyway, more idiots just like yourselves? I'm going to the cops and stop this." His face went deep red, and by the time he jumped in his truck and ground gears in a jerky takeoff, he was beet purple.

"That guy might just explode if he's not careful," Winch said, picking up an amplifier.

Howard did go to the cops, who diligently filled out a report but ripped it up and tossed it in the wastebasket before Howard even went out the door.

"That guy has severe cabin fever—365 days a year," said the sergeant to the constable. He put Howard on his mental list of people not to turn his back on.

On the morning of the registration, more than four hundred people crowded into Diamond Tooth Gertie's. Brian and Winch were beside themselves with happiness. Hotels and restaurants threw their complete support behind them, now that their rooms and restaurants were packed full. The Occidental and Downtown hotels offered sponsorships, which Brian collected and added to the growing coffers.

Professor Alexandru Anca had brought his daughter from Romania, and she was a real looker. With flaming red hair and emerald green eyes, she was a classic beauty. I made a point of introducing myself.

"Welcome to the Yukon," I said.

The professor bowed slightly at the waist and in the heaviest accent introduced his daughter.

"I am Professor Anca and this is my eldest daughter, Camelia," he said.

Camelia took my hand and gently shook it.

"Are you a communist?" she asked in the most cultured English with a British accent.

I was attracted by her charm but at the same time taken aback by her directness.

"No, but my father is a socialist," I said.

"All my boyfriends are communist," she said and walked away.

"I could convert," I yelled after her.

Maude and Lulu got word of the success and proudly showed up, decked out in the finest Halloo women's fashions with matching dresses and hats. Maude was now a full-patch member of the family.

The din subsided as Brian and Winch, dressed in tuxedos, stood nervously side by side at the microphone. Brian wore a black top hat; Winch wore a brown derby that clashed with his suit but matched his rubber boots. Brian took off his hat, collapsed it and tucked it inside his jacket. There was a smattering of polite applause before they spoke. Holding his papers at arm's length because of nearsightedness, Brian spoke loud and clear. "Welcome! Welcome, everyone, to the first annual Dawson City Alien Research Convention."

A murmur swept through the room, and then everyone stood up. Thunderous applause gave way to cheers, yells and more applause. Brian and Winch looked at each other and shook hands. Then, with beaming faces, they waved to the crowd.

I was surprised to see Richard Cooper, front row and centre, having a great time. I asked him how he was doing. He grabbed my arm and told me, "*Star Trek* convinced me that Spock is real. No amount of makeup could make pointy ears that perfect. I seen him at a convention in Las Vegas and took a real close look. They're real, all right! Nope, there are aliens out there, or maybe I should say in here." He laughed heartily, still holding on to my arm.

Sitting next to Richard was Chief Daniel with a large contingent of his family, which took up two rows of chairs. Chief Daniel got up onstage next, and after a prayer he said, "God bless you all and safe journey to you all." Then, with a rhythmic beating of his drum, he chanted in his own language a greeting to all the visitors. He then climbed down and took his seat.

I had been asked to read a prepared message, but I turned it down and suggested that Uncle Zak, as an elder and a war veteran, be given the honour. He enthusiastically took the assignment.

Zak wore his army uniform, decorated with three rows of medals and still fitting after thirty years. He took the mike. "Dear travellers, who have gathered here today from all points of the globe and universe, we welcome you with open arms and minds. It is a rarity that such a gathering as ours is taking place when so many naysayers abound—"

Then Zak left the text and started to interject his own thoughts. "—especially that damn no-good Howard Bungle, who should be tarred and feathered and driven out of town on a rail."

There was a scuffle at the back of the room, and Howard rushed up the aisle shouting the foulest language. Zak stepped back from the mike, pulling his sleeves up his bony arms to welcome Howard in whatever encounter he wished.

"Come on, come on, you dirty rat. I'll Popeye ya," he shouted over the microphone.

He didn't have to worry, because Lulu deftly stepped into the aisle and hardly had to throw her fist, as Howard ran directly into it. His head snapped back, and he fell dazed onto the floor. Lulu stood defiantly over him, smiling and brushing her hands together, while Howard was grabbed and ushered quickly outside by a group of Brian's volunteers and an RCMP officer.

"Come on, Howard, you're spoiling the party," the constable said. He locked up Howard for the weekend.

I snapped the perfect picture of Howard flying back with no part of his body touching the floor and Lulu standing with her fist out like Mrs. Rocky Marciano.

Maude was delighted and hugged Lulu. "Thanks, Lulu, you don't know how much that punch means to me."

Zak took the mike once again, grinning, and announced, "And that, folks, is why Halloo men never have to fight."

The crowd roared its approval.

Zak finished his message without further personal interjections. Then Winch read the agenda and introduced the speakers, who stood and bowed respectfully to the participants. Professor R.P. Austin was the chief expert on alien abductions. Author Glen Smarting wrote *Aliens and Beyond*. Researcher Dr. Min Yan Ming had flown in from Formosa. Elder Joseph Copper represented Dawson City. Professor Madame Merch lectured at the university in Metz, France.

Doctor Ming was first to show his film, *Look to the Skies*. Example after example of oddly shaped silver objects flashed across the screen, eliciting *oohs* and *ahs* from the rapt audience in the darkened room.

Some objects looked suspiciously like pie plates glued together. The pictures were fuzzy and out of focus, but the audience didn't seem to mind. When someone asked about the lack of clarity, Dr. Ming said, "All these pictures were taken without any advance notice, and the camera holders had only the briefest second to react. It is impossible to get any better pictures unless the aliens stop and pose."

A smattering of laughter followed his response.

Then the spokesman for the Sasquatch Believers Club, which had sent a contingency of observers, said, "We know better than anyone how difficult it is to take pictures of the Sasquatch and aliens." The discussion ended there.

Elder Joseph Copper sat quietly in the audience, waiting for his turn to speak. When Brian finally invited him onstage, he didn't rise from his seat but waved his hand and said, "At this time I won't speak. Maybe later." With that he got up and left the room, head down and frowning.

Madame Merch spoke at length, in fractured English, about crop circles. Near her home in Metz in northeastern France, people had discovered these circles numerous times. Professor Merch believed that crop circles were the greatest proof that aliens exist and were attempting to communicate. "We must decipher their meaning, as they contain important messages."

"So far," she continued, "I have deciphered a complicated message that involved the study of six individual circles that collectively said the Earth is round."

Her theories and her slide show were warmly received, and numerous questions followed.

At the back of the room, from a darkened corner, a man asked,

"If these beings are intelligent, why do they have to wait for harvest time to communicate with us? And why crop circles? Don't they have any regard for the farmers? Why don't they write us a letter or send us a postcard?"

Madame Merch pretended not to understand, apologized for her lack of English and moved on to the next query. It was quite complicated, but she answered without any difficulty.

And so the conference went, with speaker after speaker convincing each other of nothing, really. They offered the weakest of proof and the barest of evidence, but their audience accepted everything wholeheartedly. It was a case of the blind leading the blind.

When Professor Anca expounded on the Venus de Milo—he said she didn't have arms because some aliens didn't have arms—there were more loud scoffs and laughter from the back of the room.

"How do they pull their pants up if they have no arms?" was a question.

"Yeah, and how do they hug their children and wives?" came another.

Winch had had enough of this, and I stepped aside as he rushed past me toward the back.

The voices asking the probing questions turned out to belong to OP and Clutch.

Winch fumed. "Saboteurs! Idiots!" he spat. "I thought it was you two. How could you embarrass me like this?"

OP and Clutch cleared out as fast as they could; they didn't want to face the wrath of Winch. Later, when they bumped into each other in the hall, Winch turned his anger on OP, believing he'd persuaded Clutch to disrupt the convention.

"How could you be so damn rude? Who are you hanging out with these days, Howard Bungle?" he snapped.

"You know we would never do that, Winch," Clutch said, not trying to hide the hurt in his voice.

OP said, "We just want our brother back."

Winch's shoulders sagged, his voice softened and he raised his palm as he nodded. "Okay, okay. I know this hasn't been easy on you guys, but we can't talk now. We'll talk later. This whole show is almost over." He patted their shoulders and walked outside.

"Later," OP called out hopefully behind him.

The convention's comradeship was inspiring, and the banquet was sumptuous. People drove and hiked up the Dome road and overflowed the summit to celebrate the summer solstice. Brian stood on the highest point to make his speech, and the midnight sun reflected off his silver hard hat and blue face as he spoke. "Thank you, thank you all, for being here in the name of science. Wonderful things have been brought to light this weekend. I'm sure we have advanced the cause of understanding our fellow inhabitants of this universe to a new level." He stretched out both arms to the crowd, then pointed to the heavens. "Let no one rest until all aliens are human, and all humans are alien!"

No one really knew what he meant by that, but in the spirit of accepting non-conclusive evidence for the past few days, everyone cheered wildly.

I saw Camelia in an animated conversation with Howard Bungle Jr., who sported a Chinese Maoist cap with the red star and all. I think he bought it from an army surplus store while on a trip to Vancouver. He wore the cap all the time. Camelia must have taken it seriously, because she was arguing wildly about something.

Howard saw me watching them, and later when he walked past, he said, "That chick is nuts."

After his speech Brian and Maude left to lock up the meeting hall for the night. Brian called to me, "Tobias, come and help us." As we entered the cool darkness, we could hear faint voices coming from the stage area. Silently we stood and listened.

Elder Joseph Copper sat onstage with his two grandchildren Gerald and Terry, talking in a quiet voice in the silent, empty hall. The boys listened, entranced with his words. He looked up and motioned for us to come over, which we did.

"You can stay and listen to this if you want. Draw your own conclusions. I don't want to hurt anyone's feelings or change what people believe in, but everyone told their stories, so now I will tell mine."

There were chairs nearby, so we dragged them over. As soon as we sat, he began.

"Long ago, when I was young like Gerald and Terry, my father Copper John and my two uncles Robert and James took me with them up the White River for an early fall caribou hunt. It was my first time and I was very young. We hunted successfully for two days and then camped beside the river. We had to smoke and prepare the meat for transportation back home. I made my first kill. I was very excited. Around the campfire my father and uncles honoured me with their stories and gave me small gifts for the occasion. I scratched my name and the date—it was 1911—on a jackknife that my Uncle Robert gave me."

With that, Joseph reached into his pocket and took out a well-worn bone-handled Buck knife and handed it to me.

"Read it and tell what's on it, Tobias," Joseph said.

I held the knife up to catch the light from the open door behind me. I could make out the faint worn scratches on the handle.

"It says, 'Joseph Copper, 1911,'" I said.

I passed the knife around; everyone looked at it, then Joseph put it back in his pocket.

Just then Professor Anca and Camelia walked in, and uninvited, pulled chairs up and joined us. Joseph didn't seem to mind.

"The work of preparing the caribou was done," he continued, "so one afternoon when my father and uncles were napping, I decided to wander off and explore the countryside. I took my Cooey .22 rifle and followed the river upstream for a while. Then I came across a small creek flowing into the river and decided to follow it up into the hills. I kept my eye out for small game and prospected along the way. I hadn't gone very far when I saw something move on the bank above the creek. I thought it might be more caribou, so I crawled up silently and lay peering through the grass to see what it was. At first I could not make it out, because it looked so strange, but then I saw small creatures walking around what looked like the boiler from a riverboat. It was shiny and made a sound like the wings of a bee. The small creatures looked like youngsters but they moved like men. Their clothes were thick and padded, and their heads were bare. I sat and watched them for a long time. I wasn't scared. Maybe I was too young to be scared. They didn't see me because I kept hidden. They seemed to be doing something ... working maybe. Finally they all walked back into the boiler and closed the door. That was when I left and went back to camp to tell my uncles and my father. They were amazed. They wanted to hear about everything. Uncle James asked, 'Did it sound like bees' wings through the air?' I told him it did.

"Have you ever heard bees' wings like that, Brian?" Joseph asked.

Brian had been deep in thought and jerked when asked the question. "No," he said with weariness in his voice. "No, I have never heard or seen anything like that." He leaned forward in his chair, looking at the ground and rubbing his hands slowly together.

"We stayed in camp, but the men asked me to point out the direction I had travelled in. So I did, and they gazed intently in that direction, hoping to see something, all the while questioning me and talking excitedly among themselves. Sitting around the fire my father said, 'This is good. These are good people. They have come here many times before … we know about them. This is good.'

"My uncle Robert explained, 'We won't go see them. They like to be left alone. They don't mind us seeing them, but they don't like being chased. We call them Small People.'

"The men remained at camp for another night. They stayed awake, sitting around a blazing fire and excitedly exchanging stories. It seemed that the sighting had opened a floodgate of history that could now be shared because the time was appropriate.

"My father, Copper John, did most of the talking. He seemed more experienced and knowledgeable than Robert or James. Everything was related to spirits, he said. 'The Great Spirit, the One who made us—who made the land and the crow and the wolf, the mountains and water and everything—also made these people.' Then he laughed. 'I think these Small People went to school longer than us. They fly with machines that are faster than our planes.'

"I asked my father and uncles how they knew about these Small People, and my father explained, 'Only those who have seen the Small People talk about them. For a long time these sightings have been passed down, so the visitors have been coming here for a long time. One ancient elder, Yugunvaq, passed on the story that he had travelled with the Small People and they had come from beyond the sun.'"

"Who was Yugunvaq?" I asked.

"That's a story I'll tell you another time," Joseph said.

"I know," said Gerald putting up his hand as if in class.

Joseph patted him on the head and laughed. He went on, "I am telling you this now because it has been too long since the Small People have been sighted. I think they stay away because of the Blue Faces. Crazy dances, crazy movies and crazy songs have nothing to do with the Small People. It makes me angry, and I think it makes the Small People angry too. They have been embarrassed to have people think of them in this way!"

Brian shifted uneasily in his chair, and Maude reached over and took his hand.

"I was going to tell these people here today about this, but I decided against it. There were too many arguments and too many lies. If they had been smarter, I would have told them everything. Guard this knowledge and respect it. Maybe someday you too will see the Small People and be able to explain them to others."

"Do you know if they were communist?" Camelia asked.

What an idiot, I thought. Suddenly she seemed plain-looking.

No one answered, and the Professor and Camelia got up and left. The professor had seemed unimpressed and aloof to Joseph's story; otherwise I'm sure he would have asked questions.

"What could these people know that the Bureau of Extraterrestrial Beings does not know?" he asked Camelia as they walked out the door.

Joseph was finished. He slid from the stage and helped the children down one at a time. We stood up. He gave Brian a hug. "You're a good man, Brian. I like you. But you let your imagination get the best of you. Stick to facts like Tobias here and listen to your wife. I think she is good for you and a wise woman. I respected you enough to tell you this. Now respect the Small People."

He hugged Maude and me. Then, taking the children's hands, he left, wishing us a good night.

Brian mumbled something about having to go, then ran out of the building and down the street, raising dust that followed his every step.

"That upset him," Maude said, looking sad.

I gave her a hug and patted her on the shoulder, and she in turn squeezed my hand.

At that moment, from the direction of the Dome, more rowdy laughter and cheers rose and drifted through the air, down the hill and into the town like a dusty cloud of misinformation.

Rambling in the Rambler

Immediately after the Alien Convention I realized I was working far too hard and needed a rest, or at least a change. I would go over to Keno City, camp out and interview some of the locals. Like Dawson City, Keno City wasn't really a city. About forty people lived there.

Before I left, I visited Dawson's elderly Indian Army doctor with a sick puppy. He was very British, still wore his army khakis and was all spit and polish. I thought of Rudyard Kipling and the heat and dryness of India when I visited him. He was easily distracted, and no matter what you were seeing him for, he usually talked about different subjects.

He looked at the dog. This was unusual for a GP, but with no vet in town, I had no one else to turn to. I think we both felt it was beneath him.

"Put bleach on the ringworm," he said.

I was experiencing sleeplessness and melancholy, so as I held the dog's leash I asked the doctor about it.

He said, "It's a phase you're going through, Tobias. All young men experience it."

"Did you?" I asked.

He had his back to me, filling out some papers.

"No," he answered after a while.

I was going to ask him how he knew what it was like if he'd never experienced it but I didn't bother.

I studied John Henry Fuseli's painting *The Nightmare* intently in a book at the library, so much so that it caused me to despair, but then I realized it was only a picture and a bad one at that. I had no idea what the horse's head sticking out of the curtain meant.

Writing seemed to cheer me up, so I wrote.

"You need a good wife to take care of you," was Mom's solution.

On the weekend I borrowed my mother's car, threw some groceries and a sleeping bag in the back and drove out of town. It was a bright sunny day, and I felt good about being alone and just cruising down the highway.

The road was dusty and in poor shape, and there was little traffic on it. Keno was a short drive of about 160 miles, so I slowed down and took my time. My mom's Rambler rattled along, hurting my tailbone when I crossed sections of gravel washboard.

At Stewart Crossing a young man and woman stood at the green-painted bridge, hitchhiking. I pulled the car over, leaned across the seat, rolled down the window and said, "Hi."

The girl was pretty and wore her brown hair in a braid.

"Hi there, are you going to Mayo?" she asked. She spoke as if we were already friends.

"I'm actually going to Keno," I said.

Her boyfriend stood behind her holding a green packsack. I couldn't see his head.

"Great! You can drop us off at Mayo," she said, without waiting for an invite. She jumped into the front seat and he jumped into the back. He threw his packsack in, spilling my bag of groceries onto the floor.

I leaned back and asked, "Could you pick those up, please?"

He gave me a surly look and threw the fruit, bread and tomatoes back into the bag. The girl broke the tension.

"You'll never guess what we just found," she said, holding up two bottles of beer still dripping wet from the river.

It was obvious what they'd found, but I didn't feel like playing along. Depression does funny things to your willingness to participate in anything. I said, "I have no idea. What did you find?"

She never lost her smile but moved the bottles closer to my face and shook them so that drops of water splattered my T-shirt. She said, "No, silly, look!"

"Oh, you found those," I said.

She seemed very pleased that I'd figured it out. I liked that she'd called me silly. I thought she was flirting.

"Yes, we found these sitting in the water just before you drove up. Someone must have been hitching a ride like us and they drove off forgetting them."

She then settled back in the seat, a little closer than when she got in. I felt uncomfortable, with her boyfriend in the back and all. He sat sullenly, not saying a word, watching me in the mirror from time to time.

He leaned over the seat and asked, "Do you mind if we crack these open while they're still cold?"

I did mind. It was my mom's car, and open booze was illegal. We could be arrested. Not wanting to sound like the police, I said as casually as I could, "Go ahead, knock yourself out." I hated that expression and wondered why I used it.

We drove on for a few miles before my paranoia got the better of me. I pulled the car over to the side of the road and said, "My leg is stiff. I need to walk for a minute. Let's get out, finish the beer and then move on."

They never suspected a thing. We walked down the road a bit, then back to the car. They chugged the beer. He burped, she laughed and we all got back in and went on our merry way. I drove in a black cloud, hunched over the wheel, shifting gears as we went up and down hills.

"I see this old Rambler has three on the tree," he said.

I didn't answer him.

"I like it. Is it your car?" she asked. "It's neat."

I couldn't tell them it was my mom's, so I said, "My buddy, Iggy Duffy, loaned it to me."

"Hey, I know Iggy. Great guy. Worked with him at Bear Creek for a summer," he said.

I didn't answer him again.

"Next time I see Iggy, I'll tell him I drove in his car," he said.

Oh no, I thought.

The girl talked all the way; I never listened, but I nodded once in a while and thought about other things that were as unimportant as her ramblings. *Rambling in the Rambler,* I thought.

Mr. Jealous asked, "Do you have music?"

I fumbled with the radio but all I got was static. He looked out of the window for the rest of the trip.

I dropped them off at the road into Mayo, and for some reason, as she got out, she leaned over and planted a kiss on my right cheek. Her boyfriend didn't see it, as he'd already gotten out and was standing with his back to the car. If she were my girl, I wouldn't want her kissing other guys.

As I drove off, I could see him walking away but she jumped up and down waving her arm. She then turned and ran to catch up with her guy. When she did, he put his arm around her.

Cheez, I thought. Not having a pretty girlfriend like Mr. Jealous got me down. Also, I didn't like to see girls drink beer.

When I arrived in Keno City, I was more depressed than ever. I had money for a room but I found a gravel pit and slept across the car's back seat. It was a hot night, and the gravel in the pit had soaked up the heat from the sun, so I kept the windows open for a breeze to flow through. I woke early the next morning with a kink in my neck; the Rambler was a little narrow for my height. I drove into town. It was still early and quiet, with no one about, and the air was still. My favourite songbird, the hermit thrush, was singing its flute-like early morning song, *chup-wee-er, chup-wee-er,* and darting amongst the willow bushes.

I parked outside the grocery store and went in. There were no other customers, and I may have been the first of the day. It took a moment for my eyes to adjust to the darkness. The place was small and packed to the ceiling with groceries and dry goods. It smelled of damp Cheerios.

The clerk behind the counter had glasses as thick as the bottom of a bottle and wore a butcher's smock tied around his waist with a string. He appeared to be rooted motionlessly in his spot beside the till, ready to serve people.

Everything around him was worn. The original white colour had rubbed off the Arborite counter in a fan shape from the groceries and money that had slid back and forth over the years. The Plexiglas display cases on either side of the till were cloudy and scratched, their original purpose forgotten; now they were full of papers, odd mitts, balls of string and everything else that needed a place. Above the clerk's head hung a faded cardboard poster advertising a brand of paint the store no longer sold. His whole life was framed by that counter. It told who he was: an ancient clerk in a mouldy store, advertising unavailable goods.

"Good morning," I said.

"Morn," he replied quickly, as if it was too much trouble to say the full word.

Being tall, I could see that the top of his bald head had those differently coloured skin patches on it.

"I was wondering if you could help me out," I said.

"With what?" he asked.

"I'm a writer and I want to interview some of the local people and get their stories." I didn't look at him while I spoke but fiddled with a package of mints impaled on a display with other packages of candy.

He looked at me, probably thinking I was too young to be a writer. "Ed" was embroidered in red thread above the pocket of his smock. I interjected before he could answer, "Look, Ed—"

"My name is not Ed," he said.

Of course it wasn't. How could I have assumed that the smock was his?

"It's Bob," he said.

I wanted to pick up a black magic marker from the counter, cross out Ed and write "Bob," maybe even "Big Bad Bob."

"Okay Bob—," I started over.

"But I heard you the first time," he interrupted.

I felt a little exasperated to have this happen so early in the morning.

When he spoke, he smiled, revealing dentures that were too big and out of proportion with his small round face. I got the sense that Bob could be trouble if he wanted to be.

"You can go talk to whoever you want. People are friendly around here. They'll talk to anyone," he said.

I'm not just anyone, I thought, *I'm a writer.*

"Ed's dead," he said.

That got my attention. I looked at him. "What?"

"Ed's dead," he repeated. Then he started to cry.

"Oh no!" I said, which made him cry even more.

He stood there, arms at his side, tears rolling down his cheeks and his shoulders shaking with the sobs.

My mind raced to put an end to his waterworks. "I know," I said.

He stopped crying immediately and said, "You knew Ed?"

"Yes, I did, and he was a fine person," I said. "We all feel your loss. He was the nicest guy."

"Ed died in a mining accident before you were born," Bob said and slammed the till drawer shut so the whole counter shook. Then he stomped past a blanket that served as a door into the back room.

I hung my head. How was I to know that?

There was a flurry of words in the back room, and a woman as wide as she was tall entered and glared at me. Her curly red hair was piled on top of her head, and her bright green eye makeup matched her green smock. "Alice" was embroidered in pink thread over the pocket.

I didn't dare call her Alice.

"I think you had better go," she said in an eerie, squeaky voice. "You have upset my Bobby."

For a moment I felt frightened. I'd seen the movie *Psycho*, and it seemed to me that if the Bates Motel had a grocery store attached to it, I was in it.

I wanted to tell her, no, I didn't upset Bobby. Bobby should move on in his life and get a new smock.

"I was just trying to help," I said.

"You didn't," she said.

I quickly bought a loaf of bread and a package of cheese, after inspecting the expiry date.

She took my money and gave me change. As I left, I could hear sobs coming from the back room and Bob crying, "Eddy, Eddy, Eddy."

I ate sandwiches for two days and walked around town, trying to find a story.

At one house I saw an old lady, knee deep in rhubarb and cabbage, tending her garden. She had her back turned, so I called from the fence. She didn't get up, but looked over her shoulder and gave a wave of her hand. Then she went back to work. That's how it was in Keno City. Everyone was busy, and no one had time to talk. Maybe they thought I was another annoying tourist and so they gave me the brush-off.

I'd heard stories from my father about people in Keno and Elsa, so I sat in the gravel pit eating cheese sandwiches and wrote what I knew.

An argument had started thirty years ago between two miners who lived in Keno City and worked north of there on a gold claim. One went into Mayo for supplies, and while he was gone a bear walked near their cabin. His partner shot it, but he was busy with other work so he left the carcass lying where it fell for the rest of the day. When the other partner came home and spotted the animal on the front lawn, he shot what he believed was a live bear. No amount of argument could dissuade him from claiming the bear was his. The discussions became so heated their partnership broke up.

If they were in the Keno City Hotel bar at the same time, one would yell from his table loud enough for the other to hear, "I shot that damn bear." The other would yell from his table, "Go to hell! That bear is mine. I shot it right between the eyes." And so it went, year after year. That was all the conversation they ever had.

As I wrote the story, lying on the front seat of the car with my feet stuck out the driver's side window, I started to think there must have been more to their relationship than that bear. They never could have gotten along, because arguing over a dead bear just didn't make sense.

The other part of the story was that one miner bought the other one out and soon had a new partner. Months later that new partner's flesh and blood painted the inside of the mine shaft. The poor soul went swiftly to his earthly end, and the RCMP reported that there'd been a mishap with some dynamite. The miner cleaned up the mess and kept on drilling and digging, though he could never find another partner.

I was determined to find at least one person to meet. I wanted to make friends and record some Keno City stories and history, so I drove back into town, parked behind Bob and Alice's store and walked about.

Sun-bleached and weathered buildings of all different types and sizes were scattered along the streets. Some had been boarded up for decades, and others had bright patches of gardens out front that showed they were occupied. As I walked past one low log structure that had settled elegantly into the permafrost, I heard jazz filtering through the screen door. An elderly man walked out carrying a large galvanized watering can.

I immediately said, "Hello."

"Hello there, young fellow," he said cheerfully. "What brings you to these parts?"

I couldn't believe my luck. I had found the opportunity I was looking for.

"I live in Dawson. I'm a writer and reporter for the *Star* and I'm looking for stories."

"Well, you have come to the right spot. I'm Arnold Nixon. I've lived and worked here most of my life."

"I'm Tobias Godwit. You might know my father, Hudson."

"Yeah, I do," he said. "Is Victor the Gypsy still up to no good in those parts?"

"Victor is still going strong," I said.

He invited me in for coffee. His one-room cabin was neatly organized with bookshelves on the walls, a colourful patchwork quilt on the bed and a table in the middle of the room covered by a worn oilcloth. A large window above the sink allowed the bright sun to light up the room. In the middle of the table sat the white skull of a grizzly. Its impressive incisors hung over each side of the bottom jaw, touching the table.

"Interesting centrepiece," I said. "What's the story behind that?"

Arnold didn't answer right away but said, "Hold on a second. I'll make coffee and tell you."

Arnold was about sixty years old. He had close-cropped grey hair, and stubble covered his creased face. His woollen shirt and pants with suspenders were clean but worn. His appearance, like his home, was typical for a bachelor miner.

Arnold set a cup of coffee and a plate of Oreo cookies—my favourites—in front of me.

He picked up the skull and handed it to me. "That, my boy, is a grizzly I shot on the front lawn outside this cabin about thirty years ago."

Bingo, I thought. I'd hit the motherlode of stories.

I never let on that I knew about the bear, and Arnold spun the tale almost exactly as my father had told it to me. It was interesting to hear it from the man who was there.

I didn't want to confront him directly about the supposed accident that took the life of his partner, so I casually asked, "After you and your partner split over the bear, did you take on anyone else?"

"I told the RCMP everything about that."

I thought it was an odd response. We talked a bit more, and after thanking him for the story, I left. I walked around town, took a few pictures and said hello once again to the old lady in her garden. She never even looked up this time.

As I walked toward the store to pick up the Rambler, I saw Alice, Bob and Arnold standing on the timber loading dock. Alice was standing between Arnold and Bob. She had her back to Arnold and her arms held out as if protecting him. They were deep in a heated argument.

As I approached, Alice was saying, "Stop it, Bob. You have it all wrong."

They heard me coming, and all three looked my way and immediately stopped. Alice stepped away from Arnold and straightened her smock. I didn't say a word but got into the car and drove to the gas pumps. Bob came over muttering curses.

"Good afternoon," I said.

"Noon," he said. He pumped the gas and ignored me.

I figured that if I became a citizen of Keno City and lived there the rest of my life, Bob and his curly-haired wife would never speak two words to me again.

I camped out another night in the gravel pit and finished up my notes for Arnold's bear story. I wanted a picture of Arnold with the skull, so I drove over about eight o'clock in the morning and knocked on the door. It opened immediately, and Arnold stood there unsteadily. His hair was messed, and his eyes were bloodshot and jaundiced. I could smell liquor.

"Morn, Arnold," I said, thinking I might as well use the local dialect.

"Morn," he said, rubbing the top of his head.

"Can I take a picture of you and the skull for a story?" I asked.

"Sure, hang on a sec while I get my slippers," he said and went back inside, closing the door partway behind him. I heard a woman's voice, and then Arnold said, "It's the young guy from Dawson."

He brought the skull outside, closing the door behind him. He stood on the boardwalk, flanked by the gardens, and held it waist high. I snapped three pictures, shook his hand and left.

I hung around until the evening, then drove back to Dawson. I slowed down at the Mayo turnoff to see if anyone was hitching a ride, but no one was. I stopped at the Stewart Bridge and walked down to where I thought the hitchhikers must have found the beer. The water was clear and swift. I could see why someone would want to cool beer in it. I looked around but couldn't see if more was stashed. If I had found beer, I wouldn't have drunk it but would have left it for the owner.

As I stood on the rocks near the waterline, I looked up and saw a body floating face down with its arms and legs outstretched. The man wore blue jeans and a white shirt, and one shoe was missing. The body bobbed along the surface with the current. In an instant it was under the bridge and out of sight. I couldn't believe I'd really seen it, so I ran up the bank and across the road to watch it float away.

I sat down on the guardrail with my back to the river. The question was what to do. I could walk across the bridge and tell the people at the Stewart Crossing Lodge, and they would call the police. Then those poor overworked and underpaid devils would have to drop everything, recruit help, load their boat and patrol miles and miles of the river for God knows how many days and still find nothing; everyone would expect it of them, and there would be hell to pay if they didn't do it. Or I could do nothing and let the rivers give up their dead, as they historically do, on a sandbar below Forty Mile.

I thought for a moment, and with a clear conscious, chose the latter. I was confident in my father's belief that everything in this universe will come to light, even to the extent of a mustard seed, and I thought surely that's true for a dead man floating down the Yukon River.

When I got home, I said nothing of the body. I focussed on my writing. I was pleased that I'd gotten Arnold's story, and when I read it to my dad, he said, "That's it, all right."

The accuracy of my father's original reporting impressed me.

My mother took her car shopping, and when she got back, she asked, "Tobias, why does my car smell of beer?"

One evening a month after I returned from Keno, my father was sitting at the table reading a newspaper as my mother prepared food at the kitchen sink. My father put his paper down and took the pipe from his mouth.

"They found a body," he said.

"Below Forty Mile. It was hung up on a sandbar," Mom said. "They were talking about it at the grocery store."

"They had trouble identifying it because of the wrong name tag on the clothing," Dad said.

"It was that poor grocer from Keno, you know the one with the little store?" Mom said. "His name was Bob something or other."

"Bob Harmond," I said as I poured a glass of milk.

"You knew him?" My mother asked.

"Well, I didn't exactly know him," I said, "but I met him and his lovely wife."

"Apparently a grizzly got him," Mom said and grimaced in sympathetic pain. "It bit his head really hard."

"Yeah, of all things. One of the bear's teeth was embedded in his skull. Must have been an old bear," Dad said. "The RCMP are saying it's the oddest thing."

"No one has ever seen anything like it," Mom said.

I'd just taken a mouthful of milk when I remembered Arnold and the pictures I had taken. I choked, and milk sprayed out both nostrils and my mouth. Coughing and spitting, I stood over the sink and washed my face and hands. My mother grabbed a cloth and wiped the fridge door, countertop and floor.

"You have to be more careful and drink slowly, Tobias. One of these days you're going to choke to death," she said.

I excused myself and hurried to my room, where I tore out the file for Keno City and rifled through the papers and pictures. There was Arnold standing in front of the cabin, looking half-asleep and holding the skull. The left incisor was clearly missing. I looked at Arnold's smile, and I knew where that tooth had gone.

I never told anyone. I had bouts of paranoia with my depression. It shook my confidence, and sometimes I questioned my own reasoning.

I went to Keno again to try to interview that old lady in her rhubarb patch but I missed her again. For some reason she stuck in my mind; I knew she had a story to tell. I slowed down at Mayo and Stewart to look for hitchhikers but I didn't see any.

The store was now managed by Alice. She was happy as a lark and looked twenty years younger. She'd changed her eye makeup and lost weight and actually looked pretty. Arnold was helping her out. He'd gained weight and now shaved every day.

"Good morning," they said.

They offered me coffee at Arnold's cabin. A Chinese inscribed sugar bowl sat where the skull once did. When Arnold saw me looking at it, he gave me that smile again.

Brian's Epiphany

I drove over to Brian's house on a sunny Saturday morning. He'd been acting a little strangely, and I wanted to make sure he and Maude were all right.

Maude answered the door in her housecoat, then yawned and stretched. "He's out somewhere. Maybe he's walking Miami down at the river."

"Thanks." I turned to leave.

"He's upset and acting real serious about something," she called after me. Slowly she stepped back inside the house, closing the door.

I wound my way through the tall stands of willows along the shore and found him sitting by the water's edge. Maude was right, he looked tired. He was throwing sticks for her small white poodle to fetch.

I sat down beside him. "I came down to see how you were doing. Maude says you might be upset about something."

Holding his head in his hands, he ignored Miami. The little dog stood in front of him stomping her feet, eagerly waiting for him to throw the stick again.

"I might be totally wrong about this alien thing. In fact, I know I am. There is no doubt about it. All I have ever done was look for the truth and I think I got off track." He stared off in the distance as if looking for an answer.

"Really?" I never thought I'd hear him say this.

Brian plucked pieces of grass and threw them in the direction of the river. The wind blew them back. Miami tried to catch them both coming and going, jumping up and snapping her teeth in the air.

"The conference attracted hundreds of people, but what did we prove? The dance and banquet were fun, and we made loads of money, but some of those people were just plain nuts." He threw his hands in the air and shook his head. "Their theories were so convoluted they came across as being weird. That Madame Merch should never have been allowed into the country. I'm embarrassed I associated with them."

"I didn't see any brilliant truths discovered either. In fact, to be honest, Brian, I thought it was a load of garbage," I said.

Miami barked as if in agreement.

"Thanks, Tobias—and Miami. I knew I could count on you to tell the truth." He didn't sound too happy about it and pulled grass with more determination. "The truth is, I was like a mad scientist in a science fiction movie. I invented everything. There were no facts. You sat there—you heard what Joseph Copper had to say. I listened to every word, and to tell you the truth, he was right. We are acting like a bunch of crazies."

"But Joseph didn't say it in a mean way."

"I know, but sometimes the truth hurts," Brian said. "When I was young, I devoted all my energies to the aliens. I was influenced by my friend Gregg, a real Lex Luthor egghead. I think he eventually went to jail for impersonating royalty in Europe. He called himself the Duke of Earl after the pop song. A real original, he was. He was convinced that aliens had opened trapdoors on their spaceships and unloaded surplus DNA into the primeval soup, and from that, man evolved. It fascinated me to think that aliens were involved in our creation. It explained everything so easily—the Egyptian pyramids, the Bermuda Triangle, the disappearance of Amelia Earhart, the Abominable Snowman, Albert Einstein and Jerry Lewis. Why didn't I listen to my parents and stay away from that guy?"

"Jerry Lewis?"

"No, Gregg."

"Amelia Earhart, eh? You figured she was kidnapped by aliens? I'm a great fan of hers. I love her," I said.

Brian looked at me. "Sometimes, Tobias, the line between truth and fiction still gets a little blurry, don't you think? Help me out. I'm trying to get some clarity here."

"Okay," I said, my cheeks burning a little for having slipped back into the world of aliens.

"Last night I reached across the dinner table and took Maude's hand. I asked her, 'Honey sugar, you're not really an alien, are you?' Do you know what she said, Tobias?"

"No."

"She said, 'No dear, now eat your salad. It's good for you.' She didn't even blink an eye—just went on cutting her steak. I'm so embarrassed. How could I carry on like that? How crazy is it that you think your wife is an alien? Eh? Tobias, how crazy is that?"

I didn't answer, because it was really crazy, and I didn't want to make him feel any worse than he already did. I couldn't imagine anyone thinking his wife was an alien. I expected to be married someday, and I made a vow to never think my wife was an alien.

"Well, it must have made for an interesting relationship," I said.

"I thought her home was the planet Yammy in the distant A1689-ZD1 galaxy." His cheeks went red. "Boy, was I off."

Trying to make a joke of it, I said, "Yeah, you were way off. She is actually from the planet Zammy in the A1689-ZD1 galaxy."

That seemed to cheer him up. When he laughed, he seemed like the old Brian again.

"The planet Yammy—where does stuff like that come from?" I asked.

"I made it up. Imagined every bit of it," he tapped himself on the head with his index finger. "I convinced myself it was all very scientific, but it's all fiction—except for the one-legged raven and three-legged dog, of course. That's true."

"Of course," I said, "and the line between truth and fiction just got blurred again, Brian."

Over the next few months, Brian carried his space library out to the garage and dumped everything in a corner. A few times I helped him pack the boxes of files out of the house. Maude had a smile for every trip he took. "Now I can put up family pictures," she said. She took stacks of pictures out of storage boxes and covered the walls with many generations of her relatives and friends.

"Brian, honey, I never realized until I saw these pictures again just how much I miss my folks back home. We have to make plans to visit them real soon. We could load up the Winnebago, and the three of us will just go." She was sitting on the couch holding a picture of her mother, and her eyes looked damp.

I was glad this was over. I'd always thought the belief in aliens was immature and showed that people weren't really thinking the whole thing through. It made for interesting stories, but the nagging thought of the folly of it all was always in the back of my mind.

Brian eventually burned his Roswell files and numerous boxes in the wood stove. The rest we piled high in the back of his pickup truck and drove to the city dump at the north end of town. Brian backed the truck to the water's edge, and we shovelled everything directly into the Yukon River. He stood on the tailgate watching the boxes float downstream.

"There goes my life, Tobias," he said raising a hand in a mock toast. "Here's to a new one, whatever that might be."

I couldn't even imagine what might come next.

Brian and Winch stopped seeing each other. Winch had enjoyed the status of working with Brian, but without him, he had no choice but to abandon the alien cause.

"Enough of that idiot stuff," he told me one day at the garage.

This pleased everyone at Rock Creek immensely, and the Halloos' family relationships started to fall back into place. OP and Clutch always seemed to be laughing. They were happy now that they had their brother back. They gleefully slapped each other on the back, thinking that they had something to do with it.

"I told you those questions we asked at the convention would help bring Winch to his senses," Clutch announced to anyone who would listen.

"Your questions were just as stupid as the answers," Uncle Zak said, but Clutch and OP didn't listen.

Two weeks after the reuniting, the Halloos organized a big, smoky barbecue to celebrate Winch's homecoming. Many folks turned out, drawn by the promise of a barbecued pig.

After dinner, people watched in horror as the three brothers leaped arm in arm across the blazing bonfire in a ritual of unity, only to stumble and crash back onto the burning logs. A cloud of sparks and smoke leaped high into the overhanging trees. With their hair, beards and clothing singed or on fire, the three men bolted for the river, still locked arm in arm and laughing their fool heads off. Patches of flames and smoke streamed off their backs as they threw themselves into the water before there was any serious damage.

"You're ruining your clothes!" Stella yelled as she ran after them down to the river.

Winch pulled her in, sputtering and laughing. Others dived in and joined the thrashing and splashing. Then, in a chorus from the water, the brothers started hollering over and over at the top of their lungs, "Yahoo hullabaloo Halloo! Yahoo hullabaloo Halloo!" as if it was a national anthem. The women who came near were pulled into the water, and soon kids and dogs joined in the fray.

I took a few pictures of it all. I was glad things had gotten back to normal—for the Halloos—and there seemed no permanent harm to the family relationships.

As the months went by, I saw less of Brian. He went from home to work, then back again. His life had toned down dramatically.

He did confide in me. "Tobias, you know how some men have women on their mind? Well, I have something on mine, and it's causing me a lot of concern."

A shiver went through my body. *My God*, I thought, *Brian is stepping out on Maude. She and that dog will kill him.*

I was greatly relieved when he said, "I've been reading the Bible, Tobias, but I can't say I understand it, especially Revelations and the Old Testament."

"I tried reading Revelations when I was about twelve," I said, "but all the stuff about the Horsemen of the Apocalypse and the destruction of the world scared me."

"I found a Quran in the library and took it out. It's interesting and understandable if you study it along with Islamic history. And Joshua gave me a Baha'i book called *The Seven Valleys and the Four Valleys*, which refers to Sufi poetry," he said.

"I don't know much about any of that but I agree it's interesting," I said. "To tell the truth, I've had an interest in the Eastern world since I was young but never pursued it."

"Reading all this, I'm beginning to think religions are from the same source but appear at different times in history. Like gold nuggets, they all came from the same motherlode," he said.

Maude wasn't happy with Brian's new-found "hobby," as she called it. Her family pictures were being replaced with new books. The post office was constantly delivering material of every description. Fritz, the postmaster, told Brian, "We're going to have to build you a bigger mailbox."

"Where the hell am I supposed to put my knick-knacks, Brian, on the floor? You're taking up all the shelf space again," she said.

"I'll put up more shelves. There's plenty of room in the kitchen yet."

"You're not putting shelves in the kitchen, Brian, don't even try it," Maude threatened.

I was staying the weekend with the Halloos when Maude complained to Stella that Brian might be becoming a religious freak. "If I had known he was going to be this much trouble, I would never have hooked up with him. Aliens, religion, what happened to life without a cause?"

"Well, you could have married James Dean," Stella said. "He was a rebel but didn't have a cause."

"I've never heard of him but I'd like to meet that man," Maude said.

Brian was reading Hermann Hesse's novel *Siddhartha* again, and he was hooked. He couldn't get out of his mind the image of Siddhartha meditating by the river.

"I like the book," he told Winch and me one day when we were having coffee at the Flora Dora Café, "but Hesse was mistaken that enlightenment could be achieved through meditation alone."

"Then why do you sit in the middle of your living room floor, looking like a human pretzel with your legs crossed over your head, while Maude vacuums around you?" Winch asked.

"I'm not saying there's anything wrong with meditation," Brian said. "All I'm saying is that when Hesse described a group of monks on a journey to visit the Buddha, I wished Siddhartha had joined them— that he had met Buddha and received enlightenment from the source."

Brian tried to encourage Winch to join him in meditation. "Come on, Winch, it will be good for you—and fun."

The thought of a four-hundred-pound man trying to get into some of those positions worried me, so later I encouraged Winch not to participate.

"You'll blow a tire, I just know it, Winch, so take it easy."

Winch's sensitive side came out. "You saying I'm fat, Tobias?"

I was in a no-win situation, so I had to be firm. "Look, if you take up yoga or whatever you call it, I'm telling Lulu."

And that fixed that.

Days later I was with Joshua, having coffee and apple pie à la mode for lunch in the Flora Dora, when Brian walked in and sat in our booth. He looked different; the anxiety was gone from his face.

"I had an epiphany," he said.

"What's an epiphany?" I asked.

"A sudden understanding," Joshua answered.

"When did this happen? What was it?" I asked, pulling out my notebook as if I was covering a city council meeting.

Brian didn't seem to mind that I took notes. He turned his head and sat sideways in the booth, looking out the window.

"A few days ago I was by the river and got caught up in the sound of the wind rattling the leaves in the trees. It sounded like the rattles that Natives shake before they speak in council."

"Right." I'd heard that at potlatches.

"Then, out of the blue, for one brief moment, the doors of perception opened wide and I saw that all of creation started from a single point. I saw that the earth is the point of intellectual life for the universe. We have been created to inherit and inhabit the universe. There is no one else here, there are no aliens. We are alone."

"That's interesting. I've heard of that type of experience before, when a friend of mine met a holy man," Joshua said.

Brian didn't seem to hear Joshua but looked straight ahead, concentrating on what was revealed to him. "We are space pioneers, and I think religion is the charter for our advancement. The universe is ours, a gift. We own it. It's an indication of someone's love for us."

Joshua nodded, clearly impressed, as I took notes.

Then he looked back at us. "I felt dwarfed by the massive energy and power around me and the sense of spirituality that domed the earth. We are a spiritual creation. God made us spiritual. Wherever I looked, I saw all things in perfect order. The universe brimmed with the sound of expansion. I sensed the massiveness of the planet turning on its axis. Then, just as quickly as it had begun, it was over. I realized I'd had a glimpse of reality. The invisible had become visible. Things are more orderly than we imagine. The epiphany was a gift."

"Congratulations," I said.

"Good work," Joshua said.

"Thank you," Brian said. Then he sighed and turned toward us. "Tobias, Joshua, I cannot believe how out in left field I was. I apologize to both of you. I've been apologizing to everyone. It seems when you don't know the facts, you make them up, and that confuses things even more." He rubbed his eyes as if rubbing years of weariness out of them. "You have to be patient. The truth deserves patience. I'm being patient from now on."

"I had an epiphany years ago," Joshua said. "It's probably why I'm here in Dawson City getting away from it all. It scared the hell out of me."

We all laughed.

"What was it?" I asked.

"I was reading a book called *The Hidden Words* that said we should ponder at all times in our hearts how we were created. It seemed like good advice, so I sat at my desk where I worked and I did just that. I thought about my parents and how they were created by my grandparents and so on. I was back about four or five generations when I skipped ahead and went to ancient man, skipped that and went to the moment of the big bang when the creation of our universe began. That's when I became terrified."

"Why?" Brian asked.

"Because I suddenly realized we are created, and it wasn't our choice. I felt that deeply. I was so frightened I yelled out loud, 'We are androids!' My friend at the next desk looked over the divider to see what I was talking about. At that moment I felt more powerless than I ever had in my entire life. Something created us, and we are held in the palm of that Being's hand."

"God," Brian said, nodding in agreement.

We said no more, as if we didn't dare say His name.

I scribbled notes and asked them, "Is that it?"

Both nodded yes.

I finished my coffee, thanked them for sharing this and headed back to see my mom, who was working at the post office. I had the feeling those two men had forged a new friendship through their epiphanies.

Later that day I walked home along Front Street and met Brian and Joshua coming the other way.

They stopped. Joshua asked casually, "Do you know why we have to perfect ourselves, Tobias?"

"I don't know," I said, taken off guard by the depth of the question.

"Because God deserves a perfect lover," he said.

"Oh," I said. We continued on our separate ways.

As I walked on, I looked at the lush green hills that surrounded the valley and the deep turquoise Klondike River flowing into the mighty Yukon River, and I sensed that the future of Dawson City and its people was bright. Smiling, I rounded the corner next to the Historical Sites building and saw Winch on the riverbank struggling to get into the lotus position.

Jealousy among Friends

I returned to Keno City that fall. I'd visited there during the summer looking for people to interview but found much more than I expected. Now I was sure that Bob, the store owner, had met with foul play. Maybe the mystery novels I'd read as a kid were influencing me more than I liked.

What would Agatha do? I asked myself, and when that didn't inspire me, I wondered what Bogie would do. I decided that Agatha and Bogie would investigate. Agatha especially would never leave this alone; she would have Hercule Poirot on this as quick as a wink. I also had the urge to write a great Klondike murder mystery, but my instincts told me to be careful; I had knowledge that could make people nervous.

Along the way I stopped at McQuesten River Lodge for gas. One of the last tourist buses of the season was parked in the yard, and the hungry travellers were crammed into the dining room enjoying a lunch of tomato soup and tuna sandwiches. The youngest children and the most elderly adults had red rings around their mouths. The lodge's pet pig, Blossom, walked around beneath the tables snuffling up scraps, some of them deliberately dropped. The owners rushed about filling coffee cups and rotating ketchup and mustard dispensers from table to table. I wasn't hungry, so I petted Blossom, gassed up and drove on my way.

I arrived in Keno City late that afternoon. It was cloudy, and a light snow had dusted the town. I walked around and found the lady gardener I'd seen on my unsettling last visit. She was walking backwards down her wooden walk, swinging a corn broom back and forth and sending clouds of snow onto the garden. Where knee-high patches of vegetables had grown a few weeks earlier, there were now rows of neatly piled soil waiting for next year's planting.

"Hello," I said, not daring to say more in case she ignored me and walked back into the house.

"Hello," she said, pausing to lean on her broom. "You're that nice young man who interviewed Arnold."

Arnold had to be aware by now that I knew something, so it was a bit disconcerting to hear that he spoke highly of me.

"I wanted to talk to you," I said, feeling cautious but pleased that a conversation had started. "Especially because you seem to have lived here a long time."

"I'm Lily Bluebell Manchester," she said holding out her hand. "Yes, I've lived here a long time—maybe too long for some people." She laughed and blushed.

Her hand was strong like a tradesman's, and her eyes were the brightest blue. I could see how she got her name.

"Pleased to meet you," I said.

Lily gestured toward the house, and we walked to the door, stomping the snow off our boots. The house was neat and tidy, and the wood stove gave a warm welcome as we stepped into the kitchen. The aromatic smell of fresh baking filled the room.

"Ginger snaps," she told me. "Do you like them?"

"I love anything home-baked. My mom bakes all the time." I hung up my coat and hat and sat at the table.

"Arnold told me Hudson and Rebecca are your parents. I met them both a few times when I visited Dawson," she said.

"I'll tell them I visited with you."

Lily reached up to lift down her best cups from a high shelf and set the table for tea. Soon the kettle whistled on the stove. She straightened her apron, then sat down.

As we sipped tea, I hungrily devoured all the cookies on the plate. She watched as if she had seen this many times before.

After two cups of tea, I took out my notebook, crossed my legs and asked her, "Would you tell me about Bob Harmond?"

Her face took on a stark expression, and she rubbed her hands nervously. "There's nothing to say. The RCMP dealt with that."

I had made her uncomfortable, so I quickly changed the subject. "What about you? How long have you lived here?"

She brightened up. I think she was glad to be asked.

"I've lived in this area all my life. My father was James Copper—Jim—the uncle of Joseph Copper. My mother was an immigrant Norwegian schoolteacher who moved from Seattle and met my father in Whitehorse. I have one brother, Twobee."

"I've met Twobee and I know Joseph. I see him all the time. He's an interesting person with good stories," I said. "I never met your father, though Joseph has mentioned him."

Lily went on. "My husband was Ed Manchester. He was Arnold's business partner until his death."

"I heard about one partner leaving Arnold over a bear, then another partner meeting an accident," I said.

"The bear had nothing to do with the partnership breaking up. It was more complicated than that," she said.

"How so?" I scribbled notes, feeling vindicated that my instincts were right. There had been more to this story than a fight over a bear.

"I'll show you something." Lily went into her back room, and I could hear her opening and shutting drawers. I glanced around the room. An antique glass-doored china cabinet had shelves filled with collectibles; I recognized some Royal Doulton pieces because my mother also collected them. I glanced at the bottom shelf, and my heart stopped. There sat Arnold's bear skull. It was partially covered with a cloth, but I recognized the empty socket where it was missing a tooth. I almost got up to leave, but the newspaperman in me kept me seated.

Lily walked back into the room, her arm full of photo albums stuffed with loose pictures, and took in the expression on my face. Then she quickly glanced down at the bear's skull and back at me. I didn't know what to say.

"Let me explain," Lily said, and dropped her albums on the table so that the pictures spilled out.

The kitchen had become a courtroom; she was the defendant, and I was the prosecutor and jury. The truth and only the truth was to be spoken. A piece of her hair had strayed from behind her ear, and she carefully pulled it back. Lily regained her composure and opened the photo albums on the table. I wouldn't have been surprised if she'd then said, "Members of the jury ... "

She pulled out a creased black and white photo with bent edges. It showed four people. Two young men in baggy pants and windbreakers leaned on either side of an automobile. Their hair was greased back in ducktails, and they had confident smiles. Between them two pretty young women sat on the hood, their hair tied with scarves, wearing long skirts that fell below their knees. One girl smiled shyly, and the other was laughing.

Lily pointed to each in turn. "Bob, Alice, me and my husband Ed. We were such good friends—we did everything together. Bob and Ed worked in the store off and on. Then Bob went to work with Arnold, and Ed started in the silver mine at Elsa. Victor the Gypsy was his partner."

"I know Victor well," I said.

She sifted through the pile of pictures and pulled out another one. "This might interest you. Do you recognize anyone?"

I took the picture from her hand. It was a group of young men with their arms around each other's shoulders. They all had big smiles on their faces.

"Victor, Ed, Bob and Arnold," I said. "But I don't know the other two."

"That's Buford and Craven when they were young," she said. "They were all friends."

"Craven and Buford were my neighbours," I said. "I liked them."

Lily laid another group of pictures on the table. They showed a group of people in parkas and hats standing around a grave on a cold-looking, cloudy day. Wreaths lay on top of the snow. The next picture was of a headstone. Chiselled into it were the words "Edward L. Manchester. Beloved Husband of Lily Bluebell. 1920–1949."

She looked up, and her eyes were teary. "Would you like to go see the gravesite?"

I looked out through the window. In the darkness, light from the kitchen illuminated the falling snow. "Now?"

Lily nodded. "I visit it almost every day at all times of day."

We put on our coats and walked toward the end of town. The moon was as bright as a street lamp. We carefully helped each other up a steep, slippery trail to a graveyard with about thirty graves. Some of the markers were wood, others stone or marble, but every one was different. Each one leaned or stood in its own direction. If it had been day and I'd had more time, I would have liked to read each stone to see what history lay there.

"Ed is over here," she said. She reached down and brushed the snow off a headstone with her gloved hand. "This granite is from what was then the deepest part of the Elsa Mine. The miners made the headstone."

I could see the stone had high-grade silver running through it. The miners chose right.

"I always say a prayer," Lily said.

We stood there as she silently prayed. She closed her eyes, and I watched her lips move. The snow continued to gently fall in the still evening air. Then she took my arm, and we walked back to the cabin and took off our coats. Lily put the kettle back on, and we sat down. Both of us had red cheeks from the cold.

"I'm sorry about your husband. It must have been a terrible time for you," I said.

"It was the worst of times. It still is. I never got over losing Ed."

"I heard it was an accident—Arnold told me that."

"It wasn't an accident. It was all because of jealousy," Lily said. "Bob was always sweet on me. He married Alice but he let it be known that I was the one he wanted. Ed was the only man I ever loved. Bob meant nothing to me. I told him that to his face."

"Did your husband know about this?" I asked.

"The whole town knew. There are no secrets here. Ed spoke to Bob on a number of occasions. Bob would show up drunk in the middle of the night, knocking on the door and wanting to talk to me. Ed would go out and push him out of the yard. One time they came to blows, and Ed beat up Bob. Alice would get upset. It was an embarrassment, especially in a small town like this."

"What about Arnold and Alice?"

"Arnold and Alice were the best of friends, nothing more than that, but Bob was insanely jealous. He accused Alice of all kinds of things. I don't know how Alice put up with it all those years, his drinking and abuse," she said.

"The argument over the bear was the last straw. It just showed how crazy things were getting. Arnold had had enough of Bob and bought him out. A while later Ed went to work with Arnold, and the mine struck a solid vein of silver. We became relatively rich. Bob never saw a cent of it, and that drove him crazy. All these years Bob has made Arnold's life as miserable as he could. I think he treated Alice the way he did to spite Arnold. He was mean like that."

"I would like to know what happened to Ed," I said, "but only if it doesn't upset you. I don't want to cause you any grief," I said.

Lily spread her hands and sighed. "Ed was an experienced blaster, having set charges hundreds of times at the Elsa Mine. Just before the accident, Arnold and he had drilled powder holes and filled them with dynamite. Arnold walked out to secure the entrance, and Ed set the fuse. The RCMP and Arnold figured there was a mix-up—a faster-burning safety fuse somehow got mixed in with the slower ones. Ed was walking out when the blast went off."

"I'm sorry," I said. I didn't know what else to say.

"It was years ago, but it seems like yesterday," she said, wiping her eyes.

"Two weeks after the funeral Arnold came over with a bit of fuse he'd found in the mine. It was the faster-burning kind. Here, I'll show you."

She got up, opened the china cabinet and reached down beside the bear's head to pick up what looked like a torn piece of short rope.

"This is what Arnold found," she said.

I held it in my hand. I didn't know much about dynamite, so it really meant nothing to me. After examining it for a polite length of time, I handed it back without saying anything.

"Months later Bob approached Arnold and wanted their old partnership back. Arnold told him to go to hell. That's how things were left for all these years. With Ed gone, Bob tried to bother me, but Buford and Victor stepped in and warned him. Victor told him, 'I put curse on you, give you headache like you never believe.' I cannot help but think that, all these years later, the tooth was part of that gypsy curse." Lily tried to be serious, but couldn't help smiling.

"That Victor." I shook my head.

Lily went on, "Bob threatened Arnold and told him to be careful or he might just end up like his partner. So that's how it's been—people living side by side, jealous, hating each other and looking over their shoulders. You know how it is in these small towns, Tobias."

Did I ever. I nodded.

"Ed was gone, but I still had a stake in Arnold's property. That's what has paid the bills all these years. I think Arnold has been more than generous," Lily said as she poured me another cup of tea.

"So no one ever worked out what happened?" I asked.

"Whenever Bob got drunk, he confessed to Alice that he'd murdered Ed. She listened to it for years, never telling anyone. When he was sober, he denied it. Late one night she called Arnold and me over, and we listened in the kitchen to Bob ranting in the living room. He confessed all right. He staggered out to the kitchen and must have caught sight of us leaving, because the next day—the morning that you first met him in the store—he was crying, really upset that he'd let the cat out of the bag."

"What exactly did he say when drunk?" I'd filled my steno pad and was now scribbling notes on a handful of Lily's paper table napkins.

"He spoke of replacing the fuse with a faster-burning one." The voice came from behind me, making me nearly jump out of my skin.

Arnold and Alice were standing in the porch. I had been so engrossed in Lily's story that I hadn't noticed them. They walked in and stood on either side of Lily, facing me. For a moment they looked like their long-ago pictures, but older and timeworn. They took seats at the table. Arnold sat close to me and put his foot up on the rung on the bottom of my chair. His brow was furrowed. Alice fidgeted with the corner of the tablecloth.

"The afternoon you met me was the same day Bob met his end," Arnold said. "Alice and Lily were visiting me for tea that evening when Bob barged in and threw a few swings at Alice, then at me."

Without hesitation Lily said, "I picked up the skull and hit him across the head as hard as I could. He looked almost comical with the bear's tooth sticking out of his forehead like a unicorn horn. Being hit on the head didn't kill him, though. He grabbed his chest and fell to his knees, then collapsed onto his back. He was having a heart attack. Then he confessed. He said, 'I did it. I killed Ed.' 'You rat,' I said, 'I always knew you killed my husband.' Bob said, 'I'm sorry,' and lifted his arm, trying to touch my hand, but I pulled it back. He died on the floor of Arnold's cabin."

"We had no proof of his confession, and the hole from the tooth would be hard to explain, so we left it in, hoping that people would think a bear attacked him," Alice said. "We drove down to Mayo at midnight and put the body in the Stewart River. None of us felt any remorse. I was a little shaken up, but at least the long ordeal was over. He was a hard man to love."

"The police questioned us when Bob disappeared," Arnold said, "but they knew he was often drunk and had heart trouble. They figured he would show up later. As time went on, they seemed glad to forget about him. Bob affected people that way. When the body turned up, they quickly closed the case."

"You surprised us when you came to take a picture of the bear's skull," Lily said. "We'd just gotten back from dumping the body. Arnold barely handled it. When he realized you'd taken a picture of crucial evidence, we could only hope the tooth fell out on Bob's trip down the river. When I saw that you recognized the skull in the china cabinet, I knew the truth would have to come out. I should have gotten rid of it. I'm not sure why I kept it."

"Actually, I put some of it together before I came down here," I said. "If I hadn't seen the skull again, I would never have mentioned it."

"What are you going to do about it now that you know the truth?" Arnold asked.

Alice and Lily sat silently staring at me. I held their future in my hands. I sat thinking for a moment.

"Do you have any more tea, Lily?" I asked, hoping to give myself more time. I lifted my cup. "And a few more of those delicious cookies would be great."

Lily got up and refilled my cup from the teapot warming on the stove, then offered tea to Arnold and Alice.

"No thanks," Arnold said, not taking his gaze off me.

Alice silently waved her hand in a no.

The three of them waited politely as I added cream and sugar, took a sip and bit into a cookie. Finally I said, "Nothing. I'll do nothing. It's not my business. I'll leave it to you to make your own decision."

They looked at each other as if to take a consensus. They seemed relieved.

Arnold studied me for a minute. "Okay, but if you change your mind, call us first."

That's how people are in the Yukon. If they trust you, they don't quibble or question.

"I won't change my mind," I said, reaching for another ginger snap.

Lily smiled. "Ed used to eat my baking like that, cleaning up the whole plate."

"I wish I'd met Ed," I said. "He sounds like a good guy."

"He was," Arnold said.

I got up to leave. As I hugged Lily, I asked her, "Do you know how I know Ed was a good guy?"

Lily Bluebell just shook her head.

"Because he had a sweetheart for a wife."

She started to cry and sat down. Alice went and put her arm around her friend.

Arnold pointed to my notebook, stuffed with the table napkins I'd written on. "Do you need that?"

I adjusted the collar of my coat. "No, I suppose not." I handed him the notebook.

"Thank you."

I shook hands and left without looking back.

That evening I'd planned to get a room and stay over but I didn't feel comfortable after hearing three people confess to assault and dumping a body in the river. The snow was still falling when I passed McQuesten River Lodge at about eight o'clock. Blossom was sitting on her haunches under the porch light by the front door, and I swear that pig lifted a front leg and waved as I drove by.

When I arrived home my father was asleep, and my mother was reading in bed by a lamp. She was excited. I'd received a letter from the admissions department of the University of Victoria.

"Did you find any good stories over in Keno?" she asked the next morning over breakfast.

"No, not one, Ma," I said. "I looked, but nothing ever happens over there. It's just a quiet little town."

"Yeah, right," my father said. He looked over his newspaper and gave me a wink and a smile.

A couple of years passed before I got back to Keno City. I held too many cards that controlled people's lives. Bob killed Ed for the worst of reasons, I believed: jealousy and hate. Maybe he'd actually wanted to kill Arnold or maybe both of them. He'd had his own reasons to hate both men. So Lily had lived all those years broken-hearted without her husband, Alice was abused every day and Arnold lost his friend and partner, then had to watch Bob hurt Lily and Alice. No one murdered Bob; his heart gave out after a lifetime of hard living. I was glad he got this Yukon justice.

Winch's Meltdown

Walter Rather was stacking shelves in his general store when he engaged Brian and me in his favourite conversation.

"More of those damn hippies arrive every day. Where are we going to put them? We'll have to support them, so our taxes will go up as well."

Brian and I did our best to ignore him. Then Winch walked into our aisle, lifting cans of food off the shelves and placing them in a shopping basket. On his big arm it looked like a child's toy.

"Picking up a few things for Lulu?" I asked.

"Yes," he said, and greeted each of us in turn. He seemed a little distracted.

"How are things at the creek?" Brian asked.

"Well, everything is fine, except that place is a madhouse at times. It's best if I get away for a few hours." He lifted the basket to show us that shopping was one way to get away.

Walter finished stocking, and still muttering, moved off to help a customer who was too short to reach a top shelf.

Brian had been telling me all week that he thought he owed Winch an apology for abandoning him during the alien fiasco. This was as good a time as any to put things square.

"What are you doing these days?" Brian asked.

"Working," Winch said. "I'm doing body work on Mrs. Godwit's Rambler. Next I'll repaint it."

"Blue," I said.

Leaning against a shelf, Brian said, "Did you hear I gave up on all that alien stuff and threw everything out? Tobias helped me."

"It was a ton of stuff we had to haul out too," I said.

"I heard about that," Winch said.

"I'm reading religious stuff right now," Brian said, pretending to read the label on a tin; he looked like Hamlet studying a skull.

Winch didn't appear happy to hear about religion. He said good-bye and turned to leave.

Brian caught his shirt sleeve. "It's not what you think."

Winch looked interested, as though he wanted to hear more and was sort of glad Brian had stopped him.

"Let me explain," Brian said. "I had an epiphany. Now I believe we are alone, there are no aliens, and the universe is a gift to us from the Creator. Religion is the guidance we need to build the future. That's why I'm interested in spiritual things."

"What's an epiphany?"

"A sudden understanding," Brian and I said in unison.

Winch's eyes widened—it was obvious that Brian had caught his attention—and he leaned against the shelves, absent-mindedly peeling the label off a tin of peaches with his thumbnail. "You know, Brian, the first thing that comes to my mind is, here we go again."

Bingo! I thought.

"I was taken in by your alien conviction; you made it all sound so real. How do I know this isn't another phase you're going through, and I'll be left high and dry again like a fool?"

"I apologize for the last time. It was wrong that I didn't support you, but it won't happen again, I promise," Brian said, placing both hands on Winch's grocery basket.

Winch sighed and patted Brian's shoulder with a huge hand.

After that, Winch and Brian started to rebuild their partnership and met at the Flora Dora or Brian's house for coffee in the evenings. They mostly discussed religion. I joined them once in a while.

"Tobias, Winch, what do you think the purpose of life is?" Brian would ask.

Winch had never considered religion before—it was organized and had rules—but independent study sparked an interest in him. Quickly he started developing his own interpretations and theories, and some of them went beyond moderation. He was already opinionated enough, but now that he had religion and God, he thought he was right on everything. Brian was patient with him, but Winch became increasingly more insistent and argumentative.

"That's it! No more coffee meetings," Brian said one night, getting up abruptly. "I'm not arguing over religion."

"You just won't listen," Winch said, and stormed off to his truck.

It wasn't long before OP and Clutch realized they'd lost their brother again, since he was becoming totally absorbed in religion. This time they were determined to do something about it. They blamed Brian and took their complaints directly to him. One evening he and I were sitting at the kitchen table having a cup of coffee and going over notes I had written about his epiphany. OP and Clutch stomped up to his kitchen door, knocked and entered before being invited in.

Ignoring their bad manners, Brian picked up his cup and pointed it in the direction of the coffee pot. "Want a cup? It's fresh."

"No, we don't," Clutch said, without trying to hide the agitation in his voice. "Look, here we go again, but now you have Winch all involved in this here stupid, dumb religion stuff."

"Yeah, why do you have to go and do this again?" OP chimed in. "He's our brother, not yours!" OP had never had an original thought in his pointed head; he usually just repeated Clutch's opinions.

"I've done nothing," Brian said, raising his palms in protest. "In fact, Winch has taken off entirely in his own religious direction. I've stopped discussing it with him altogether."

"He's on his own?"

"Yes, all on his own, as I said. I have nothing to do with his involvement in religion."

They fidgeted for a moment, then Clutch turned and pushed OP toward the door, and both of them blustered out. I heard them arguing all the way out to their truck.

"Why didn't you know that?" Clutch shouted at OP.

"Assuming makes an ass out of you and me," OP yelled back.

They climbed into their truck, gunned the engine and tore off down the street, leaving a cloud of dust in their wake.

About a month later I was visiting the garage to see about Mom's Rambler getting an oil change.

"This is one weird-looking car," Brian said when he lifted the hood. "But nice paint job. Have you seen Winch lately?"

I shook my head just as Winch walked in. His face looked flushed. He didn't bother to say hello but just started talking. "I had an epiphany!"

No, you didn't, I thought.

"An old dust-covered gold miner in a wide-brimmed hat, tattered shirt and carrying a gold pan. Said he belonged to some committee of miners or something. He came to me in a dream and said I was special. He said, 'You're a real piece of work.'"

Brian caught my eye, then said, "That's not an epiphany, Winch, that's a nightmare."

I remained silent but studied Winch's face to see his reaction.

His face went red, then redder, and he blew the words out of his mouth like a tornado. "It wasn't a dream, it was my epiphany! You're not the only person to have them."

"You were asleep, and it was probably Lulu snoring in your ear," Brian laughed.

I cringed. Winch was in no mood for Brian's kidding. He wanted his own epiphany so badly that he was willing to accept anything and call it that. When he wheeled around and left without another word, I felt as if an angry bear had left the room.

Joshua came out of the back of the garage, wiping his hands on a grease rag, to watch Winch drive away. "Uncle Zak was in town the other day and stopped by the house. He told me the family thinks Winch has gone zealot. He wants the adults to gather in the living room while he stands and preaches. He tells everyone the world was created in six days, all of creation died in a flood and only a fixed number of people are going to heaven. He's gone real kooky. Where's the seven-sixteenths-inch wrench?"

"Keep your pen and paper handy, Tobias," Brian said with a chuckle. "If he keeps this up, he's going to give you plenty to write about. When I tried to talk sense into him, he got angry and pounded the kitchen table with his fat fist until the cups jumped out of their saucers. Maude grabbed his ear and told him, 'Thump my table one more time, and you'll find out what a real thumping is about.'"

"He's a big guy. When he gets physical, it's intimidating," I said.

"To us maybe, but not to Maude. She would pile-drive him."

Joshua wiped the grease off the wrench. "I don't like to analyze people, but I'm guessing he thinks an epiphany means leadership or something."

With his zeal to be special, Winch continued to spread his message. He cornered me a few times, and I listened politely.

One time he was explaining his theory of "the return" when I asked him, "How could a person descend on clouds when clouds float up?" It seemed like a simple and logical question to me.

"Everyone knows that's how it will happen. The Lord will be standing on a cloud coming down to earth." He then pulled up his hand like a six-gun quick draw, squinted like Robert Newton playing Long John Silver and stuck a cracked and grease-stained finger in my face. I expected him to say "Aargh, matey!" like Long John, but instead he said, "Don't be a heathen unbeliever, Tobias. The wages of sin is death."

I had to cross my eyes to see his finger, he held it so close. "Winch, it's me, Tobias, your friend. Why are you getting so worked up? There's no call for this."

He growled and walked away.

Winch had become a different person. I believed in the good of religion, but his type of religion had ruined him. He had slid past zealot to become Mr. Fire and Brimstone. It made me uncomfortable to hear him talk about sin, especially my sin. I always thought sin was supposed to be private, between you and God. It also saddened me to realize that there was nothing but trouble down the road for Winch and his family, but I felt powerless to help.

I told my dad about Winch. He laughed and said, "Son, I grew up with that. It's abuse. Ignore it. Those guys burn themselves out in time. Brimstone doesn't last forever. I shouldn't laugh, because it is serious, but those guys are such hypocrites."

Everyone in town was talking about Winch. His endless preaching was like a noise that couldn't be turned off. Most waved him away and didn't hide their annoyance.

Halloo family members met in private, concerned because he was the head of the family. Lulu told me about it later.

"There could be a coup d'état if things don't straighten out soon," Zak announced. "I was first in at Dieppe. Taking Winch down will be a piece of cake."

The Halloos didn't buckle under Winch's religious insistence and become a closed sect. I attributed this to their fierce disregard for authority. The women seemed to take the lead in that area.

"To hell with him," Stella said. "Who does he think he is, some television evangelist?"

"Better watch out, Lulu. Those guys end up in some sex scandal sooner or later," Olive laughed.

Lulu shot her sisters a glance that stopped their joke in its tracks. "I'm really worried. This is serious."

Winch argued so much that she made him sleep in the barn. Lulu was afraid he might get into a punchout with other members of the family, and she knew that would be disastrous. "Don't argue with him. It will only make him worse," she advised everyone.

Winch continued his bullying ways. Members of the family stopped talking to him and left the kitchen when he sat down.

"I can't enjoy my food while hearing about when King Rehoboam went to Shechem, and feeling someone thinks he's better than me," Uncle Zak complained. He took his plate and joined the others eating on the front porch.

On some weekends I would stay over at the Halloos; my mom always loaned me her Rambler. I got along well with Lulu and her sisters, who made me feel at home. They were the sisters I never had, and I enjoyed their company immensely. It also gave me an opportunity to interview family members, especially Uncle Zak, who'd been in the secret service and had interesting war stories to tell.

"Tobias, you're welcome here anytime. You're the only guest who makes his own bed and helps with the dishes," Lulu told me as I was leaving one time.

"Now if we could just get him to cook and do laundry," Missy said, washing vegetables for dinner in the sink.

Early one Monday morning, I was eating breakfast before heading into town. People were grabbing coffee and toast to eat on their drive in to their jobs or to take the children to school. Winch strolled in wearing his work overalls and took his place at the head of the long plank table. Resting one elbow, he pointed a finger at the children and said, "Say grace before putting one more scrap of food in your mouth."

Lulu scoffed, and the adults started to clear the room. A child choked and started to cry. I lost my appetite and pushed my plate away but hung around to see what happened next.

Stella's twelve-year-old daughter started to protest, "But Uncle Winch—"

Winch cut her off sharply and launched into a tirade on obedience. When he got to "spare the rod and spoil the child," Lulu decided she'd had enough. She walked around the table and hovered over him. Winch sank in his chair and tucked his head between his shoulders.

I slid down the bench to the other end, thinking that maybe it wasn't such a good idea to stick around.

Lulu stuck her index finger in his face and growled, "Don't upset the kids!" When he didn't answer, she roared, "Stop it!" so forcefully that spittle left her lips.

Winch began to stutter, but a hard slap on the back of his head silenced him. He raised his beefy, tattooed arms in defence. Lulu drew her face closer, so that her chin almost touched his nose, "If you so much as criticize one of these children again, you'll be sorry for the rest of your life … I swear," she snarled.

Stella and Olive walked into the room and stood with their backs to the wall and their arms folded, glaring at Winch. Stella tapped her foot rapidly.

Lulu straightened slowly and walked around the table, maintaining eye contact, but Winch glanced away and muttered under his breath, "Yeah, yeah … right."

It was a grave mistake. Lulu heard him and instantly boiled over. She scanned the table for something to throw and spotted a large wooden spoon sticking out of a bowl of steaming porridge. She grabbed the spoon and swung it at his head, missing completely, but a great glob of porridge came loose and struck him squarely in the right eye. Winch cursed and clawed at his burning face.

I got up and stood in the doorway, ready to run if I had to. Stella and Olive stayed where they were against the wall.

"Stupid religious idiot! Freak! You made more sense as an alien!" Lulu screamed.

The small children cried and hollered. Their mothers rushed in to lift them from their chairs and ran out to avoid the battle. Winch was still cursing.

"Stop swearing, you brainless twit!" Lulu ran around the table and beat Winch's head until the spoon snapped in two.

Winch scrambled under the table. Unable to see through his watering eyes and barely able to fit under the table, he raised it on his back and dragged it toward the door. The tablecloth caught, and plates of food and pitchers of milk crashed to the floor. Avoiding the broken glass, he scooped up the cold milk and splashed it on his face. Crawling closer, he reached up, opened the door and threw himself out onto the porch. A sleeping dog woke suddenly and turned to growl at him. Scrambling to his feet, Winch sprinted across the yard with his head tucked into his shoulders as if expecting something to hit him at any time. He jumped into his truck, and with the door half open, sped off in a cloud of dust, grinding the gears all the way. Lulu and her sisters stood on the porch, shaking their fists at the departing truck.

I stuck my head through the doorway. I didn't know whether to laugh or cry. Olive walked past me into the house. "I'm sorry you had to see that kind of family business, Tobias."

Soon after that Brian told me, "OP and Clutch paid a visit to our house. They were really polite this time. They knocked on the door and waited to be invited in. Then they stood with their hats in their hands and begged me to take their brother back and talk sense into him. They said, 'Please help us, Brian. This is ten times worse than anything alien. We are in a heap of trouble.'"

OP and Clutch needn't have bothered. Winch had made up his own mind. He'd decided he was living among the ignorant and had to leave before they influenced him totally. He stayed away for two weeks, then went home to pick up his belongings. I caught a ride out with him, and for once he was silent all the way. His face still bore a red teardrop around the right eye.

When we walked into the kitchen, a three-year-old in a high chair with food covering his face said brightly, "Uncle Winch looks like a clown, Mom!" To make his point even more clearly, he told Winch, "Your eye looks like a clown eye!"

This deflated Winch's dramatic moment of announcing his departure, but he still made his speech standing in the middle of the kitchen. It sounded rehearsed. "I'm going up Hunker Creek for the winter. Don't try to stop me and don't come looking for me. I intend to spend the winter alone," he shouted into the house for all to hear.

Zak yelled back from a distant hallway what everyone wanted to say. "Go! And when you're alone and freezing your ass off, think of us. We'll be warm and cozy here in our nice, peaceful, happy house!"

Winch could see he wasn't going to get one ounce of sympathy, so he threw his duffel bag into the truck along with tools from the barn and food supplies. "I had an epiphany too," he yelled one last time before driving off.

Lulu was heartsick. Winch had never treated her like this before and had never been so mean to so many people. "A man alone on Hunker Creek will either come to his senses or drop off the deep end of reality," she told her sisters.

Olive and Stella tried to comfort her, but everyone was worried.

"What will he do all alone … all winter?" Missy sounded worried. Winch had always been her favourite uncle.

"Your guess is as good as mine," Lulu said with a sigh, "but I can tell you he's in for a hard time."

Over the next weeks, things settled down around the house. Uncle Zak and OP wanted to go up and get Winch, but Clutch disagreed. He'd recognized that with Winch gone his place in the family hierarchy had moved up a notch. "Maybe this really is what he needs, some time alone. Leave him where he is."

Shortly after that, winter set in, and Hunker Creek Road became impassable, ending all discussion about bringing back Winch.

Looking out in the direction of the hills and the falling snow, Lulu wiped her hands on her apron and said, "Well, Tobias, that's that. What spring will bring no one knows."

Life returned to normal in the Halloo house. Things calmed down and were more pleasant. No one said a word about the improvement, I noticed on my next visit, but a few made a point of offering their support and condolences to Lulu. She appreciated that but hardly needed it—she was strong—and never skipped a beat in caring for the household and the children. I was surprised how quickly life went on without Winch. It seems people aren't as important as they think.

Hunker Creek Hideout

Winch spent the winter up on Hunker Creek and came home a changed man. For one thing, he had fewer toes on one foot. He wouldn't talk about it, but I never let up asking him.

"Winch," I said, "I know you're holding back on my story."

"Your story?" he huffed. "When did it become your story? I'm the one who was up there."

"You know what I mean. You lost your toes, and I want to hear how you did it."

I also wanted to hear what had changed him. He had gone up the mountain angry and closed-minded and had come back a humbled new man. I was curious as hell.

"If you can figure it out, Tobias, I would like to hear it too," Lulu said.

After a week of my pestering, he finally told me what happened.

"I appreciate you wanting to record people's history, Tobias, but the main reason I don't talk about it is that every time I do, my foot hurts. The doc tells me it's all in my head, but I ask him, 'How can it be in my head when it's my foot that hurts?'"

We talked out at Rock Creek on the front porch, where an occasional child ran in and out of the kitchen, making the maximum of distracting noise. Winch rubbed his knee as he talked, and when he stopped rubbing, the interview was over. It would take three meetings over three months to piece the story together.

Uncle Zak walked by just as we began and asked, "What are you fellows talking about?"

"Winch's lost toes."

"I don't know what the hell is wrong with a man who leaves home and comes back without his toes. In my day we kept our toes, we didn't lose them!" Zak shuffled off into the kitchen.

Winch rolled his eyes and began his story on the day he left Rock Creek. "As soon as I drove out of the yard with my gear and supplies, I knew I was making a mistake. I hardly said goodbye to Lulu and the kids. But what could I do? I was angry, my pride was hurt and no one would listen to me. At the time I figured I was right.

"It was raining and snowing, so the road was slick. I drove like a madman from hell. I couldn't see, and I almost slid off into the Hunker Creek Valley more than once. My knuckles were bone white from clutching the steering wheel. I pounded the dash and dented it. I pushed my feet so hard on the floorboards that I lifted myself off the seat, bumping my head on the roof of the cab and hurting my neck. I yelled curses until my throat was sore."

He laughed in embarrassment and shook his head, recalling his rage.

"My gut feeling told me I was wrong. I remembered what my mother taught us: 'It's better to have a handful of patience than a bushel of brains.' I didn't want to spend the winter alone on Hunker Creek. I wished someone had stopped me."

"They wanted to stop you, Winch, but no one knew how. No one dared to say no to you. I was there the day you left and I saw how upset everyone was. I would have tried, but you're a big guy. You intimidate people."

Winch looked stricken. I realized he now understood how much trouble he'd caused.

"Do you know Lulu's final words to me as I left?"

"No," I said.

"She said, 'Some of the things you say are right, Winch, but you say them ugly.' It was true. I was right about some things but I was ugly about it. I argued too much, and it bought me a winter alone on Hunker Creek. How stupid is that? I really wanted no part of it. On the drive up I slapped the side of my head a couple of times, trying to knock some sense in, but all I got was a headache. Never let your pride or anger run away with your life, Tobias. If you do, you'll be sorry."

I didn't fully understand what he meant. I never had a problem with anger, and what influence pride had on a person I knew only from the downfall of characters in Shakespeare's plays.

"I reached the cabin by late afternoon. It was on the crest of a hill overlooking Hunker Creek, which ran hundreds of yards below. It should still be there today, if you care to drive up and take a look."

"I might someday," I said.

"A more forlorn sight never greeted a man in all his life. You know that song by Hank Williams, 'I'm So Lonesome I Could Cry'? That's how I felt, like crying. I stepped out of the truck and I imagined that the wind coming up the valley was saying, "Go home, go home." But I ignored it. That's what anger and pride does to a fella, Tobias, shuts out the feelings of his heart." Winch stopped rubbing; the knee of his pants was shiny. "That's all I have time for today. My damn foot hurts. Phone me later on, and we'll talk in a few days."

I phoned a few days later from the pay phone in the Flora Dora, but Winch was busy repairing the barn. It would be a week before we sat down again.

I was enjoying the meat loaf special when Joshua walked in with the prettiest girl I'd ever seen, a brunette. He waved and walked over to my booth, and the girl followed. He let her slide in first. I'd forgotten to chew my mouthful of meat loaf, and I almost choked when Joshua introduced her as Flora.

I took a drink of coffee and shook her hand. They both ordered the special.

Flustered, I thought of something to say. "After the restaurant, no doubt."

"What?" she said.

"Flora, like the Flora Dora."

"Flora after my grandmother." She cast me a look as though I was simple. "The first woman lawyer in Ontario."

Great first impression I made, I thought.

"Flora is dancing and acting in the Gaslight Follies at the Palace Grand this year," Joshua said. "Tobias is a reporter heading off to the University of Victoria this fall to study English."

"Great, I'll have to come and see you."

"And I'll have to read your newspaper articles," Flora said.

I couldn't take my eyes off her.

She looked up and gave me the sweetest smile. "What are you staring at, writer boy?"

Joshua bent his head over his plate and laughed so hard his shoulders shook.

That Saturday Joshua and I joined the tourists at the historic theatre, paid our admission and took our seats front and centre.

The melodrama *Love and Heartbreak on Gold Bottom Creek* had its moments. The piano player pounded away enthusiastically like Schroeder from the *Peanuts* cartoon strip. The barbershop quartet was okay, though the tenor's voice cracked, and the slapstick clowns were amusing. Flora played in the melodrama and danced in the can-can chorus line. No one applauded and cheered more than Joshua and I did. Flora gave a cheery wave and blew a kiss our way as she left the stage. I didn't know if the kiss was for Joshua or me.

After the show the three of us met and went to a party. Flora and I talked all night as though we'd known each other all our lives.

Winch called eventually and invited me to hear more of the story. When I got there, he started right in as though we hadn't left off. At first I found it hard to concentrate; I was thinking about Flora.

"It took me all week to repair the cabin. I lived in the truck in the meantime. I missed my bed; it had been a long time since I slept in the cab of a truck. I repaired the plank door and broken window and put up some shelves. I chinked the logs with stuffing from an old mattress lying out back in the fireweed. Except for squirrels and the occasional hunter stopping to make a cup of coffee, no one had lived in the place for years. Firewood was plentiful on the hills, and over the next month I gathered enough for the winter. A week of hot fires in the rusted stove drove out the dampness, and once the supplies and odds and ends were moved in, it was home sweet home. It was not as nice as Rock Creek but liveable just the same."

"Did you think the cabin was winter-ready?" I asked.

"No, it was a shack, to tell the truth, but I found the area peaceful. It was a quiet place to be. It felt good to be away from all the turmoil. I could relax. My plan was to study the Bible, meditate and become more spiritual, so that in the spring when I headed back down the valley, my family and friends would see a new reborn Winch. The old one would be gone—all my troubles would be gone—and I would be a happier, smarter man." Then Winch let out a sigh. "That was the plan, anyway."

"'The best-laid schemes o' mice an' men gang aft a-gley,'" I said.

"What?"

"It's a quote from Robbie Burns, the great poet."

"Oh," said Winch. Then he plunged on. "It surprised me that winter came early. The temperature dropped, the ground froze, the snow stayed and windswept drifts blocked the road. I welcomed the closing, since it meant I was unreachable. For some reason it made me feel stronger."

"You were probably happy Mother Nature was making a decision for you," I said.

Winch didn't seem to appreciate anyone, even Mother Nature, being involved in his decision making.

Lowering his voice, he said, "Just remind me, Tobias, this is a friendly interview, right?"

I said, "You're right, this is a friendly interview."

"Good." He leaned back. "I wouldn't want to read something that made me look like a wuss, now, would I?"

I nodded in agreement, having just learned a lesson that would assist me for the rest of my life as a journalist: never anger your interview subject. Years later, when I lectured at the University of Victoria, I kept a framed sign posted behind my desk for my students to read: Never Anger the Winch. Some asked what it meant. The less imaginative ignored it. I favoured the inquisitive ones.

"I had a combination short- and long-range radio I'd bought at Sears. I took the battery out of the truck to run it. With a long copper-wire antenna I was able to pick up music and weather stations all over the North. Most days the reception was excellent. There was a good rock 'n' roll show out of Vancouver DJ'd by a young guy named Rockin' Red Robinson. I saw his picture later in a magazine, and he really did have red hair. After a few weeks I felt like I knew him.

"I also dialled in on Russian fishing boats off the coast and listened to ship-to-ship patter. I couldn't read Morse code, but listening to the dots and dashes was soothing and put me to sleep. How many nights I went to sleep with dots and dashes rather than Lulu, I don't know.

"In early December the weather stations reported that an Arctic front was extending down from Old Crow into northern British Columbia, plunging the entire Yukon into sub-zero temperatures. There were no animals to be seen, and nothing ventured out except the ravens. The cold went on for weeks. I figured there was a seventy-degree separation between the cabin's temperature and the temperature outdoors."

Winch told me that he read the Bible. He liked the Gospel of Matthew but had difficulty understanding a lot of things. The basic Christian teachings were clear—love one another and so on—but he didn't know if he had that kind of commitment and discipline. He just wanted to be enlightened.

"Isn't the purpose of enlightenment to find love and knowledge?" I asked.

"I don't know. That's it for today, Tobias." When Winch stopped rubbing his knee, he looked tired. I'm sure that recounting some of those times was painful. He got up and limped stiffly into the kitchen, holding the top of his leg.

At home I had barely gotten in the door when my mother called out, "Tobias, come here this instant!"

It sounded like trouble. Ma was sitting in the living room smoking a cigarette. She didn't smoke, so whatever it was had to be serious. She appeared agitated.

As casually as I could, I sat on the arm of her chair and asked, "What's up, Ma?"

She didn't look at me but touched her thumb and forefinger nails together and looked at that. Her legs were crossed, and she bobbed her foot up and down. "What's this I hear about you going out with a dance hall girl? The whole town is talking."

I almost fell off the chair, so I moved to the couch where it felt safer.

"Who told you that, Ma?"

"Is it true?"

"No, it's not true. She isn't a dance hall girl, she works in the Follies for the summer and goes back to school in the fall. We're friends."

"I knew it! Wait until I tell your father." Without further words she ground out the cigarette, stood up, straightened her apron and marched into the kitchen. She never looked at me once.

Oh my, I thought.

Mom and I didn't speak for the next few days. I heard her and Dad arguing in the kitchen after I went to bed. It might have been about Flora, but my dad never said a word.

Although Flora asked to see me, I had to get Winch's story. I spent the next weekend at the Halloos' place.

"How is your leg feeling, Winch?"

"My foot still hurts. I get a pain across where the toes used to be, then it goes right up my spine. My friend cut his foot in a pond where a family of swans lived, and every time he saw a swan, his foot hurt. Go figure." Then he asked, "Where did we stop the last time?"

I wanted to say, when you were beginning to show the first signs of cabin fever, but I didn't.

"Yeah, yeah, right, I remember now. I exercised to keep busy. When the temperature dropped, I walked in circles around the table for hours and read the Bible. I dragged my thumb around the table-top until I developed a callous and the paint on the table wore down to bare oak. I calculated that each time around was twenty-five feet. From that I figured out the mileage from Rock Creek to the Dempster Highway, then on to Gravel Lake, McQuesten River, Moose Creek and finally Stewart Crossing. I was halfway to Mayo when disaster struck."

"Disaster? What sort of disaster?" I asked, my interest picking up.

"People get all sorts of cravings in the winter. I've known some to hunger for oranges, tomatoes, pickle juice and other things. I knew one guy who lived thirty miles up the Yukon River who wanted pork. He hiked into Dawson at forty below, took the best room in the Eldorado Hotel and had the cook fry him up twenty chops. He ate them in one sitting, pork chops and nothing else. It took him two hours—scraped his plate clean. He then instructed the cook to make gravy from the pan drippings and pour it over a loaf of bread. It worked for him. He was a lot happier the next day when he left.

"I had plenty of food and vitamins, but my craving was for clear, cold water. I had been melting snow, but snow tasted flat and dusty. I wanted fresh water, but the creek was at the bottom of the valley. I thought it over for a few days and made up my mind I was going anyway."

The trip down to the creek from the Hunker Valley rim was steep and long; I'd seen it on a wood-cutting trip. I couldn't imagine anyone hiking it in the middle of winter through four feet of snow.

Winch waited for it to warm up. When the thermometer read thirty-six degrees below, fifteen degrees warmer than it had been, he bundled up and set out. He took a small axe and slung six plastic milk jugs, tied together, over his shoulder. It was a tough slide through the snow, and when he reached the creek, he was exhausted.

"I stood among the willows beside the creek to catch my breath. It's hard to breathe when you're sucking in cold air. I rested a moment, then walked out on the ice. I could see the creek running about a foot below where I stood. It took a few smashes with the axe to make an opening big enough to dip a jug in. I removed one glove and kneeled down to reach the water."

"I would never go on creek ice like that," I said.

"Yeah, well, you were home in your nice, snug bed, and I was on Hunker," Winch snapped.

Never anger the Winch! Any kind of criticism made him testy. I thought he was going to get up and leave, but he continued on. I was feeling testy myself. I didn't appreciate Ma's interference with the friends I chose.

"I filled three jugs and set them in a row. I was dipping the fourth when the ice cracked and I felt it drop a few inches. That was a weird feeling. I should have gotten off the ice then but I wanted to fill the rest of the jugs just in case I never got back down there.

"I was getting used to that scare when there was a louder crack and bang! I dropped into the water. I cracked my forehead on the way down and went right under, dropping my axe. The shock caused me to suck in mouthfuls of water. I jumped up and banged my head on the bottom of the ice. I was coughing and spitting when I slipped and fell under again. I got to my feet and steadied myself. I was stunned, and my eyes burned. It was actually warmer in the water than in the frigid air, but I knew I had to get out as soon as I could. I was bleeding badly and heavy drops of blood dripped into the water, diluted and flowed downstream.

"I waded toward the opening and reached up to grab a handful of willows. It took all of my strength to swing my legs up and pull myself onto the ice. I barrelled up the hill. My coat and pants began to freeze and stiffen, making it hard to move. In minutes my beard and hair were covered in ice. I must have been quite a sight, with frozen ice and blood covering my face and the mist rising off me as if I was on fire.

"Both of my gloves had floated away, so I tried climbing by alternating one hand in a pocket at a time, but I needed both hands for balance. My scarf froze around my neck, making it hard to look down. I panicked and started to pray, 'Please God, save me, help me! Please help me!' My hands and face stung. For every two steps I took forward, I slipped back one. It took forever to reach the crest of the hill. By then I was completely exhausted. I crashed into the cabin and threw myself down on the floor, kicking the door shut behind me."

"Wow, you were lucky," I said.

"I crawled to the stove, packed the firebox with wood and left the flue wide open to get as much heat as possible. I struggled to remove my clothes. My frozen pants stood by themselves in the middle of the room until they thawed and slowly tipped over. I climbed into bed shivering uncontrollably, pulled the sleeping bag over my head and fell into a deep sleep.

"When I woke up, the fire was almost out, and the cabin was cooling. In the next instant a pain like a thousand needles shot up through my limbs. My fingers and toes had frozen. They burned so badly it felt like they were on fire. When I swung my legs over the edge of the bed, it hurt so much I threw up. My first instinct was to beat my hands on the headboard to shake off the feeling that they were asleep. When I did that, it felt a hundred times worse, because they weren't asleep. I wished I had a bottle of whisky."

"I've never seen you drink," I said.

"I don't drink. None of the Halloos do. It was for medicinal purposes, Tobias, purely medicinal. For several days all I could drink was hot tea with milk and sugar. I walked on my heels and carried things with the palms of my hands. My pants and shirt hung undone because I couldn't fasten buttons or pull a zipper. If it wasn't for suspenders, my pants would be at my ankles. I had to crawl outside on my knees and elbows, pushing a few pieces of wood ahead of me. I tried to stand, but my head spun, and I became nauseous. There was no relief. I actually cried and groaned in pain. I wished I was back at home with Lulu looking after me. My fingers grew fat like cocktail sausages and then slowly returned to normal. The skin peeled off, but I could see they would recover."

His toes were another matter. Every morning he pulled back the covers to inspect them and each day he dreaded it more. His left foot was recovering, but the toes on his right foot continued to swell until a tinge of bluish black ringed the nails. He could smell almonds.

"I'd seen this before on a fellow at Pelly Crossing who froze his feet working on his trapline. It was gangrene!"

"Did the fellow at Pelly survive?" I asked.

"He survived the gangrene but later on he died of scurvy. Life is tough." Winch shrugged. "I started losing weight. I couldn't eat. My toes continued to blacken, and red streaks appeared under the skin halfway up my calf. I was stressed and depressed, which didn't help any."

"Red streaks mean blood poisoning," I said.

"Yeah. I was scared but I was thinking what I might have to do. I left it as long as I could, but reality is reality, Tobias, and I had to do or die. There was no way I could go for help.

"I had another axe, but it was dull, full of nicks and chips. It had never been sharpened, and I'd used it mainly as a wedge for splitting wood. Fortunately I had a heavy machinist's file in the truck's toolbox. It was rusty but still sharp. Sitting by the window to catch the light, I braced the head on the edge of the table and filed for hours. The blunt edge became as sharp as a razor, and I was able to shave my arm with it. I put a pan of water on the stove and boiled the axe. That made it nice and clean and sterile. At least I hoped it did!"

I knew what was coming next, and it horrified me. I began to understand Winch's psychosomatic feelings about his foot.

"I rolled the heavy chopping block in and covered its top with my cleanest dishcloth. Seeing it sitting there in the middle of the floor made my stomach flip. It made me think of how those poor folk must have felt during the French Revolution when head chopping was popular. I stoked up the fire, trimmed the lamp and tied a tourniquet around my leg. I still wished I had a bottle of whiskey, but then if I was drunk, I could really mess things up.

"I sat down, pulled my knee up and placed my right foot on the log. Then I drew a pencil mark across the base of my toes."

"Cut on dotted line," I said.

Winch laughed. "The pencil mark was purely for my peace of mind, because to tell you the truth, I wasn't sure how accurate I was going to be. I didn't want to cut too far into my foot. Using my right hand on my right foot was awkward, so I took a few practice swings. My skin was cold and clammy. I sat a while, knowing what I must do and wishing I didn't have to. I blocked all thoughts out, gripped the axe near the top, raised it, aimed and brought it down as hard as I could. The last thing I saw before I passed out was a spurt of blood and my toes flying across the room."

I started to laugh—the image of his toes flying across the room seemed hilarious—and Winch realized what he'd said and started laughing with me. We laughed until tears came to our eyes.

The kids came out of the kitchen and gathered around. "What's so funny, Dad?"

Winch couldn't tell them; they were too young. "Go back in and see your mom. When you're older, I'll tell you." He wiped his eyes. "And to make it even funnier, Tobias, before everything went black, I heard one bonk off the wash basin!"

We laughed some more.

"Ahhh," he said, still laughing, "and then I had my first vision."

I waited. Would this be another so-called epiphany?

"I was in a smoky dome-like structure where a small open fire cast yellowish light and dark shadows on the walls. In the background a group of almost naked men beat a large drum and sang in high-pitched voices. They looked like Plains people from around Edmonton where we used to live. In the foreground a young man was barely swinging back and forth, suspended above the hard-packed floor from ropes attached to pieces of white bone inserted through the flesh of his chest. His arms hung limply at his sides, and his head was thrown back as far as it could go. His long black hair hung down to his legs. Rivulets of blood streamed down his body and dripped off the end of his toes, forming a dark reflective pool into which the light from the fire flickered. I knew I was seeing the sun dance. A Native friend had told me about it, and I'd seen pictures of it in history books.

"When I came to, I could still hear the singing. But this time it was joined by another voice. It took me a moment to realize that it was my own. I was screaming my lungs out from the pain in my foot as I lay twisted on the floor. To my horror the axe pinned my foot to the stump, and I couldn't move. I got up on my elbows and stared in disbelief at the incomplete job. The blow had detached the four small toes but only half my big toe. I wrenched the axe from the stump, aimed and struck again.

"The second vision was in the same place. The drumming continued, but the young man was no longer suspended and now stood facing me. He had a broken-toothed smile and looked friendly. His face was sweat-streaked, and his hair was matted on his forehead. A look of total calm shone from his features. The ropes hung loosely down his bloodied chest, still attached to the bones piercing his skin. He reached out his right hand and placed it on my left shoulder. He looked me in the eyes and spoke clearly. "Winch, the pain you feel in your heart and mind will lead you to better things." He then nodded and released my shoulder, stepped backward, turned and danced toward the drummers.

"When I came to, I was no longer tethered to the stump. I wrapped bandages around the wound, staggered to the bed and passed out. When I woke up, great clots of blood had soaked through to the mattress. I felt weak and nauseous. I could hardly sit up and flopped over on the bed. After a few attempts I managed to sit at the kitchen table. Surprisingly I was hungry and I wolfed down cups of hot cocoa and thick peanut butter and jam sandwiches."

"How did your toes look?" I asked.

"They looked okay. Bloody, but okay. I was successful." Winch hesitated. "Tobias, he knew my name."

"Who?" I asked.

"The young fellow in the vision. He knew my name."

"He probably looked you up in the phone book."

"I wish sometimes you would get serious, Tobias."

"Sorry," I said. "So what happened next?"

"Cleaning the wound was difficult. I soaked my foot in warm water and removed the coverings. I was pleased to see the red streaks retreating down my leg.

"I'm going to be okay, I thought. I'm going to be okay. I was laughing and weeping at the same time. 'Yahoo!' I yelled, 'I am going to be okay!'

"I had two grey not-very-clean rags for bandages but I needed to change the dressing at least twice a day. I'd heard that printer's ink had antiseptic qualities. The only book I had was the Bible. I cut out sections and tied them around the end of my foot like a butcher's package. I felt terrible and guilty for using it, but what was I to do? My next dilemma was what to keep for reading. I picked through the books of the Bible, leaving my favourites and cutting out the rest. I saved Exodus, Psalms, Isaiah, Zechariah, Luke, John, Matthew and Revelations. The paper was dry and clean and helped the healing. Soon the bleeding and seepage stopped."

As he got better, Winch wondered what to do with the severed toes. The Eldorado Hotel had a sourtoe cocktail, but they were selective about the toe they used. A drunk had swallowed the toe one time, and they were very exclusive about choosing a new one. He thought about making a necklace, but that was too gruesome. People would think he'd flipped out and avoid him more than they already did. So he threw the toes onto the roof for the ravens. But the ravens knew better; they never touched them.

"The pain and agony I went through made my problems seem small, and I forgot them as time went on. I spent another two months up on Hunker.

"One day a D-8 Cat came up the road. Just as well! I was running out of supplies and wanted to go home. It was Henry Cougar, a placer miner, getting an early start on the gold-mining season. He was surprised to see anyone up there and stopped for coffee. Henry was the first person I spoke to in seven months. The road was now cleared, so the next day I wasted no time in getting my things loaded in the truck. The battery was dead from my using it all winter with the radio, so I coasted down the hill a bit, popped the clutch and away I went.

"It was beautiful down in the valley. The sun was melting the snow, and water ran everywhere. The Klondike River was starting to thaw, and the roads were all muddy. Lulu, the kids and the dogs must have recognized the sound of the International Harvester coming up the drive, because all of them were out waiting for me. Lulu said later that her intuition told her I was coming home that day. The kids ran screaming and yelling. They were happy to see me."

Winch's eyes were tearing over. He sniffed a couple of times, blew his nose and went on.

"Damn, Tobias, what a person does to avoid love, eh? I hugged the kids close and couldn't believe I was such a fool as to leave them. Lulu was standing on the porch wiping her hands on her apron. She stared at me. I knew she was looking to see how I was. I set the children aside and limped up to the porch. She was standing on the second step so we were the same height. I said, 'Hi, Lulu.'"

Lulu told me later, "I could see Winch was a changed man. His face was bright, and his eyes were clear. He'd lost so much weight that his clothes hung on him. The straps that cinched up his overalls, which normally hung at chest level, now fit under his chin. Not since our wedding day had he looked so thin."

"Lulu gave me the biggest hug and said, 'Welcome home, Winch.' I loved the fresh smell of her clothes and the warmth of her body. I buried my head in her shoulder and told her how sorry I was." She said, 'Now, now, we won't have any of that, will we? It's over.' She hugged me again and we went inside.

"We sat at the kitchen table, since the children wouldn't let me out of their sight. They were waving every crayon drawing they'd made since I left and telling me everything that had happened in the past months. One of the dogs had pups and my lap was soon covered in puppies.

"You know, Tobias, sitting there in the kitchen with my wife and kids, I realized then and there that when you come right down to it, all there is is love. Love is all that matters."

I began to understand more clearly what had changed Winch.

"I told Lulu again that I was sorry I left, because I felt so bad. She started to cry and sat on the edge of her chair with her elbow on the table and her chin resting on her hand. I knew I had hurt and worried her. I swore I would never do it again for as long as I lived.

"The news spread that I was home, and everyone came to the kitchen to see me. I hugged and greeted everyone individually to make sure each person knew I was happy to see them. I apologized where I had to and put other things straight when it seemed appropriate. Uncle Zak gave me the once-over a couple of times, looking to see which Winch had really returned, but I won him over. 'I was organizing a coup d'état, Winch,' Zak said. 'You were lucky you left when you did, otherwise by now I'd be running this show. Clutch thought he would make his move, but if brains were dynamite, he wouldn't have enough to blow his nose.' Zak didn't care that Clutch was standing next to him.

"They all wanted to know about my toes, so we chased the younger children out of the room, and amid gasps and groans, I showed them what I'd had to do. Where the toes were, there was now a row of fresh pink stubs, cleanly healed. There was a little jog where the big toe took a second hit, but it was pretty straight overall. Holding up my leg, I couldn't help but feel a little pride at the fine job I had done."

That was the end of Winch's Hunker Creek story. It became a running joke around the house from there on in that if anyone froze their toes, they should see Doctor Winch.

About a month later the Halloos threw a combination birthday-welcome-home barbecue for him. OP only got a birthday party, but he didn't care. He and Clutch were glad to have their brother back, and they hugged him every chance they got.

Winch told them, "I'm here to stay, boys. I'm not leaving physically or mentally. What you see is what you get."

I talked Mom and Dad into going to the party with Flora and me. Dad was all right, but Mom balked.

"Come on, Becky, you can meet our son's friend." Dad called Mom Becky when they argued.

"Okay, but I never thought my son would date a dance hall girl."

"She's not a dance hall girl, Ma. I told you that already."

Mom and Dad sat in the back of the Rambler, and Flora and I sat in the front. In the rear-view mirror, I saw Mom pull out her pack of cigarettes, and I said, "Mom!" She put them back in her purse.

"When did you start smoking?" Dad asked.

"Never you mind," Mom said.

Somehow a conversation got started about school. Flora was heading back to Simon Fraser University in September, and I was off to my first year at the University of Victoria.

"What are you studying, dear?" my mom asked.

"I'm studying education," Flora said.

In the mirror I saw my mom's cheeks blush.

Once Mom realized Flora was a hard-working student "and a very bright, pretty one at that," the ice was broken. By the time we reached the party, they were inseparable.

Winch and I stood together drinking punch, watching people enjoy themselves.

"This is what it's all about, Tobias, friends and family being together, supporting each other, giving each other confidence."

"I will never forget that," I said.

We shook hands, and Winch hugged me like a bear.

"I love you, man, like a brother," he said, then moved on to sit with Lulu and the children.

I sat with Flora, my parents and Zak, who was spinning tales. I never felt so good in all my life.

Uncle Zak took the axe and mounted it on a varnished and stained plywood plaque. It hung on the living room wall in a place of honour, over the couch among family photographs. If you looked closely, you could see a reddish stain on the handle. Winch put his condensed version of the Bible in the drawer beside his bed and read it at night before sleeping.

"I never did feel comfortable using a holy book like that," he told me, "but it saved my life."

Lulu helped out by putting things into perspective to ease his worries. "If God didn't make things to help man, well then, what's the use of having them?"

Years later I helped Dad get a load of winter wood up on Hunker Creek. We drove the rattling two-ton stake truck up the winding road a few extra miles to visit Winch's cabin. The door was open; no one had lived there since Winch had left. I stood on a stump, maybe the one Winch used, to look for the toe bones on the sod roof. I couldn't find them. Rodents must have spirited them away to gnaw on for the minerals. Inside the cabin sat the old stove, and next to that, bolted securely to the wall, was a metal bed frame sans mattress. On the third log above the bed, carved in deep letters, I read these words:

> God's gifts to man
> He has chosen to ignore
> So in pain he will walk
> Through reality's door.
> – Winch

My father went to the truck, and I took a moment to look out over the valley. Hot summer days had infused the bushes and trees with more energy than they could possibly hold, and with the approaching winter, the plants were burning out their life in surreal, vibrant colours, paying homage to the retreating sun. The wind came up and blew the grasses on the valley slope like waves on the sea. For a moment I heard something and strained to hear it again. From somewhere above, below or across the valley came the unmistakable sound of many drummers beating one drum.

Dawson City's Ditch Digging Authority

I returned home after completing my first year at the University of Victoria, leaving daffodils in Victoria for snow in Dawson City. There was a summer job waiting for me at the Flora Dora Café—washing dishes—and I started in right away.

It was great to be home with my parents. The first couple of days, my mom wouldn't stop crying or feeding me.

"You've lost so much weight! Did you forget to eat?" she asked.

My dad was more interested in my marks and life on campus; we talked for hours.

I visited the Halloos at Rock Creek as soon as I could. We had kept in touch by writing a few letters during the year. The lunch table was packed when I walked in, and I was greeted with yells of surprise and bone-crushing hugs from both the men and the women. I was seated at the head of the table; Winch gave up his spot for me.

"Look here, you're all grown up and educated," Lulu said, beaming with pride. She'd hugged me repeatedly and now set a plate of boiled cabbage and beef in front of me.

"I'm only first year," I said.

"Nonsense," Stella said. "You're probably smarter than all the other students."

I went along with her and said, "Well, I am pretty smart."

That brought about a chorus of laughter. OP, in his exuberance, put a headlock on me and gave me a knuckle rub. "That's our boy!"

It hurt, but I'd learned to laugh these things off.

I straightened my hair and enjoyed the rest of my lunch. I was happy to be back with the Halloos; they were truly my brothers and sisters, and I'd missed them. Sitting there, I admired how uncomplicated their life was compared to Victoria and university.

Lulu was pregnant with a boy. The baby's gender had been determined by the tried-and-true method of needle-and-thread dowsing. Her pregnancy must have influenced fertility in the other women, because Olive, Stella and Missy were all due about the same time.

"It's going to look like spring lambing around here in a few months," Uncle Zak said. "Better line up the midwives, hot water and clean towels."

"It's doctors, nurses and hospitals these days, Zak, but thanks for the advice anyway," Stella said.

Winch had gotten over his obsessions with aliens and religion, and this lack of a cause allowed the brothers to pay more attention to their music. They pulled guitars, amps, and a drum kit out from under tarps and dusted them off.

An assortment of colourful electrical cords was stretched from the barn to the house, and the music began. The electrical circuits soon overloaded, so the children were trained to run up the hill and reset the breakers when they tripped.

Late at night, when the house slept, the men themselves had to reset the breakers. No one volunteered, so the brothers developed an elaborate contest of paper, rock and scissors combined with straw-drawing and coin-flipping. It took more time to come up with a loser than it did to reset the breaker. Through some sleight of hand, Zak's turn never came up. The men would run up the hill, bending over to rest a number of times with their hands on their knees, and arrive back at the barn out of breath and too tired to immediately pick up their instruments.

I sat in on one of these midnight practices, when the shouts from the house were changing from "Knock it off!" to pleas of "We are trying to sleep here."

One night, very late, all three sisters—Lulu, Olive and Stella—marched down to the barn with their nightgowns flowing out behind them and pushed over the amplifiers, forcing the brothers to quit.

"Why don't you ever learn who is boss around here?" Stella yelled, as the chastened brothers clutched their instruments and bit their tongues so as to not make matters worse.

The band needed a new name. With their father in mind, they called themselves the Dawson City Ditch Digging Authority.

"Why that name?" I asked after a practice one evening in the barn.

Clutch started to explain, and his brothers joined in. All three pulled up paint-splattered sawhorses.

"It's like this," OP said. "Our names are not our real names."

No kidding, I thought.

"We changed them to change our lives," Clutch said.

"OP's name is Leonard, Clutch's is Bernstein and mine is Chopin," Winch said.

"I never would have guessed." I was now mystified, especially because of Chopin.

"Our parents were amateur musicians and played a bunch of instruments," Winch went on. "It was an unusual day when the radio or the record player wasn't crooning out Armstrong, Sinatra, Holiday and others. They were both big people like us, and Mom was always cooking and baking."

"They met at the Southern Alberta Institute of Technology. Ma was studying nursing, and Dad was studying architectural technology," OP said. "It was love at first sight, they told us. Soon after graduation they married, bought a house and started a family."

"Winch and OP arrived first; my parents didn't expect twins, and neither did the doctors, so that was a big surprise. I was born a year later, but I've always been ahead of my brothers in school because I skipped a few grades," Clutch said. "From the start they encouraged us toward music. When the Bolshoi Ballet performed *Swan Lake* in Winnipeg, Dad took us out of school, and we made the three-day journey in our '58 Cadillac. During the summer holidays, we practically lived at Banff National Park where the School of Fine Arts produced plays and concerts. We attended so many of these that the people of Banff thought we lived there. We were easy to spot because we wore suits with white shirts and ties, and our brown Oxfords shone. Ma always made sure we were spotlessly clean. We used to play around the stages and meet the stagehands. This was more interesting than the performances themselves."

"Leonard and Bernstein took piano lessons, while I practised the violin," Winch said. "Dad invested in a violin—not a Stradivarius, but an expensive one just the same. From the start we showed talent. Day after day, mornings and afternoons, we practised Beethoven, Vivaldi, Mozart and Bach. We were the best in the school band. The teacher featured us as an ensemble at concerts, and our parents would sit in the front row beaming with pride. I showed enough promise that Dad said I was a prodigy.

"But we got older and went through puberty, and everything changed. We started to get interested in girls and cars. We skipped school and failed our grades. Dad shook his finger in our faces and warned us over and over, 'You'll be the kings of the ditchdiggers if you don't take your education seriously.'"

Now I knew where they got the name for the band.

"We grew our hair and beards and developed this badass attitude. It's just a show! We aren't really as bad as we seem, we're just actors," Winch said with a smile.

"I don't believe you're acting," I said.

"We'll get you for that later," Winch said.

"So did you dig ditches?"

"We got part-time jobs pumping gas, changing tires and pulling wrenches at Mike's One-Stop Auto Garage on Main Street. That was far more interesting than school or concerts! We were good mechanics and we could fix anything. 'Bunch of professionals,' Mike told his customers. We doubled his business."

"We pooled our $1.25 an hour earnings and bought a '52 Buick, which we had running perfectly. Cruising around town and the surrounding countryside, we became popular with the girls. We started playing rock 'n' roll and called ourselves the El Caminos."

"Our neighbour Taffy has a green 1959 Chevrolet El Camino parked in his backyard under a tarp," I said.

"Yeah, we know," said OP. "We tried to buy it so we could relive the good old days, but he wouldn't sell."

"We asked him to put it in his will for us, but he told us to go to hell," Clutch said. "Apparently his gypsy neighbour is going to get it."

"Life was good back then," OP said. "We were free. We had money, friends, rock 'n' roll and each other. We quit school and were rarely home. Ma was upset, and Dad was angry when he saw us throwing everything away."

"It was sad," Clutch said. "We loved them, but things went sour. Dad was a control freak."

"The thing that hurt most was the name calling," Winch said. "He called us stupid, idiots and punks. We moved out and rented a farmhouse on the outskirts of town. Our friends moved in, and it was one big party. We went home to see Ma, and on one occasion we told Dad, 'The only reason we visit is to see Mom.'"

"That hurt him badly," Winch added.

"In the meantime we met the Robinson sisters—Lulu, Stella and Olive—and got married together on the same afternoon," Clutch said. "We thought we were the luckiest men in the world to land such beauties. Mom came to the weddings. Dad didn't."

"You should have seen that wedding," OP said with a grin. "It went on for four days and almost wrecked the house. The cops were called twice to shut us down. That's when Winch spent his wedding night in jail. Lulu was not impressed."

"Yeah, that's the first time I realized I married someone with a temper," Winch said. "We bought Mike's garage and ran it for a few years, but it seemed we were always in some sort of trouble with the townsfolk and our neighbours. A friend living in the Yukon spent some time with us and convinced us to move here. We packed and left, bringing with us whoever wanted to come along. When we left

Alberta, there were grandchildren our dad had never seen. I think he lost the thing he loved the most, but he was unable to accept the lifestyle we had chosen."

"We were musicians, but not the type Dad wanted us to be," OP said. "We played rock 'n' roll and knew its history from front to back. We knew that the guitarist of Stone the Crows was electrocuted on stage, that Deep Purple's original drummer Harvey Shields was replaced by John Kerrison in 1967 and that Mott the Hoople was named after Willard Manus's novel by the same name. We made up our own version of Trivial Pursuit. We could play thousands of songs by heart and harmonize as well as anyone."

I found the brothers' history intriguing, and I was pleasantly surprised to hear it was rich in music and talent. It was sad about the family split, but it can be confusing when another direction is forced upon you.

"You have to be yourselves. You have to follow your calling," Lulu said over Winch's shoulder.

Everyone has a story, I realized. At that moment I knew what kind of journalist I wanted to be, one who sought the facts from the past and the present to do justice to someone's life. If the brothers hadn't told me their story, I would never have known it.

Discovery Day weekend near the end of June is the big event in Dawson City. I was helping out as the manager for the Dawson City's Ditch Digging Authority and got the word out that the Halloo brothers were available to play dances. The city council discussed the possibility of bypassing the perennial favourites, the New Tones from Whitehorse, and asking the brothers to play. Some councillors were adamant that the Halloos shouldn't play here or anywhere else on the planet. Walter Rather was the most outspoken. "Those people have been nothing but trouble since they arrived here. Why encourage them to stay? They'll only buy more goats with the money we give them!"

Walter's argument had weight, but the Halloos' price was less than the New Tones'.

"We have to be responsible to the taxpayers and take the best price," one councillor said.

"Even *you* have to admit it's a bargain, Walter," Richard Cooper scolded. "And last time the New Tones played, their conductor got so drunk he fell in the river and never showed up for half the night. When he did, he looked like a cross-eyed Cab Calloway on steroids. He didn't even face the band when he conducted!"

The council voted for the Ditch Digging Authority.

At about eight in the evening, the brothers tuned up for the dance with a Beethoven overture. A crowd had filled the hall to capacity in eager anticipation of a night of dancing. The lights were dimmed except for the stage, and Winch launched into the searing opening chords of Chuck Berry's "Johnny B. Goode."

Out of the dimness, a sea of orange and beige rushed toward the stage. The Halloo women, every last one of them from a six-year-old to Zak's sixty-year-old wife, wore matching ankle-length printed dresses. Their rubber boots had been traded in for new white tennis shoes, but they still wore knee-high woollen socks. The women hooted and hollered encouragement, and Winch duck-walked across the stage. It would've made Chuck proud.

Other men did not dance with the Halloo women. No one dared. I too stayed clear, though Lulu tried to drag me onto the dance floor. I dug in my heels all the while, yelling, "I can't dance! I can't dance!" Much to my relief, she gave up and left me alone.

The girls danced with their legs together, moving up and down, back and forth, in a Chubby Checker-style twist. I was a little surprised that anyone still danced like that, with the pony and the monkey being so popular.

After the first song more couples made their way onto the dance floor. By the third tune nothing could stop the infectious urge to dance. In one wave the crowd rushed forward. Everyone was having a great time.

By the end of the evening the brothers were accepting multiple compliments. Winch was standing on the stage, holding his guitar and bending over to shake the hands of people congratulating him from the dance floor.

People liked the Halloos' music. The Dawson City folk seemed eager to embrace them as friends. Even Walter Rather went up and shook their hands. He and his missus danced almost every dance, though I'm sure Walter invented some of them.

By 3:00 a.m. the equipment was loaded into the trucks, and I drove back to Rock Creek with Winch and Lulu. The pale sun was rising from its lowest midnight-sun setting. The air was cool, and the mist rising from the dredge ponds clung like cotton balls to the rock piles.

I could see Winch was happy with the evening's performance. Lulu sat beside him, linking her arm in his and laying her head on his shoulder. I looked out the passenger window, wondering what to do with the time I had left before returning to school. I thought I should spend more time with my parents.

"That was so much fun," Winch said. "Can you believe it, they actually paid us to do that? I would have played for free."

When Winch pulled the truck into the yard, Uncle Zak came running out the kitchen door, missed the last porch step and crashed to his knees. He stood up, wobbled, swore, and holding onto one leg, limped to Winch's side of the truck.

Rolling down the window, Winch asked, "What's up, Zak? You okay?"

"Come in really fast," Zak wheezed. "Your ma called last night after you left. Said it's really important. You got to call back right away."

"But it's 4:30 in the morning," Winch said.

"No matter," Zak instructed. "Your Ma said as soon as you came home I was to tell you to phone. I've been waiting up all these hours to tell you. Way past my bedtime."

"I appreciate you staying up, Zak," Winch said.

We rushed into the house as the rest of the trucks pulled into the yard and emptied out behind us.

The phone rang only once.

"Hi, Ma, it's Chopin. Is everything okay?"

Winch listened intently for three or four minutes, not making a sound, and the colour drained from his face as he turned to the crowd. He took the phone from his ear, held it to his chest with both hands and said sadly, "Pa's gone. He died. Passed away last evening. He was walking the dog. Just fell over. The neighbours tried to help, called the ambulance, but the paramedics said he was gone before he hit the ground. Heart attack. He cut his head on the sidewalk when he fell."

I heard gasps and wails as people ran through the house and back outside to tell those who were still arriving. In minutes the kitchen was so crammed we could barely move. People hung on every word that Winch exchanged with his mother.

"We're coming down, Ma. Just as soon as I get off the phone, we'll pack." With that Winch hung up and turned to the crowd. "Pack everything. We're going home."

The room emptied, and for the next two hours drawers and doors opened and banged shut as people finished their packing.

I got caught up in this whole thing and phoned my mom, who really didn't like being awakened at five in the morning, to tell her I was going with the Halloos to their dad's funeral. She was half-asleep, and I didn't say where the funeral was, so she said, "See you when you get back, dear, and take care."

A cavalcade of trucks and cars snaked out of the yard and onto the Klondike Highway, passing those who were headed into Dawson for their day's work. People must have known something was up when they saw all the Halloos in one long procession.

Down the dusty gravel road we travelled, driving night and day. We stopped only to repair tires and to sleep at a small motel, where we rented all six cramped cabins and lined up for showers.

The first day, with Winch in the lead, we cruised through White-horse stopping only for gas. We made Watson Lake early the next morning. At Fort Nelson the guy in the restaurant filled forty-six orders of burgers and fries to go—he'd never done that before. Fort St. John was next, then we pushed on to Dawson Creek, then turned south for the Halloos' home town of Fort Saskatchewan, which was north of Edmonton. We arrived at dawn, four tiring days after leaving Rock Creek.

Their father's siblings planned the funeral, so there was little the Rock Creek family had to do but contribute funds. Ma was heartbro-ken but glad to see her family, especially the new grandchildren.

It was a bright sunny day at the gravesite. Winch, OP and Clutch, dressed in clean blue-jean bib overalls with white shirts and black bow ties, stood arm in arm by the grave and wailed like babies. Their massive shoulders shook with sobs, and their eyes were bloodshot pools of tears. Their noses ran, and they gasped for breath. Tucking their hands up their shirt sleeves, they wiped their faces on the cuffs, and soon wet stains smeared the cloth.

The family tried to console them, but they were inconsolable.

"Pa's gone! Pa's gone!" they wailed over and over again. "He won't be back. We will never see him again." And they hollered even more, so much so that we were fearful they might become distracted and tumble into the open grave. Their wives came forward, took their arms and led them away to the chairs set out on the cemetery lawn. The children started crying too, upset at seeing their fathers in such distress, and clung to their mothers.

The Rock Creek family overflowed Ma's house, so they set up tents in the yard. The neighbours must have thought that an occupying army had come to town. Being respectful of the funeral, they complained little except when the children trespassed onto their properties. During the week the Rock Creek clan re-established its ties with the family and friends they had left behind. Everyone could see that the boys and their families were doing well, so they asked about the Yukon. So many invitations were extended that if everyone arrived on the Halloos' doorstep at the same time, there would be no place to put them all.

On the last evening of the visit, Alice led her sons Chopin, Leonard and Bernstein into the parlour. I got up to leave, but Winch motioned for me to sit down again. "He can stay, Ma. Tobias is like family. He's the little brother we never had."

I was taken aback by the unexpected adoption into the Halloo family. All I could say was, "Thank you."

Ma took a letter from the pocket of her apron and held it in her hands. "Sons," she said, "your father wrote something for you just before he died. I think he had a premonition." She handed the folded paper to OP—he was the best reader—and told him to read it out loud.

OP unfolded it, glanced at its contents and read, "My Dear Chopin, Bernstein and Leonard, when your mother gives you this letter you will know I'm gone. I want to tell you what has been in my heart and on my mind for some time. I want you to know that I love you, and along with Alice, you are my most cherished possessions. I thank God that you were my children.

"I deeply regret not having seen how important it was to support you in what life called you to be. This is my most regrettable mistake. I wanted only the best for you. In another world, in another time, this will all be put behind us, and we will be together again. Look after your mother. Love, Father."

OP wiped away a tear, folded the letter and handed it back to Ma. "Keep it," she said.

Clutch and Winch cried silently.

The next morning as they packed to leave, Ma Alice called her boys into the parlour again. She was holding a violin case, and in it was a Romeo Antoniazzi violin. "Your father bought this many years ago. He told me, 'When the time comes, give it to the boys.' He put all his savings into it with hopes that one of you would play it for a living."

Winch took the violin and bow out of the case, tucked it under his chin and tuned it in a minute. With a nod of his head he indicated to Clutch to sit at the parlour piano. "This is for Pa," he said. He and Clutch played Chopin's "Fantasie-Impromptu" from their hearts.

I slept all the way on the drive back home, which was completed in typical Halloo fashion, as quickly as possible. A week after arriving, the three brothers and I sat with Uncle Zak on the worn living room couches and stared at the violin case sitting on the oversized coffee table. Zak opened the case and laid the violin on top of it.

"It's got to be worth some money," OP said.

"It's a gift, for heaven's sake!" Clutch said. "We can't sell it."

"Like hell we can't! It's ours to do whatever we want with," Winch said.

"I'd rather have a new truck," Zak said. "You can't drive a violin."

Zak's opinion held weight, and no one argued with him.

Months later Lulu did some research and contacted Sotheby's auction house in New York. Winch crated the violin and sent it via Canadian Pacific to Vancouver, and Brinks delivered it to the dealer.

Shortly after that a cheque arrived in the mail made out to Lulu Halloo for a little more than US$70,000.

When the Halloos opened the envelope, the hooting and hollering could be heard a mile from the house, and the men and women linked arms and danced a hoedown in the kitchen.

Within days two new trucks appeared in the yard, and one of them was for Zak. Everyone had new clothes, and the brothers took turns driving an ATV all over the hills behind the house.

A carpenter was hired to repair and renovate the house. He built new cabinets in the kitchen, but the walls and floors were so uneven and out of plumb that he took twice as long as usual and charged twice as much to complete the job. A bathroom with an oversized Jacuzzi tub was added on to Lulu and Winch's bedroom. They tried to keep it private, but the kids lined up in their bathing suits with water wings and snorkels, and soon everyone was using it.

"Turn on the jets for us, Auntie Lulu," they sang in chorus.

"Looks like a damn swimming pool in there," Winch complained.

Lulu had another way of looking at it. "At least we don't have to drag them in to take a bath."

Zak booked every Friday night and lay back in a bubble bath smoking a cigar, filing his calluses and humming softly to himself.

Simpsons-Sears was kept busy bringing in furniture, kitchenware, blankets, lamps, tools, musical instruments, toys and auto parts.

Every last penny was gone within four months. No one cared, in fact they were happy. The brothers and their wives believed money was to be spent. Pa was gone, and now so was the money.

The three new baby boys were named Chopin Winch Bruce Halloo, Bernstein Clutch Bruce Halloo, and Leonard Oil Pan Bruce Halloo. The "Bruce" was in honour of the Rock Creek boys' father. Missy and Joshua called their baby Hunker Joshua Tobias Halloo Shackelton.

Ma Alice visited Rock Creek often, staying several months at a time before heading home to rest. When she was at Rock Creek, she poked around the rooms and closets in the sprawling house. The boys would catch each other's glance and raise their eyebrows. They knew she was looking for the violin. No one said anything, and Alice never asked. The boys figured she knew what had happened; all the new things they'd bought made it obvious. Why say anything?

Their dad's passing inspired the Rock Creek boys to reflection, and each brother—in his own time and way—accepted his father's letter. The compensation they received from the sale of the violin influenced their acceptance. "Pa paid us back for all those unkind words and hard times," OP said, and Winch and Clutch agreed.

"It's all over," Clutch said. "Pa's gone, and we should remember only what was good about him from now on."

"It's funny how you start to remember only the good things about a person as time goes by," I said.

"You're right, Tobias. We should remember only the good things."

"Yes," I said. "Remember only the good things."

Acknowledgments

I acknowledge the magnanimous spirit of the people of the Yukon and thank them for giving me so much to write about. I also thank Josephine Holmes, Alison Kalnicki and Susan Mayes for their encouragement, editing and thoughtful suggestions.